1st
Edition

P9-BZU-042

Avery's Knot

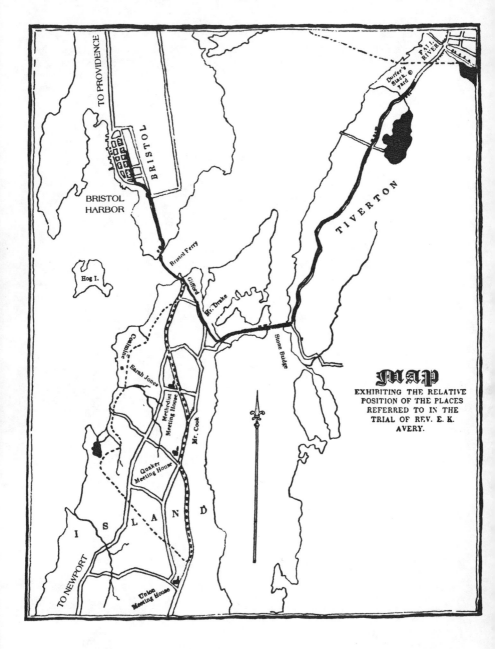

TO PROVIDENCE

BRISTOL

BRISTOL
HARBOR

Hog I.

Bristol Ferry

Gifford

Mr. Drake

TIVERTON

FALL RIVER

Durfee's
Black.
Yard

Coalmine

Sarah Jones

Methodist
Meeting House

Mr. Cook

Quaker
Meeting House

Stone Bridge

TO NEWPORT

ISLAND

Union
Meeting House

MAP

EXHIBITING THE RELATIVE
POSITION OF THE PLACES
REFERRED TO IN THE
TRIAL OF REV. E. K.
AVERY.

Avery's Knot

Mary Cable

G. P. PUTNAM'S SONS
New York

The author wishes to thank the staff of the Providence Athenaeum; the Redwood Library, Newport; the Fall River Historical Society; the New-York Historical Society; and the New York Public Library for their help and interest.

Library of Congress Cataloging in Publication Data

Cable, Mary.
    Avery's knot.

    1. Avery, Ephraim K., d. 1869—Fiction. 2. Cornell, Sarah Maria, 1802–1832—Fiction. I. Title.
PS3553.A27A95   1981   813'.54   81–8672
ISBN O-399-12569-8   AACR2

Printed in the United States of America

Foreword

Much of this story is true. Ephraim K. Avery and Sarah Maria Cornell were real people, and the principal events of their lives occurred very much as I have described them. Where the facts are not known, I have made educated guesses.

Contents

Ye virgins all a warning take.
Remember Avery's knot;
Enough to make your hearts to ache,
Don't let it be forgot.

Rhode Island poet, 1833

Avery's Knot

I

The Walking Stranger

On the blustery, cold afternoon of December 20, 1832, on the Island of Rhode Island, several local citizens noticed a tall stranger, striding along past their farms. In that stony, salt-water country, farm people had so much work to do that they seldom did anything just for pleasure. Certainly not walking. When they walked, it was because they had to get somewhere right away and no horse or horse-and-wagon was available to carry them. For this reason, when they saw anyone on foot they were likely to take note of it, particularly if the person was a stranger.

That day, the sky was scattered with fast-blown clouds that kept rolling over the sun, and whenever they did it was clear that true winter was setting in. The few apples left on bare boughs were black and withered. The orchards had no more to give, and neither did the stone-walled fields, where the cornstalks stood like brittle bones, wearing rags. In the woods, the fallen leaves that had been so prodigally red were faded to ochre and dull brown. Even when the sun shone, its warmth was parsimoniously given. The stranger walked with his collar up and his hat pulled down. He carried his head a little on one side.

William Anthony and his young family lived within sight of the Bristol ferry-landing. William had turned his cows out of the barn to water themselves at the pond, and was sharpening axes,

15

when he saw the stranger, taking a shortcut across a field of corn-stubble.

"There goes somebody in a hurry," William said to himself. Later, he estimated that the time must have been about half-past two.

The stranger was wearing dark clothes. A black surtout, or it could have been a box coat, and a wide-brimmed, black hat. When he came to the bar-way and climbed over it, William saw his height. A tall man. The bars were five feet high, and the man must have been a foot or more taller. After climbing the bars, he headed round the pond, went over a stone wall, and disappeared into a woodlot.

William was sure of the day, he said later, because he had a child down sick. The doctor had come that morning and had left a bill, dated Thursday, December 20.

The Carr boys—Billy and his little brother, Charles—had driven to Fall River market with a wagonload of apples. They had started home to the Island about one o'clock, had crossed over from Tiverton on the Stone Bridge, and had then taken the main road to Portsmouth. About a hundred yards on the Island side of the bridge, they met a man, walking fast. He wore a black, broad-brimmed hat, and he had a handkerchief tied over the lower part of his face—to give protection from the wind, the boys presumed. They greeted him, as country people were wont to do, but he did not answer. Young Charles said to his brother, "*He* is rather proud. He didn't even look 'round."

Billy Carr said afterward that, after all, when you don't meet many people on the road, you like the ones you do meet to be civil, at least. Yes, he added: the stranger was a tall man. That he'd swear to.

Old Peleg Cranstoun lived by the Stone Bridge and was the tollkeeper. By midafternoon that day, he later recalled, eleven people had crossed—most of them in wagons—and he knew ten of them. The one he didn't know must have crossed not far from three o'clock: a tall man, of dark complexion, and dressed in dark clothes. He had his fourpence ready in his hand when he came up to the tollgate.

"A pretty cold day," he said.

" 'Tis," Peleg said. "You're welcome to step inside and warm yourself."

But the stranger shook his head, paid the toll, and walked on over the bridge. Peleg didn't see him again.

After sundown, foot-passengers could avoid the toll by scrambling down on the beach, walking around the tollgate, and then climbing back to the bridge or the road. In the morning, Peleg was in the habit of checking to see how many tracks there were in the sand, so he would know how much he'd been cheated. On the morning of December 21, he found one set of tracks, coming from the bridge and headed toward the Island.

Annis Norton, a young girl of sixteen, lived in a gray-shingled, saltbox house on the mainland side of the bridge. About three o'clock that same afternoon, she was at the kitchen window, watering pots of lemon geraniums, when she saw the walking stranger.

"Who's that, I wonder?" she said to her mother.

Mrs. Norton took her hands out of the bread-dough she was kneading and came to the window.

"Never saw him before," she said. "Wonder what his rush is."

"If he keeps walking at that rate," Annis said, "he'll be in Ohio afore nightfall."

"Some sort of a minister, is what I'd say," Mrs. Norton said.

"I've seen Methodist ministers wearing those big, black hats," said Annis. "More'n likely he's going to preach in Fall River."

"Well, don't let me hear of you listening to Methodists, Annis," said her mother.

"Why not?"

"They have camp-meetings and scream and fall down and act all crazy."

"What do they do that for?"

"I dunno," Mrs. Norton said, returning to her bread-dough. "And they say there's other goings-on, too, at those camp-meetings. You stay away from 'em."

At Robinson's farm, along the road to Fall River, two young farmers named John Durfee and Abner Davis had spent the day blasting rocks. They had their explosives packed in a cart, in bags sewn up with heavy string. About sunset ("Not much difference from sunset," was the way Abner later told it), they set their last charge and were running away from it when they noticed a man they didn't know, sitting on a wall near the cart, some eighty yards away from them. As soon as the man saw them, he started off across the field, holding up the tails of his coat as he walked through the long, withered grass. John and Abner sang out to him to mind the flying rocks. He then stopped in his tracks, and they could tell that he was a man above the common height and kept his head tilted slightly to one side. But he was too far away for them to see his features.

"He can't be from here," Abner said.

"How do you know that?" John asked him.

"If he were, he'd want to know how the rocks broke. He'd be over here, looking at 'em."

Instead, after the rocks had stopped flying, the stranger went away at a rapid pace, heading toward Fall River.

John Durfee, driving home after sunset, saw him again, this time on the Durfees' own farm. The man had paused on a little rise of land from which he could see the whole countryside, with its neat fields and woodlots sloping down to Narragansett Bay. He was staring intently at the Fall River road. As the color drained from the landscape, his clothes looked very black, and John later said that such a tall, black figure gave him a queer feeling. He considered shouting at him to get off the Durfee property, but being hungry for supper, he drove on home instead. When he looked back, the man was no longer to be seen.

At George Lawton's tavern, between the Stone Bridge and Fall River, there had been few customers that day. Late in the afternoon, a clock peddler came in with a friend, and they ate supper. Then came a gentleman, who took his supper alone. He did not linger over it. Margaret Hambley, the barmaid, said that as soon as he had finished he stepped to the barroom door, asked her for a half a tumbler of brandy, and drank it neat. Was he tall? they asked her later. Yes, unusual tall. What did he look like? Oh, well-favored—blue eyes, curling dark hair, clean-shaven. She had not seen him with a hat, but he might have left one in the entry. She was shy and hadn't looked at him full in the face, but she'd had the impression of a very well-favored man.

Soon after the stranger left the tavern, night fell. Candles and a few whale-oil lamps glimmered in farmhouse windows, and in the houses on the outskirts of Fall River. There was no moon, but a few stars were shining through tattered, fast-moving clouds. Nobody who could help it was out-of-doors on such a chilly evening. A woman named Zeruiah Hambley, the barmaid's mother, needed a spool of gray darning thread and ran over to her friend Mrs. Owen's house to borrow one. On the street she overtook a tall man, walking with a woman much shorter. Because it was so dark and she was in a hurry, she hardly glanced at them, but she did happen to notice that the woman was wearing a cloak, and a calash instead of a bonnet. The pair turned down the lane that passed by Mrs. Owen's house. Zeruiah went into the house and stayed to chat a while. Just as she was getting ready to leave, the meetinghouse bell began to ring, and Mrs. Owen set her clock by it, as she was accustomed to do. In winter it always sounded at seven-forty-five. When it stopped ringing, both women became aware of another sound. "A screeching," Zeruiah later called it, as of a woman in distress.

The Owen house was on the very edge of Fall River. Beyond

was Durfee's farm, and it seemed that the cries were coming from that direction. As the women stood and looked at each other with alarm, the cries ceased.

"Must have been a cat," said Mrs. Owen.

One other person, that evening, heard unusual sounds. This was a harness-maker, William Hamilton, whose wife had sent him to buy a loaf of sugar. At the store, he lingered by the stove with three or four acquaintances, reading the *Fall River Monitor* and discussing a speech Governor Haynes had made. Because Fall River was on the border of Massachusetts and Rhode Island, the politics of both states interested people there. Then they talked about what time it was. One man had had his watch regulated three weeks before, and in spite of that it was still gaining. He had set it that evening by the factory whistle at the new mill in Fall River, but William Hamilton was of the opinion that the whistle often went off as much as twenty minutes late. The other men took out their watches and compared them. Finally, they agreed that the right time was seventeen minutes before nine, and Hamilton said good night.

As he walked along the road near Durfee's farm, he heard screams and stifled groans.

"I thought, 'Someone is beating his wife,'" he later said. "I heard the groans off and on for three or four minutes. It crossed my mind to go and see what was going on, but then the noises stopped."

Hamilton thought it was better not to know who in the neighborhood beat his wife. Hastening his steps, he continued homeward with his loaf of sugar.

The evening became more cloudy, and the wind blew sharper. Over on the Island, near the Bristol ferry-landing, an elderly ferryman named Jeremiah Gifford was snoring in his bed when he was abruptly aroused by the sound of knocking. He waited a minute or two, hoping his daughter, Jane, would hear, but (as he remarked later) that girl could sleep through anything. He then went downstairs barefoot, in his nightshirt and nightcap, and peered out the front door. No one. Then he went through the kitchen and into a combination mudroom and sink-room, where there was a pump. Jeremiah, short and frail, was somewhat alarmed to find a tall figure looming over him. Then he recognized him as a man he had seen earlier that day when one of the other ferrymen, William Pearse, had brought him over from Bristol. There had been no other passengers, and Pearse had charged him double—sixteen cents—for the private trip.

"He was bent on coming," Pearse had told Jeremiah, adding that the man's name was Reverend Ephraim Avery, and that since July he had been the Methodist minister in Bristol.

Now, Reverend Avery was washing his hands at Jeremiah's pump.

"How soon can you dress?" he asked. "I must go over to Bristol right away."

The wind was roaring over the Bay and stirring up whitecaps. Waves breaking on the rocks beside the ferryslip sounded like the ocean.

"No, sir, this weather is too cussed," Jeremiah said. Although he was frail, he was stubborn, and nobody told him what to do. He looked critically at the minister.

"It ain't no time of the year to be on foot."

"I've been up-Island on business," Avery said. "My wife is unwell and I need to get home immediately."

"Well, you won't go tonight," Jeremiah told him. "It's too tedious out there and it's way too late."

"Not so late as you think for," Avery said.

"It's more'n half-past nine, and I ain't going to take you," Jeremiah said. "You can sleep here and we'll go over in the morning."

He gave the minister a candle and showed him to the spare room.

Before dawn, Avery was up and pacing the kitchen. The ferryman's pretty daughter, Jane, came down yawning, and baked him some johnnycake at the hearth fire. She asked how come he was making such a long foot-journey in such cold weather, and he said he had had business with Brother Cook, the Methodist minister in Portsmouth.

Jane, a pert and lively girl, liked knowing what did not concern her. She noticed that Avery kept one hand wrapped in a bandanna, and asked what was the matter with it.

"A dog bit me."

"Brother Cook's dog?"

"No."

"Did you stay for supper with the Cooks?" she asked.

"You ask very idle questions," Mr. Avery said in an intimidating tone. He put on his surtout and hat and went down to the wharf. The wind had quieted and the tide was right. Gifford put aboard the two horses that provided power for the paddlewheel, and the little ferry thrashed its way over to the Bristol landing in less than an hour.

During the crossing, Gifford, who was nearly as inquisitive as his daughter, said to his passenger, "Was there a Methodist meeting last evening down Portsmouth way? I didn't hear of one."

"There was not," Avery replied. "I went up-Island on business of my own."

"My Jane, she's a Methodist."

"You surprise me," Avery said curtly.

"Yesterday was a cold day," Jeremiah observed. "And you had a far walk."

"I am fond of a good ramble," Avery said. "There is nothing like a good ramble in cold weather."

"Is that right," Jeremiah said. "Well, now, my father always told me, 'Jeremiah, never walk when you can ride, never stand when you can sit, never sit when you can lie.' I cal'late that's why I'm a ferryman." And he laughed wheezily.

Mr. Avery did not appear to be in a mood for humor, and the rest of the trip passed in silence. The sun came up and cast a frigid light on the gray waves and on the gray, rocky shores of Narragansett Bay.

* * *

Over near Fall River that morning, the farms were under a heavy frost. The stubbled fields, the long brown grass, and, in the woodlots, the bare trees, were sheathed in ice crystals, which, as the sun rose, turned to diamond. John Durfee, who lived at the Durfee homestead with his wife, four young children, his elder brother, William, and his widower father, rose earlier than the rest, hitched the team, and set off to meet Abner Davis for another day of rock-blasting. He found he needed his cap well over his ears, even though yesterday's wind had mostly died down. He and his horses puffed white breath into the fresh dawn air.

The dirt track led past a large haystack, which had a fence around it to protect the hay from animals. John thought how strange the stack looked, blinding bright and glittering with frost. He had heard an old sailor describe igloos he had seen in the north while seal-hunting, and wondered if the ice-encrusted haystack looked like one.

The sparkling of the frosty stack at first prevented John from seeing anything else. Probably the horses saw first; John felt a change in the way they were walking, a tensing of the reins.

Then he saw. He felt a sharp chill grip his body, deeper and colder than any winter weather could produce. The newly risen sun was showing him a terrifying sight. It was the body of a woman, hanging from a stake in front of the haystack, and moving slightly whenever the wind blew.

His heart thudding, John Durfee climbed down from his wagon and looked closer. The woman's hair was in wild disorder and hung over her face, so that he could not see whether he knew her. He guessed she was not old, for her hair was thick and black. On her head she wore a calash, pushed awry, and she had on a cloak, fastened except for one or two hooks. She was not very tall, for the stake was not much over five feet high; and her legs were bent so that the knees nearly touched the ground and the toes just did touch it. Her skirt was tucked back beneath her legs in an incongruously fastidious way. Beside her on the ground were a pair of shoes, carefully placed side by side, and a crumpled handkerchief.

Something about the neat skirt and the meticulous arrangement
of shoes that would never again be needed intensified the chill
inside John Durfee, so that he had difficulty in breathing. He
walked up to the body, and, with a trembling hand, raised the
hair from the face. Open eyes stared at him, unseeing. The brow
was fixed in a frown, and the tongue protruded slightly between
swollen lips. Nevertheless, John could see that this had been a
pretty girl; but one he did not know and never would.

Close to panic, John ran back to his wagon, turned the team
around, and drove as fast as he could to spread the news and find
Elihu Hicks, the coroner.

It was the middle of the morning before Elihu Hicks arrived at
the stackyard, accompanied by five men for a coroner's jury.
Hicks lived only a half-mile away, but he was very old—over
eighty—and doddering. It took him several minutes just to climb
down from his wagon and totter into the stackyard, where he
contemplated the body.

"Ain't had a suicide since way back," he said, shaking his
head.

"What makes you say it was a suicide?" John Durfee
asked.

Hicks looked at him scornfully. "I been a coroner going on
fifty years," he said. "But 'tain't for me to say. We'll have to ask
the jury and the doctor. Cut her down."

The other Durfee men and several neighbors, who had con-
verged on the stackyard out of curiosity, now approached the
body and discussed how to take it down.

"She tied a good knot," John's older brother, William, said.
The cord was a narrow one, almost like string; it went twice
around the girl's neck and was so tight that it was embedded in
the flesh. Someone produced a pocketknife and cut the cord from
the stake. Then they laid the body on the trampled grass. It had
to be laid on its side, because the legs had stiffened in a bent
position.

They all could see that beneath the fastenings of the cloak, one arm was at her side and the other was raised, the gloved hand at chest-level and palm out, in a warding-off gesture.

"Anybody know her?" Hicks asked.

No one did.

"She must be from one of the mills in Fall River," one of the men said. "Them gals come from all over."

"Reckon she was more of a sailor than a weaver," William Durfee said. "That knot's a sailor's knot. They call it a clove-hitch."

"Put her in the wagon, boys," Hicks directed. "Take her up to Durfee's. Dr. Wilbur will be along soon, I cal'late."

Dr. Wilbur was Fall River's most respected physician, an old Quaker. He arrived at the Durfee farmhouse in his shay. Not far behind, in a wagon, came three old women, sisters-in-law, all named Borden and all widows. Hicks always sent for them when a body needed laying out and there was no family to do it.

"We don't need nobody here right now excepting the jury, the Borden ladies, and the doctor," Hicks said irritably. "Women and children, go visitin'. And all you fellows, ain't you got work to do?"

In the house, the body was laid on the best-bedroom bed, and the five men selected for jury duty stood sheepishly in one corner. Ruth Borden stepped forward and began to unbutton the young woman's dress; signs of embarrassment among the jury.

"What do you have to do, Dr. Wilbur?" one of them asked nervously.

"I'll do what has to be done, so that we get justice," Dr. Wilbur said. "And as for thee, thee must do thy duty." He lifted the hair away from the face of the corpse. "As I thought," he said. "I know this girl. She was my patient."

Hicks had pen, ink, and paper ready for writing his official report.

"Write this down, Elihu," said the doctor. "The body is that of Sarah Maria Cornell, a mill-girl, lately of Fall River. Twenty-nine years old, five feet one, weight probably about one hundred and fifteen pounds."

"Wait up," Hicks said, dropping the quill pen. "What's the girl's name?"

"I see this will take a while," Dr. Wilbur said. "While we're busy here, why don't somebody go and see to her belongings? I know she boarded with Mrs. Hathaway."

"She'd probably like to be buried in her Sunday-best dress," Ruth Borden put in.

John's father, Richard Durfee, who was one of the jury, went to the kitchen and suggested that John should go. He was glad to get away and do something, in order to stop thinking so hard about that lonely death, almost within the lamplight of his house. He and his family had heard nothing, but that was not strange, because there was always a good deal of noise in the house, and anyway the stackyard was on the parlor side. The Durfees never used their parlor, unless there was a funeral. They would be using it tomorrow.

Mrs. Hathaway, a motherly widow with a daughter, Lucy, who worked in the weaving mill, had heard what had happened before John Durfee reached her house. She came to the door with tears running down her face.

"You came for her things? She didn't have much, the poor little creature. They're saying she did it herself, but I don't believe any such a thing."

"The coroner's jury is deciding that now, I guess," John said.

"I just don't believe she was the sort to kill herself. A plucky girl she was. Always pleasant, even when you could see she didn't feel cheerful. Yesterday, she was in good spirits. Said she was going to Durfee's."

"I'm John Durfee," John said, "and I didn't know her. None of us Durfees knew her."

"Well, that's queer," Mrs. Hathaway said. "She surely told us she was going to Durfee's farm. Says she, I don't care if it storms all winter, so long as it don't storm today. Might not be back till after nine, says she, and I shouldn't sit up waiting for her."

John thought, if only she had really come to Durfee's house, knocking at their door, she would not be dead now.

"Here are her things," Mrs. Hathaway said, pointing to a very small trunk. "And here's her bandbox, where she kept her bonnet. Like I told you, she never had much, but what she had was neat and tidy."

"Is there anything of value?"

"No, indeed, she never had jewelry or such things. She was a Methodist. They are very plain, you know."

Mrs. Hathaway opened the bandbox and removed a bonnet, a knitted shawl, and some unfinished crochet-work: a sacque for a baby. At the bottom of the box was a scrap of paper with writing on it in pencil. This Mrs. Hathaway held up and read:

> If I should be missing, inquire of the Reverend
> Mr. Avery. He will know where I am gone.
> S. M. C.

"Why would she think she would be missing?" John asked.

"She never talked anything about herself," Mrs. Hathaway said. "And she never mentioned any Reverend Mr. Avery. Maybe he's a Methodist preacher."

Sarah's little trunk was locked.

"She always carried the key," Mrs. Hathaway said. "Did they look in her wallet?"

"I didn't hear about any wallet," John said. "I don't think she had one."

"Oh, she always had her wallet. If she didn't have it, it must have been stole." Mrs. Hathaway's face lit up with a new idea. "Maybe she was robbed and the robber killed her."

John thought about it and shook his head. "Nobody's going to murder a poor mill-girl for what she'd have in her wallet. Coroner Hicks thinks it was suicide."

"Never," Mrs. Hathaway said. "Not Sarah Maria."

* * *

By the time John got home again with the bandbox and the
locked trunk, the doctor and the jurymen had left and the old
women were in the bedroom, laying out the body. John's father
had been one of the jury. He was taking the day's ordeal hard
and was now soothing his feelings by the kitchen fire with a mug
of hot buttered rum.

" 'Twaren't a pretty business, I can tell you, son," he said.
"Dr. Wilbur, he wanted to cut her open, but we wouldn't let
him."

"Cut her? What for?"

"Why, to take out the baby. Fetus, they call it. The girl was in
a *certain situation*, son, you see. Looks like that was why she did
away with herself."

John poured himself a couple of ounces of rum and noticed
that his hand was shaking. "Is that what she did?"

"That's what the jury says."

John swallowed straight rum. He said, "I don't see why he'd
have to cut her."

"And that's not all he wanted to do. The ladies put a napkin
over her *parts*, and he wanted to take it off. We jurymen, we
didn't want him to. 'Twaren't decent. So he left it alone."

John, setting his mug down hard, went to the best-bedroom
door and asked the Borden ladies if they'd found a wallet or key.
One of them handed out a key, which had been in the girl's pocket. No wallet had turned up.

The key opened the trunk, which John had carried into the
kitchen. Inside were a few clothes, a Bible, and a druggist's bottle—full—labeled "Oil of Tansy." There were also three letters,
all of them open.

"You'd better read them," Richard Durfee said. "It's legal, I
reckon. I'm a juryman."

"I don't feel right about it," John said.

"I don't feel right about this whole business," Richard said,
and poured himself another hot rum. "But somebody's got to

read those letters They might say something we need to know, like, if she wanted to kill herself. Or if somebody wanted to kill her."

John at once sat down by the fire, the letters in his hands. One was on pink paper; one on straw-colored; and one on white. The earliest postmark was on the buff one. It had been mailed in Warren, Rhode Island, on November 13, 1832. The handwriting was slapdash, with periods that looked like dashes, and elongated crossings of the *T*s. It read:

Miss Cornell:

I have just received your letter with no small surprise, and will say in reply, I will do as you ask, only keep your secret. I wish you to write me as soon as you get this, naming some time and place where I shall see you, and then look for an answer before I come. And I will say whether convenient or not and I will say the time. I will keep your letter till I see you and wish you to keep mine, and have them at the time. Write soon: Say nothing to anyone.

Yours in haste.

The second letter, on pink paper, was dated November 29, 1832, at Providence, Rhode Island, and it was much longer:

Dear Sister,

I received your letter in due time, and should have answered it before now, but thought I would wait till opportunity. As I told you I am willing to help you, and do for you. As circumstances are, I should rather you would come to this place, *viz.*, Bristol, in the stage, the 18th of December, and then stop at the hotel, and stay till six in the evening, and then go directly across the Main street, to a brick building near the stone meetinghouse, where I will meet you and talk with you.

When you stop at the tavern, either inquire for work, or

go out in pretence of looking for some. Say nothing about me
or my family. Should it storm on the night of the 18th, come
on the 20th. If you cannot come, you might meet me at the
Methodist meetinghouse in Somerset, just over the ferry.
Or, if you cannot do either, I will come to Fall River one of
the above evenings, back of the same meetinghouse where I
once saw you, at any hour you say, when there will be the
least passing; I should think before the mill stops work.

I will come if it does not storm very hard. If it does the
first, I will come the second. Write me soon and direct your
letters to Miss Betsey Hills, Bristol. Remember this. Your
last letter I am afraid was broken open. Wear your calash,
and not your plain bonnet.

Yours, etc.

The third letter, on a half-piece of white paper, was dated
December 8, 1832, Fall River, and was very brief:

I will be here on the 20th, if pleasant, at the place named,
at six o'clock; if not pleasant, the Monday evening. Say
nothing.

John Durfee read the letters aloud. It took him quite a while.
When he had finished, he and his father sat in silence, trying to
piece together the meager scraps of information. Presently, Mrs.
Meribah Borden came out of the best-bedroom. She was the
oldest of the sisters-in-law, and was in her late seventies.

"You juryboys," she said to Richard Durfee. "You said she
done away with herself. 'Tain't so."

"Why not?" Richard Durfee demanded.

"Because rash violence was done that girl. Bruises, very cruel
bruises. Her life was bruised right out of her."

"It's all been decided," Richard said crossly. "Juries don't
change their minds. Anyhow, it's clear enough. She did away
with herself because of her *situation*. She was a bad 'un. That's
the simple fact of it."

Next day, they had the funeral. John and Richard Durfee dug a grave in the Durfee burying-ground, down by the Bay shore, and William made the coffin. It wasn't their responsibility, of course; but Richard said that since the Lord had allowed the death to take place on their property, He would want them to take care of the rest of it.

The ground was not hard-frozen yet, and the earth was black and rich; better for planting than for burying, John thought.

When Sarah was laid out in her coffin, he went to look at her. The old women had done their work with care. The girl's hair was tidy at last, lying in curls around her marble face. The Bordens had not been able to smooth away the frown, but in spite of it, John was aware of her good looks: a short, straight nose, full lips, a strong chin. She was small and delicately made, and she seemed much younger than twenty-nine. A frill had been added to the high collar of her Sabbath dress, hiding the ugly marks on her neck. And the women had closed her eyes. The long lashes lay dark on her cheeks.

John turned away, reminding himself that she must have been a bad one.

News of the death and of the letters found in the trunk had spread fast, and nearly two hundred people, about half of them mill-girls, came out from Fall River to the funeral. The only people who had known Sarah were Mrs. Hathaway and her daughter, Lucy, Dr. Wilbur, and a few girls from the mill. Mr. Bidwell, the Methodist minister, declined to officiate, or even attend, saying that the girl had not been chaste and had he known it he would have expelled her from the Fall River Meeting.

The Congregationalist minister from Tiverton said a few prayers, and after John and his brother, William, had shoveled the earth on the coffin, everyone stood about awkwardly. It was not the sort of funeral they were used to, the comforting kind where family and neighbors of the deceased gathered in the parlor to shed tears and reminisce, eat funeral meats, and drink rum.

As the gathering slowly dispersed, someone asked Dr. Wilbur

what he thought had happened. The old Quaker maintained a pensive silence, and finally said that he didn't think it was for him to say, since the law had taken its course. But as he stepped into his shay and clucked to his sorrel mare, he apparently could not resist speaking out. His voice was low, but John Durfee and a few others who were close by heard him.

He said, "I am as certain she was murdered as I am of my own existence."

"But who? Who did it?" John asked.

Paraphrasing the note found in the bandbox, Dr. Wilbur replied, "Inquire of the Reverend Mr. Avery."

He shook the reins and the mare carried him away, toward Fall River.

II

Bristol

At about the same moment that John Durfee was making his discovery in the stackyard, the Reverend Ephraim K. Avery disembarked from the horse-ferry at Bristol landing. The landing was more than a mile from the town, and as he walked along the road, several people recognized him and took note that he had a bandanna wrapped around one hand. When he arrived at the house on Wardwell Street where he and his family boarded, his wife, Sophia, immediately demanded to care for the wound, but he refused to let her look at it.

"I have told you before, do not fuss at me," he said, pushing her away.

"Oh, Mr. Avery, I have been so worried," Sophia said. "You did not say you meant to be away all night. You know you are not supposed to worry me in my condition. It is worry that makes women miscarry."

"You are as strong as any ox when you want to be," her husband said.

"But where were you? Where did you go?"

"I went up-Island on business," he said. "And now I am very tired. I walked as far as the coal mine and back. Leave me alone and keep the children quiet."

He went upstairs to his study.

Sophia Avery was well-accustomed to her husband's moods

33

and tempers, and most of the time she was resigned to them. Her mother had told her that putting up with a husband's unreasonableness was a natural part of a wife's duties, and that she ought to underline, in her Bible, "A soft answer turneth away wrath." Sophia had done that, and she also frequently reminded herself how proud she was to be the wife of this handsome man who preached so strikingly. She exulted when she saw the adoring expressions on women's faces, gazing up at him in church. She herself had been one of his adorers ten years ago, when she was seventeen; and he had put out his hand, as it were, and raised her to his level. She and only she had achieved his love and the privilege of being his consort.

Now they had three children and a fourth six weeks from being born. In addition, there had been one stillbirth and several miscarriages. From a graceful, sweet-faced young girl, Sophia had changed into a drab woman with a martyred air. Childbearing had deprived her of several teeth, leaving gaps in her wistful smile. Her brown hair was thin and lackluster. They had moved seven times, from one New England village to another, all mill-villages or ports: East Greenwich, Duxbury, Scituate, Eastham, Lynn, Saugus, Lowell, and now Bristol. The Methodist Church always rented them quarters in someone's large house, and they never had a home of their own. The trouble with mill-towns and ports was that they always had more women than men, and from the point of view of a wife with a handsome husband, this could be a source of anxiety. "Thank Heaven he is a Man of God," Sophia often thought. Ephraim was particularly eloquent in denouncing carnality.

Although he sometimes slapped, pushed, or cuffed her, he never blackened her eyes or broke any of her bones, as some husbands she knew of did. He beat the children regularly, but so did most fathers, believing with the Bible that it was a parental obligation. Sophia dared not disagree with such high authority, even though she wept to see the cut and bruised bottoms and frightened faces of her children. But when Ephraim was affectionate or lustful toward her, Sophia's heart lifted with happiness and with the excitement of anticipated caresses. She was in love with him.

The Averys had come to Bristol the summer before, following two years in Lowell, Massachusetts. Two years was longer than the Church usually allowed ministers to remain in one place, for they were not supposed to become attached to any place or possession here on earth. Those who were unmarried went about as circuit riders, constantly traveling from town to town. Only married ministers were "located." In Bristol, the family lived in part of a large, old house owned by a Mrs. Rebecca Dimond, who lived there also. The Averys had the ground floor, plus a second-story front room for Ephraim's study, and a garret, under the eaves, for Sophia's unmarried, forty-year-old niece, Betsey Hills. Betsey, daughter of a much-older brother of Sophia's, was crippled and walked with two canes. She spent her life helping various relations with chores and childcare. This year, she had passed September and October with the Averys and had then been boosted into the stage for East Hartford, where she would help one of Sophia's sisters with sorting apples and pressing cider, molding candles, mending the featherbeds, and baking Thanksgiving pies. She would return to the Averys in January, in time to assist at the lying-in. Her absence gave Sophia more housework, but Betsey was so dreary and querulous that Sophia did not miss her. Sometimes, when Ephraim was particularly moody, Sophia would retreat to Betsey's garret and enjoy the luxury of tears, unthreatened by her husband's truculent, "What are you crying about? *I'll* give you something to cry about."

The morning of December 21 wore on, dinnertime came and went, and there was not a sound from Ephraim's closed study. Sophia guessed that her husband had fallen asleep, and sent Edwin, Catherine, and Maria to play very quietly in the yard. Glancing out of the window about three o'clock, it struck her that there was an unusual number of people in the street; not enough to call a crowd, but perhaps a dozen. As she watched, she saw that they were not passing to and fro but standing in front of the house. Presently, five-year-old Edwin came in, saying that some gentlemen were asking where his father was and when he was going to show himself.

"Show himself? Why should he show himself?" Sophia asked.

"Because they want to ask him some questions," Edwin replied.

Sophia began to sense trouble. Ephraim's absence all night, his aroused temper, and now these strangers, both men and women, gathering before the house and staring up at the windows. All these things were, perhaps, connected.

"Call your sisters," Sophia said. And when the children were inside, she bolted the doors.

Soon after that, a sudden sleet storm drove the bystanders from the street. Ephraim came downstairs and ate the pork and turnips she had kept on the fire for him.

"What time would you like to start for Mrs. Gladding's?" Sophia asked.

"Damnation," said the minister. "I'd forgotten about that."

"She wanted us yesterday," Sophia said. "I'd have preferred to go yesterday, but, no, you said Thursday wouldn't suit you, it had to be Friday. So now, Mr. Avery, it's Friday."

"Then, of course, we'll go." Ephraim glanced out of the window and saw that the sleet was coming down hard.

"We'll go now," he said.

"But, Mr. Avery, she don't want us so soon. And, besides, why not wait for the storm to let up?"

"We are going *now*," he said, his voice rising. "Why must I always be contradicted?"

When the family arrived at the home of Mrs. Nancy Gladding—she was an elderly Methodist who lived several streets away—they were considerably wet, and much time was spent in drying shoes and cloaks before the fire. Three young and comely women of the Methodist flock were there as well, and Ephraim forgot his ill temper and became charming. He inquired for their health and spiritual welfare, and listened as if fascinated to their detailed replies. He told of a long ramble he had taken the day before on the Island of Rhode Island. He had visited, he said, a coalmine near Portsmouth, to find out if coal were any cheaper there than in Bristol. And he had gone to a place called King Philip's Chair, an interesting rock formation overlooking the Bay. His father had been an officer stationed on Rhode Island during the Revolution, and had often spoken to Ephraim of this pretty place. Ephraim had always longed to see it for himself, and now, at last, he had done so.

While he talked, he held one hand—the wounded one—inside his waistcoat. This gave him a Napoleonic air, and also hid the bandanna, so that the ladies did not exclaim and commiserate. The family remained until after dark, enjoying Mrs. Gladding's sponge cake and damson preserves. Before they left, Ephraim led them all in prayer.

That night, in their small and uncomfortable bed (too short for a man of Ephraim's height, so that he always slept with his knees intruding on his wife's narrow space), Ephraim suddenly embraced Sophia and rolled over on top of her distended belly. Pleased but frightened, Sophia reminded him that she was prone to miscarry, and that the doctor had warned against what he had called "indulgences" at this time. Ephraim stopped her mouth with kisses, which she loved, and was in and out of her in a couple of minutes. Then he began to cry.

Sophia was amazed. She had never known him to cry before. She held him like a child, and he responded like one, resting his head on her bosom, not as a lover but as a small boy. She was still sexually aroused—for he never troubled to satisfy her—and she pressed his rough, dark head against her swollen breasts.

"You are a good little woman, Sophia," he said in a broken whisper. "Pure and good. You are an angel."

Such words were what she lived for. "I love you, Ephraim," she said. In the darkness and privacy of their bed, she used his Christian name.

"Sophia," he said, "if people say ill of me, you must promise me you will not believe them."

"Ill of *you?* Of course not."

"You know I am incapable of evil."

"Absolutely incapable." Inwardly, Sophia hoped the Lord would overlook what she was saying, because she was quite aware that Ephraim could be evil. She had experienced it. But she was made happy now by his weakened state and his mood of dependency, and she forgave him.

"You are perfect, Ephraim," she said, taking his hand and passionately kissing it.

"I have so many hardships," he said pitifully.

"Yes, my dear. Too many."

"My life is very hard."

"You are right."

After that, he fell asleep in her arms. Not to disturb him, she lay in an awkward position, with not enough covers on her shoulders, until, at last, he turned about and left her yearning body alone.

All day Saturday, there were more and more people gathering on Wardwell Street. Ephraim forbade his wife and children to go outside, and he himself kept to his study, with the blinds closed. Sophia dared not question him. His soft mood of last night had disappeared and he was once more bad-tempered and aloof.

Late in the day, he sent Edwin out through the back alley to run to the stage-stop and summon Stephen Blodgett, a fellow-Methodist and crony, who was a driver for the Fall River Stage-coach Line. Blodgett came and the two men spent half an hour in private conversation. Meantime, Sophia could hear shouted comments in the street, and make out part of them.

"Come out, Avery!"

"Tell us about the girl."

"Where were you on Thursday, Avery? Where did you go?"

And, for the first time, Sophia heard the word:

"Murderer!"

When her husband emerged from the study with Brother

Blodgett, Sophia cried, "What is it? What is happening, Mr. Avery?"

"Brother Blodgett has brought grievous news," Ephraim said. "A Fall River mill-girl has hanged herself, and certain anti-Methodists and anti-Masons of that town are looking for a scape-goat. Alas, alas, they have settled on *me*. They are accusing me of killing her!"

The child within Sophia gave a sharp motion, and Sophia clasped her hands tightly around her belly.

"Who was the girl?" she asked faintly.

"A wicked girl, and, as it happens, Sophia, we knew her in Lowell," Avery said. "You will perhaps remember her, because I was obliged to expel her from our Meeting."

Sophia found a chair and sat down, feeling faint. Several girls had been expelled from the Lowell Meeting, but without hesitation she said, "Sarah Cornell."

"I believe that was her name. Is that not correct, Brother Blodgett?"

"Sarah Maria Cornell. Apparently, an individual of extremely bad character," Blodgett said. "Brother Bidwell says he heard . . ." he glanced diffidently at Sophia . . . "heard she was afflicted with a foul disease. Pray, excuse me, Mrs. Avery."

"It sounds as if she was a common prostitute," Avery said.

"I must be getting back to my stage," Blodgett said. "I will bring you news from Fall River."

He went out through the alley, to avoid the crowd, but now there were people there, too, who clustered around him and wanted to know when Avery would come out.

Before dawn on Sunday morning, the Reverend Mr. Bidwell arrived on horseback from Fall River. He had ridden all night to say that because of the hue and cry that was rising in Fall River, Avery would be wise not to preach that day, but to stay at home. Bidwell had sent to ask advice from the Church elders in Boston. He added that a public meeting had been held on Saturday evening, resulting in an overwhelming vote to demand both an arrest

warrant for Ephraim K. Avery and an autopsy on the body of
Sarah Cornell. The body was to be disinterred on Monday under
the auspices of Dr. Wilber.

All Fall River, it appeared, now knew the contents of the three
letters found in the girl's trunk. Furthermore, the old women
who had laid out the body had been telling everyone that there
were bruises on the girl's private parts and her knees and thighs
were grass-stained and cut. A comb had been found, broken, in a
field near the haystack—a high, tortoise-shell comb, such as the
mill-girls usually wore to fasten their hair. People who had seen
a tall, ministerial stranger on Thursday afternoon were coming
forward, and two farmers who had been blasting stone that day
had found string missing from their sacks of explosives—string of
the same type as that used in the clove-hitch knot around Sarah's
neck.

Christmas Eve and Christmas Day were traditionally ignored
by Yankee Puritans, and shops remained open. However, not
much business was done in either Fall River or Bristol on December 25, 1832, because about a hundred Fall River citizens
traveled by ferry to Bristol harbor, and marched to the house on
Wardwell Street.

Sophia closed all the blinds and sat in the kitchen with the
terrified and weeping children. Ephraim kept to his study, occasionally lifting his voice in loud psalm-reading.

"Judge me, O God, and plead my cause against an ungodly
nation," she heard him say. "O deliver me from the deceitful and
unjust. . . . Why go I mourning because of the oppression of
the enemy?"

In the midst of all this, two Methodist ministers, elders of the
Church, arrived by private carriage from Boston, elbowed their
way through the throng, and embraced their beleaguered colleague. The two were Abraham and Joseph Merrill, and they
were brothers—in the flesh as well as in the spirit. Reverend
Joseph cheerfully reminded Ephraim of a passage in the New
Testament, in which a band of Jews conspire to kill Paul.

"What an amazingly similar situation to your own, Brother
Avery!" he said, and proceeded to quote: "And there were more

than forty which had made this conspiracy. And they came to the chief priests and elders, and said, 'We have bound ourselves under a great curse, that we will eat nothing until we have slain Paul.' "

Ephraim smiled wanly, as he heard one or two voices outside, persistently calling out, "Let's go in and get him!" But not long thereafter, the urgent tooting of the ferry-whistle, warning that the steam was up and the ferry about to return to Fall River, suddenly caused the street to empty.

Sophia, still huddled in the kitchen, was delighted at the effect of the ferry-whistle, but it did not put a stop to the dismayed thoughts that were tumbling through her head. She remembered Sarah Maria Cornell, whom she had considered pert and forward. In the Lowell Methodist prayer-meetings, or Love Feasts, as they were officially known, Sarah had once stood up and "exhorted," just like a man. Women were permitted to exhort on such occasions; the privilege was one of the Methodists' best drawing-cards among the mill-girls. And people said that Sarah Maria did it well. But Sophia had thought this girl tossed her curls about and gestured with her pretty little hands more like an actress than a pious Methodist.

Another thing that troubled Sophia was that, sometime in November, a letter had come for Ephraim from Fall River, addressed in a suspiciously feminine-looking hand. Sophia had been so curious about it that she had steamed it open. It had not said much—simply that the writer urgently required to see Ephraim and suggested several times and places. Sophia had regretted the trouble she had gone to and had felt guilty about it; especially since the steam had left stains on the paper. But now, looking back on it, she remembered the signature: "S.M.C."

After an hour's lull, which, in the wake of so much commotion, seemed almost unnatural, the Reverend Bidwell reappeared and with him came two lawyers: a Mr. Bullock, of Bristol, and a young man from Newport, Mr. David Randolph.

"I can't afford lawyers," Ephraim exclaimed impatiently, when these visitors were introduced to him.

"Don't fret, Brother. The Church will provide," Brother

Abraham Merrill assured him. "Mr. Randolph is an experienced trial lawyer."

"No more trials, surely!" Ephraim exclaimed. "Of course I am as innocent now as I was innocent before, but what a cross for my beloved Church to bear!"

"We are not going to mention those other trials," said Joseph Merrill. "Mr. Randolph tells me that there is no reason for you to mention them. After all, they were trivial. Slander is hardly as serious as murder."

Sophia, who had come into the study with a tray of tea for the visitors, overheard all this. She agreed, silently, that of course slander was not as serious as murder, but she would not have called it trivial. The trials the gentlemen were referring to had certainly caused great distress. In the first instance, Ephraim had verbally attacked a fellow clergyman from the pulpit; had lost his temper and said things that were clearly slanderous. The clergyman brought suit in civil court, and was awarded $190 and court costs—a sum the Avery family could ill afford. Ephraim had promised Sophia then to govern his temper, but a year later he flew into a rage with a maiden-lady parishioner in Scituate, and insisted that she be tried before the Church for lying and cheating. The woman had many friends and a reputation for piety and charity. Nothing could be proved against her, and the only result of the trial was that Ephraim looked foolish.

"I will endeavor," said Mr. Randolph, "to keep all mention of the defendant's previous legal involvements out of the court proceedings."

"Defendant? Court proceedings?" Ephraim stared gloomily at Randolph. "Will it come to that?"

Mr. Bullock explained that at a second public meeting in Fall River, the people had voted to request Bristol authorities to summon Ephraim for examination.

"It is purely voluntary, and you need not agree to it," Mr. Randolph added.

Avery frowned and turned to the Merrills.

"Indeed, I will not agree to it," he said. "Surely, that would be highly undignified and quite unbecoming to a clergyman."

"Brother, I would strongly advise you to attend," said Reverend Joseph Merrill. "You have nothing to hide and it will clear the air. Right now, there is such a stir, and I do believe it is all caused by anti-Methodists. There is always much prejudice against us, and also against Masons. You happen to be both."

"God help me if the judges are neither."

"God *has* helped you, Brother Ephraim," Reverend Joseph said, with a gentle smile. "Mr. Howe and Mr. Haile, the justices of the peace who will adjudicate your hearing, are both Masons, and Mr. Haile is a recent convert to Methodism."

"The Lord's hand is in this," Brother Bidwell said. "Put your mind at ease."

"And now, sir," said Mr. Randolph, "we have no time to lose. We must prepare your statement."

"Statement?"

"Yes, Mr. Avery, you will open the hearing with a full, honest, and open statement of the facts."

"And eloquent," added Bidwell. "Eloquence, as I am sure you know, Brothers, is our Brother's greatest gift."

Early on the morning of December 27, in spite of a cold sea-fog, the streets of the town were crowded with people walking, driving, and riding in the direction of the courthouse. Many had come from Fall River, spending the night with friends or putting up at the hotel. Bristol had been seriously joggled out of its customary placid engrossment with fishing and shipping; only during Fourth of July parades had it ever seen so much excitement.

There were not many women in the crowd, because details of murder and illegitimate pregnancy did not interest (or were not supposed to interest) female minds. Mr. George Howe and Mr. Elihu Haile, the two magistrates, had forbidden their own wives and families to attend and had urged their friends to do the same. Avery himself had barred Sophia. But men who had daughters in the factories were out in force, and so were any workingmen who

could take a day off. Sailors, stablemen, fishermen, and farm-
hands crowded the courthouse steps, waiting to get in. A news-
paperman from Boston asked one of them why he was there.

"Just want to know if he's guilty. Find out what they're really
like."

"They? You mean ministers?"

"All I want to know is, do they practice what they preach," the
man said. "Or are they just like other folks. Maybe worse."

"You don't like ministers?"

"Who said that?" the man said.

The others laughed, and one of them called out, "Oh, we love
'em. Especially Methodists."

Ephraim sat beside his two lawyers. Opposite them was Mr.
Staples, of the attorney general's office, to present the government's evidence. There was no jury, the two presiding magistrates being responsible for rendering a verdict. Although Avery
was not under arrest and was not being tried, but only "examined," the atmosphere in the courtroom seemed as tense and
highly charged as if it had been a trial for murder.

After the court was called to order, Ephraim arose and read his
statement. He wore the same black surtout he had worn on December twentieth, and he also had on spectacles, which made him
look older and less handsome, but more imposing, than he usually looked.

"My first acquaintance with, and knowledge of, the deceased
was in July, 1830," he began. His delivery was measured and
solemn. He seemed to be holding himself under a tight rein, and
people who knew his preaching missed his usual eloquence. "I
then resided in Lowell, Massachusetts. At this time, she called at
my house and wished for employment in my family. Mrs. Avery
not being pleased with her appearance, she was not employed. In
August, she again came to my house and stated she was going to a
camp-meeting and requested a certificate of regular standing in
the Methodist Church. Having previously heard her accused of
profanity, I hesitated to give one, but consented to give it condi-

tionally—if I heard a good report of her conduct. Some weeks later, the overseer of one of the Appleton factories, where she worked, came to see me and stated that this girl's character was very bad, and that, from her own confession, she had been guilty of illicit intercourse with two or more."

Ephraim paused, with an expression of disgust on his face, as if he had just detected a bad smell. Many in the courtroom mirrored this look, especially the many Methodists present.

He went on. "One or two days after this, she herself came to converse with me on the subject. She confessed she had done wrong, and had been a bad girl. She said she had had unlawful connection with a certain man, but with him only. I told her there must be a trial in the usual way, and advised her to go immediately to her friends. I told her that as the subject was of a delicate nature, she had better be with her friends at the time of her trial than in Lowell; that if she was dissatisfied with it, she could have an appeal to the quarterly conference. At the time, I asked for the certificate I gave her. She said she had lost it. She finally consented to go to her friends, agreeable to my advice, and immediately left town.

"Previous to her trial, a physician in Lowell asked me if one Sarah Maria Cornell was a member of our church. I told him there had been, but she was not then in town. He said he felt it his duty to inform me of the character of this girl—that she had applied for his professional assistance for a *foul disease*; that her case was as aggravated as any he had ever known; that she could not sit or stand still, and walked with difficulty."

Ephraim's speech was here interrupted by exclamations and murmurs of shock from many of the spectators, and a call for order from Mr. Howe. Ephraim was accustomed to sizing up the effects of his speeches as he went along, and now, the look of repulsion on Mr. Howe's face gave him encouragement. George Howe was one of the most respected gentlemen in Bristol: an owner of ships and real estate, a Federalist, a Congregationalist, and the senior member of a large, irreproachable family. Ephraim dared hope that he would take the side of a clergyman, even though Methodist, against an allegedly promiscuous mill-girl.

In a firmer, louder voice, Ephraim continued: "The doctor told me he had reproved her for her conduct and that she had replied she was not as bad as he thought; that she was a member of Mr. Avery's church. And she showed him the certificate. I soon learned that the young woman had gone to work in Summersworth, New Hampshire, using my certificate as a proof of her regular standing in the Church. I immediately wrote to her, demanding a return of the certificate, alleging that if the demand was not complied with, I should publish her in the papers as an impostor. I also wrote to the minister there, Mr. Storrs, cautioning him of her character. In reply, I received a letter from her, enclosing the certificate, and another, from Mr. Storrs, inquiring the nature of the charges against her and the course taken at her trial; to which I replied that she had been expelled from the Church. I also informed him that, since then, she had been suspected of *theft*."

Ephraim said this last word with great emphasis, and then paused for a sip of water. He wanted his hearers to fully grasp the suggestion that this girl might have been dishonest as well as loose. Then he went on.

"A week or two later, she wrote to me again, saying that she had heard a sermon on confession and was constrained to make a yet fuller acknowledgment of her crimes—that she had been guilty of all the crimes charged upon her and that she had been afflicted with the foul disease, though ignorant of it at the time. She also admitted to having been treated, in Lowell, for this disease, but charged the physician who treated her with an attempt to have intercourse with her.

"I did not answer this letter, and did not hear from her again until some time later, when she called at my house in Lowell of a Saturday morning and asked my forgiveness. She said she had come on purpose for that, and wanted it in writing. I gave it in writing—adding, forgiveness from me is nothing, she must seek it of the Lord. She went away, and I heard nothing more of her till

August of 1832—last summer—when, being at Thompson, Connecticut, at a camp-meeting, I was informed by Brother Abraham D. Merrill that she was on the ground. The brethren were cautioned of her, at my suggestion. I did not speak with her.

"In the month of October last, I attended a four days' meeting at Fall River. Reverend Ira Bidwell told me that a Sarah Cornell was attending meetings there, and that someone had told him of my difficulties with a girl of that name in Lowell. At his request, I described Sarah Maria Cornell and told him that she had been expelled from my church. Mr. Bidwell thought the girl he referred to was the same. In the evening after preaching, I was invited to stay through the night at Mr. Edward Mason's. As I was entering his house in company with Mrs. Mason and some others, someone pulled me by the elbow and expressed a wish to speak with me. I immediately recognized Sarah Maria Cornell, and asked her what she wanted. 'To see you a moment,' said she. I told her I wanted nothing to say to her. But she replied, 'I *must* speak with you.' I then told Mr. Mason I would be in the house in a moment and turned to the girl and again asked what she wanted. She said, 'I have come to live in Fall River where I am not known, and don't want you to expose me.' I told her I had no disposition to injure her, and it would depend upon her behavior whether I exposed her or not. 'Don't,' says she, 'ruin me here, you have ruined me in Lowell and Dover.' I told her it was entirely up to her, and she went away. I never saw her again."

When Ephraim sat down, Mr. Howe nodded to him pleasantly, and Mr. Haile thanked him. He felt relieved. The procedure was not as distressing as he had feared, and he was confident that it would soon be over. But he had not then any idea of the parade of witnesses waiting to be heard.

The hearing went on for ten days, and during all that time Bristol continued in a turmoil. The local newspaper remarked that there were enough Methodist ministers in town to save every soul in Bristol twice over. There were also hundreds of visitors from Fall River, many of whom had taken part in the town meeting and were eager to see justice done. More than fifty witnesses had been called, some from as far away as Lowell and Dover, and many of these arrived with an escort of relatives. Besides, a surprising number of persons came from nearby towns—ordinary citizens who had nothing to do with the case, but were either curious ("Prurient," said the Methodists and the Bristol folk who stayed away) or genuinely concerned about the safety of millgirls and the morality of ministers. The crowds became denser as the days went by. On Wardwell Street, every time Sophia Avery looked out of the window, she saw twenty-five or thirty strollers.

The first witness called by Mr. Staples, for the government, was the discoverer of the body, John Durfee. He had never been in a courtroom before, and he was extremely nervous. Taking the oath seemed to render him almost inarticulate. His favorite responses seemed to be, "I don't rightly remember," and, "I think so, but I wouldn't swear to it." Afterwards, he said that he had been in great fear that he might swear to something that wasn't true and go to Hell for eternity.

Mr. Staples became impatient with him.

"You *did* find a body in your stackyard, did you not?"

"Yes, you might say that."

"Do you say that?"

"I cal'late so."

"Then please describe what happened next."

"William and I, we took her down, and laid her on her side. We couldn't lay her on her back so well, because her knees was bent."

"How was she dressed?"

"A calash, pushed back on her head, and a cloak, hooked up. And gloves. Her shoes was off."

"Had you seen any strangers in the vicinity?"

"I saw a man I didn't know, the day before. It was just afore sunset, and he was about twenty rods from the stack, standing still."

"Can you describe him?"

"If I remember rightly, he was tall and he had on a dark surtout. Oh, and one of them black hats with a high crown and a
wide brim."

"Is that the man?" Mr. Staples indicated Avery.

John Durfee glanced toward the prisoner's bench and then
quickly looked down.

"I hadn't better swear to it," he murmured.

John's older brother, William, was called next, and was asked
to describe how he had cut the cord from the girl's neck.

"It was real deep in," William said. "I had to pick it out. It
went 'round twice, horizontal. No higher, front nor back."

"And how was it tied?"

"With a clove-hitch knot, sir. It's a sailor's knot. I know
because I have followed the sea."

"Is it used only by sailors?"

"Well, I reckon farmers'll use it. I've seen farmers bind a flail
with a clove-hitch."

"And could a woman have hanged herself with such a
knot?"

"I don't see how. Not with her hands under the cloak. The
cloak and calash were all in proper order, just as though she had
been living."

This "proper order" of the girl's clothes, in contrast to her
violent death, seemed to have made a deep impression on those
who had been in the stackyard. The next witness, a husky young
farmhand named Benjamin Manchester, had helped take the
body down. When Mr. Staples asked him to describe the corpse,
he spoke very slowly, as if getting something heavy off his
mind.

"She looked well-dressed, neatly dressed," he said. "As though
she *was* somebody. But her hair! It was in the most frightful way
as ever I saw."

Manchester went on to say that after the body had been placed
on the wagon, he had gone to his labor, across the fields.

"A little west of the stackyard," he said, "I found a piece of a turtle comb. It was just off the cowpath, in among rosebushes. I stopped and looked around some more and I found the other two pieces."

Abner Davis was next, the young man who had been blasting stones with John Durfee on the afternoon of December twentieth.

"We was blasting, you see, and we had a cart with some bags on it, bags of powder. The bags are sewed with such stuff as was around the stake and the girl's neck. Next day, I noticed some of this string was missing."

"Was the string like this?" asked Mr. Staples, holding up a piece.

Manchester peered at it, and said, "Exactly like."

Staples turned dramatically to the presiding magistrates.

"Gentlemen," he said, "this is the string that caused the death of Sarah Maria Cornell."

The spectators, craning their necks to see, made a stir, and Mr. Howe had to bang his gavel for order.

Staples turned again to the witness and asked him to recount what he remembered of the late-afternoon of December twentieth.

"Well, sir, we had set a charge and lighted the train and we was running away from it. We seen a man walking, in the field, going in a direction where he was liable to be in danger. We hollered at him, and just as he halted, the powder took fire."

"And then?"

"When the rock had blown up, he went off. He went east, toward Fall River."

"Do you see the man here in this courtroom?"

Davis hunched over and looked upset.

"Well, he were tall, and wearing a surtout like Mr. Avery's got there, buttoned snug around. But I couldn't see his features. I wouldn't like swearing."

After the noonday dinner hour, old Elihu Hicks, the coroner, was called. Slightly deaf and more than slightly irritable, his testimony took most of the afternoon. He could not remember whether he had properly sworn in his coroner's jury. He had had to replace two jurymen, because they were not property-owners, as the law required. He had written out the verdict and the jury had signed it, but then he had lost the paper.

"I will go home and look for it," he told the magistrates. "But if I can't find it, I won't bring it."

"Well, what was the verdict, Mr. Hicks?" inquired Mr. Howe.

"Died by committing suicide upon herself, with the assistance of a married man."

Mr. Howe and Mr. Haile looked at each other impatiently.

"But, now I'm not so sure," added Hicks. "I'm beginning to believe . . ."

"Thank you, Mr. Hicks," Mr. Howe said. "You may step down."

Next day, the three Borden women, Ruth, Meribah, and Lucy Ann, were brought to Bristol from Fall River in a private carriage. One literary-minded reporter who saw them arrive in their black bonnets and best dresses of black bombazine, wrote that they looked like a trio of Yankee Fates.

Word went around Bristol that the evidence they would present was of a shocking nature. Meribah Borden, the oldest and most voluble of the three sisters-in-law, testified first.

"Yes, we three laid her out," she said. "And we seen the whole body. Most every part of her had some mark on it."

"Describe these marks, please," requested Mr. Staples.

"Well, there was a dark spot on the back just above the hip bone. And marks or prints of an open hand or of someone's fingers on the right side of the belly. *Spots,* as of the four fingers and the thumb, as if there had been a *grab* there." Mrs. Borden spread out her hand and made a grab. "Ruth Borden applied her fingers to the spots and they fitted. The bottom of the belly, near the private parts, was very dark. Below that . . ." (Mrs. Borden lowered her voice) ". . . there was the appearance of violence—very black clear across, not a white spot to be seen. For decency, we put a cloth over her, up to the hips, before the coroner's jury saw her. The body was very stiff. We applied hot cloths, wrung out in water as hot as could be, to the arm that was raised, but could not get it down. The knees were darkish, cut, and grass-stained. The tongue was just catched between her teeth, not out of her mouth. I have assisted in laying out many corpses before but I never saw such a sight as this."

Ruth Borden corroborated Meribah, adding that she had examined the clothes of the deceased and had found a little blood on the linen—not much—and feces stuck to the linen, as if mashed on.

"She must have died lying horizontal, not hanging vertical," said Mrs. Borden, "or the feces would not have been mashed. I said at the time, 'There has been rash violence,' and I still say so. This girl was very much abused."

Meribah Borden, recalled to the stand, agreed: *very much abused.*

"To what end?" asked Mr. Staples.

"Could be abortion or could be rape," Meribah said. "But she was bruised to death."

Lucy Ann Borden, a shyer sort, testified in a whisper that she, too, had seen the bruises, but would not care to say what caused them.

"I don't wish to express an opinion," she said, close to tears. "I never did hear such things talked about in public, and I ain't a-goin' to do it."

In the afternoon, Dr. Wilbur was called, followed by his young assistant, Dr. Hooper.

"Dr. Wilbur, you examined the body of the deceased on Monday, December 24, after it was disinterred?" Mr. Staples inquired.

"I did, sir, with my colleague, Dr. Hooper."

"You examined the *entire* body?"

"We did, sir."

"And what did you find?"

"A great many marks and discolorations. Incipient putrefaction may have caused some of this, but assuredly there were many severe bruises."

"And what would you say caused them?"

"Sir, I must assume an abortion attempt. The *os tincae,* the womb entrance, was open, and the vagina was discolored. However, the fetus had remained undisturbed. We removed it and weighed and measured it. It measured eight inches long and weighed five ounces. We were able, although with some difficulty, to determine the sex. It was female."

Mr. Haile asked, "How old would such a fetus be?"

"I have little personal experience in this field," Dr. Wilbur said. "But according to books I have studied, such a fetus might be between three-and-a-half and four months old."

Many people in the courtroom, including Mr. Howe, knew Dr. Wilbur and trusted him. A rigid look came over Avery's face as the doctor continued, firmly insisting that the deceased could not have hanged herself, because a clove-hitch knot had to be tightened with equal pressure on the two ends of string. The fact that her hands were inside her cloak, and gloved, made it even less likely.

"If the girl had died by hanging," the doctor went on, "the string would have been higher in back. In my opinion, death was caused by strangulation with the string while the victim was in a horizontal position. The murderer hanged a corpse."

Dr. Wilbur went on to say that the deceased had consulted him several times about her pregnancy, and had showed him the bottle of oil of tansy, which she said had been given her by the defendant.

"I told her it would not only destroy her infant," he said, "but that it would destroy her life as well."

Dr. Hooper came next, corroborating the older doctor's testimony. After he was excused, Mr. Howe recessed the court, saying that although it was still early, the evidence all day had been so repellent to listen to that he was sure everyone needed a rest.

The next day's witnesses were Fall River people who had been acquainted with Sarah Maria Cornell and had seen her on her last day.

Amy Durfee was a very young, rawboned girl who could hardly speak for shyness. In a whisper, she managed to tell the court that she had worked near Sarah in the weaving room and that Sarah had been planning for some days to leave early on Thursday afternoon, December twentieth. Sarah had asked Amy to tend her loom, and had also lent her a small sum of money to buy cotton goods so that Sarah, Amy, and Lucy Hathaway could make themselves some aprons.

" 'We'll have them just alike,' says Sarah," offered Amy. " 'And,' says she, 'we'll wear them next week.' "

"Did she tell you when she intended to make her apron?" asked Mr. Staples.

"We were going to sit together and make them next day. At our dinnertime."

"Would you say there was anything in her demeanor to suggest that she was planning suicide?" Mr. Staples said.

"I never met a person planning suicide," Amy said cautiously. "I wouldn't think so, but I don't know."

Mr. Staples sighed and called the next witness, Mrs. Hathaway, with whom Sarah had boarded. Mrs. Hathaway was a better witness and was quite willing to swear that Sarah had said nothing to suggest a wish to do away with herself.

"She was a nice, quiet girl. She never went out, except to Methodist meetings," Mrs. Hathaway said. "She never had men visitors."

"Tell us what she did on Thursday, December twentieth, if you please."

"She was more cheerful than usual that day, I'd say. She came home early and had tea by herself. Says she to me, 'It don't seem right, me eating when you're not eating, but I have an appointment.' She had three letters lying in her lap—one straw-colored, one pink, and one white. I'd seen her before with these letters.

She seemed to set store by them. She said to my daughter, Lucy, that they came from Bristol."

"Did she say what was in them?"

Mr. Randolph objected that this would be hearsay, and Mr. Howe sustained him. The question was withdrawn, and Mrs. Hathaway continued:

"Between candlelight and dark, Sarah went out. Said she was going to Durfee's. She was neatly dressed, as she always was, but she'd changed her factory dress for a better one. I left the door unfastened for her, and I sat up until after ten. The later it got, the more uneasy I felt. I was fond of her."

"What was your estimation of her character?"

Mrs. Hathaway answered firmly, "I never knew her to do or say anything that was improper."

Lucy Hathaway, a quiet-spoken girl of twenty, was the next witness. She volunteered a recent bit of conversation between herself and Sarah.

"Sarah says, 'Lucy, don't you think it is possible for an innocent girl to be led away by a man that she has confidence in and rather looks up to?' I says, 'I don't know,' and she says, 'But what can an innocent girl do, in the hands of a strong man and he using all kinds of argument?' "

"Did you see the deceased on the afternoon of December twentieth?"

"Yes, sir, a few minutes before she left the mill, she came to the window near where I sit. She took the comb out of her hair and combed it, and put the comb back."

"Was it broken?"

"No, sir, it was all in one piece. Then, just as she was leaving, she asked me to wind some waste yarn so that she might take some home to knit. We girls may wind as much waste yarn as we wish. She says, 'Lucy, next week I'm going to knit your mother a shawl.' "

The government now called Annis Norton, William Anthony, Peleg Cranstoun, and the others who had seen a walking stranger on Thursday afternoon. But when it came to swearing that Avery was the man, no one was quite willing to do so. They thought it was he; they were tolerable sure about it; they would almost be ready to swear it; but they did not.

The same situation prevailed among the postal clerks who were asked what they could recall about the straw-colored letter, postmarked November 13: nothing could be established. Several witnesses swore they'd seen Avery in a Fall River general store on December 8, buying a half-sheet of white paper and writing on it at a desk there. But Iram Smith, owner of the store, was not so sure.

"There is very few things of which I should be certain," said Mr. Smith.

Avery exchanged a slight smile with his attorneys, but his face fell again when the government, in connection with the pink letter, called John Orswell, a steamboat engineer, who swore that Avery had come aboard the steamboat *King Philip*, at its wharf in Providence, and asked Orswell to hand-carry a letter to Fall River.

"It was in the morning of November twenty-ninth, between eight and nine o'clock," Orswell said. "I told him I was not allowed to carry letters, and advised him to put it in the letter box. He said he did not want it to go in the letter box, but wanted it delivered as soon as it got there. He said it would do him a great favor if I carried it and he took the letter from under his cloak, and handed it to me with a ninepence. I consented to carry it. A few days ago, after I heard about the death, I went to Bristol, because I had a curiosity to see if Avery was the same man. The sheriff let me go into his house to see the gentleman, and I recognized him. I had looked directly in his face on board the boat, while he was persuading me to take his letter. There is no doubt in my mind as to the man."

Orswell identified the letter, saying that he remembered smudging it, because his hands had been dirty from "fixing the works." He held up the pink letter so that everyone could take note of the smudges.

This testimony created a small sensation in the courtroom, during which Ephraim kept his eyes on the ground. His lips were trembling, and he seemed to be chewing the inside of them. But now the government closed its case, and next morning Mr. Randolph began to present evidence for the defense.

For most of the day, one Methodist clergyman after another took the witness stand, each expressing strong praise of Ephraim K. Avery: his blameless character, his affection toward his family, his exemplary Christianity. Reverend Joseph Merrill said he had been Avery's presiding elder for six years and had never once found fault with him.

In cross-examination, Mr. Staples asked about the slander trials, but Mr. Randolph objected that they were irrelevant, and was upheld.

Many of the clergymen who testified had either been with Avery in Providence, in late November, or at the August camp-meeting in Thompson, Connecticut. They were confident that he could not have sent a letter from Providence, pink, or any other color, nor could he have been alone with Sarah M. Cornell or any other woman at the camp-meeting. One or more of these gentlemen had been at his side continually on both these occasions.

Ephraim became less tense as minister followed minister, sustaining every point in his alibi. Reverend Holway, a silvery-haired old man who headed the Methodist Meeting in the neighboring town of Warren, testified that he had known of Avery's planned excursion to the Island of Rhode Island. Avery's father had been on the Island as a Revolutionary soldier and had often spoken of the interesting rock formation called King Philip's Chair. And Holway himself had advised Avery to visit the coal mine and inquire about prices.

"He is a young man who loves a solitary ramble," concluded Reverend Holway. "He thinks nothing of walking many miles in an afternoon."

"Who saw him near the mine?" shouted a voice from the back of the courtroom. Mr. Howe had the shouter ejected, but his question went unanswered. The defense called three persons

who, on December twentieth, had seen a stranger in the vicinity
of the mine, but, when cross-examined, it developed that they had
seen him in the morning, not the afternoon. And according to the
testimony of William Pearse, a ferryman, Avery had not arrived
on the Island until about two o'clock.

Next came a doctor, who testified that in August he had set a
broken ankle for Avery, and that while he might have walked to
the coal mine and back—twelve miles—he would have been unable to walk as far as Fall River, which meant covering another
eight miles.

Apropos of Avery's physical condition, Mr. Staples wanted to
know how he had hurt his hand.

"I will gladly explain," Avery said. But Mr. Staples interrupted him, saying to the magistrates, "I don't want to hear *his*
story. What I want is a court-appointed physician to examine the
injury."

The court declined to appoint one, however, and Mr. Staples,
inexplicably, let the matter drop.

Reverend Joseph Merrill was recalled by the defense to testify
that none of the three letters could have been written by Ephraim
Avery. Merrill was well-acquainted with Avery's handwriting
and it was quite different.

While the hearing was in progress, an enterprising printer got
hold of the letters and published facsimiles of them, along with
the comments of handwriting experts, who identified the handwriting as Avery's. This slender volume sold briskly all over New
England and even as far away as New York, where news of the
case was attracting great public interest.

Mr. Randolph saved for last the testimony of half a dozen
young women who had known Sarah Cornell at various mills
and had nothing good to say for her.

"Oh, yes, her character was bad. Everyone said so," said a
Miss Catherine Blake, who had known the deceased in Lowell.
"She behaved improperly. She kept company with young men.
She was unchaste."

Mr. Staples objected that these remarks were irrelevant hearsay, but he was overruled. Miss Blake continued.

"I asked her how she could do it without being discovered at
her boardinghouse. She said she did not do it there, she went
down to a village nearby, Belvedere, where she had been invited
to come and stay nights. She said once a young man carried her
out in a chaise to a tavern. They had wine, and went into a
chamber."

"Did she mention the *day of the week?*" asked Mr. Randolph
pointedly.

"Yes, sir, it was on a *Sunday*. And Sacrament Day, too."

Clearly pleased with Miss Blake's contribution, Mr. Randolph next called Miss Mary Ann Barnes, also of Lowell. Had
the deceased ever confided her?

"Oh, yes, sir, she confessed to me on the evening before she left
town, that she had conducted improperly. She confessed that Dr.
Graves had doctored her. She said she didn't know if it was the
bad complaint or not, but, she says to me, 'This much I know, I
have a very bad disorder.' "

"For how long a period did you know her?"

"It was during the summer of 1830. In September she left
town because she was expelled from the Church, but later she
came back for a day or two. Dr. Graves heard she was there, and
got the sheriff to go with him to collect a bill for doctoring. She
got away from them and was in another house. She sent for me,
and asked me where would be the best place to wait for the
stage—not the regular stage-stop. Then she went off."

"Did she, at any time, Miss Barnes, mention Mr. Avery?"

"Yes, she told me she didn't like him. She said she had a certificate from him and he asked her to give it up. But she told him
she had lost it. She said, 'I have got it and I can go and join
anywhere I like and he may help himself.' "

Another Lowell girl, Lydia Pervere, testified that she had
known Sarah Maria Cornell about four years. Sarah had told
Lydia that she didn't want to see Avery—didn't want to go to

meeting or to a camp-meeting nearby, or anywhere "where Avery is."

"She didn't want to see him," said Miss Pervere, "because he had talked to her about some complaints that had been made to him against her."

"Did she tell you what these complaints were?"

"Yes. They were lying and fornication. She told me they were true. She said she had been with three different men, and in a tavern, and on the Sabbath Day, too."

"What was your opinion of the deceased?"

"Well, sometimes I thought she was crazy. She cried a lot. I heard one day she came to the mill dressed all in white. Folks took it to be craziness."

After hearing similar testimony from young women who had known Sarah in other mill-towns, the defense rested. Since this was a hearing, not a trial, there were no summations from either side.

The two magistrates took a day to prepare their opinions. On the morning of January sixth, they were ready to present them, and the courtroom was packed well beyond its proper capacity. Fishermen had beached their boats, farmers had put off work, ship captains had contrived to delay sailings; and a large number of people waited outside the courthouse in the cold for news of the decision to be relayed out to them. They had a long wait. Mr. Howe, who spoke first, took over two hours to give his reasoning, but it was apparent almost at once which way he would go.

"Let us look first at the manner and circumstances of the death," he began, "with a view to the simple question whether the death was caused by herself or another. She was found hanged by a string probably found at a cart not far distant, or procured from the factory at which she worked, to a stake, in an advanced state of pregnancy, being unmarried. The stake was about of her own height. Her cloak and calash were on, the former being fastened at the top and at one or two or more other places, but admitting of her putting her arm out. The right hand

was raised, and whether prevented by the cloak from falling soon
after death, having been used under the cloak to tighten the string
on the neck, or not, is perhaps uncertain. The string, somewhat
like those used in loom harnesses, was small and tied with a
clove-hitch knot.

"The ladies who examined her say that she must have been on
her knees in the grass and that there were appearances of violence, probably to produce abortion. The medical gentlemen who
have appeared in this court had no doubt that the death was
caused by the string on the neck; leaving it undecided whether
applied by herself or another; and if by another, whether before
or at the time of suspension."

Mr. Howe now turned his gaze toward Ephraim. "Let us consider whether it was done by the respondent." (Ephraim was
encouraged to hear himself called "respondent," and not "defendant" or "prisoner.") "If we believe it was done by the respondent, we must accept that it was done near a much traveled
road, within sixty rods of the Durfee house and within half a
mile of the three thousand citizens of Fall River village, before
seven o'clock in the evening. Because at about half-past nine, the
respondent was quietly retiring to bed, eight or more miles away,
at the ferry-landing, having come there on foot (we must believe)
with one ankle lately fractured or dislocated.

"If he strangled her in the open field, where her broken comb
was found, we must believe that he then conveyed her dead to the
stackyard, found a suitable stake in the dark, and fixed the string
over the stake with one hand, while holding her up with the
other. We must believe that he then arranged her shoes and pocket handkerchief beside her, put up her right arm, and hooked the
cloak. All this while exposed to the possibility of momentary discovery by people or dogs. Can we give credence to all this?"

Mr. Howe looked around at the solemn, upturned faces.

"I, for one, cannot. My opinion is that there is no reason to
doubt that the deceased destroyed herself. And this was the general opinion until certain letters were found. These letters have

become the grounds of wild rumors, suspicions, and surmises, undoubtedly exaggerated and carried verbally and by the public newspapers through all parts of the country.

"The bruises attested to by the ladies were without doubt self-inflicted, in an effort to produce abortion. The cries and groans heard that evening would also have been a result of this self-inflicted violence."

Ephraim now began to feel relieved, but he wished Mr. Howe would stop talking. Having once decided that the girl had committed suicide, why was there anything more to be said? But Mr. Howe plainly did not see it that way.

"Let us now consider," he continued, "the evidence of those who saw a walking stranger. After suspicions became rife, indeed, two or three persons recollected to have seen Methodist minister-looking folks, variously described so that they might be almost anybody that was tall and wore dark clothes. But no one has ventured to swear on oath that this stranger and the respondent are one and the same.

"I understand that some people find it implausible that a clergyman should spend an afternoon rambling about the shores and coal mines of Rhode Island. It may strike businessmen as strange, but I cannot think it very improbable that a professional man, of a contemplative turn, a newcomer in this region and something of a naturalist, should devote a pleasant afternoon to such an expedition."

Mr. Howe now indulged in a ramble of his own, praising the beauties of the country roundabout Bristol until a noticeable restlessness among his listeners recalled him to the matter at hand.

"As for the letters, if Mr. Avery wrote them at all, which is certainly to be doubted, they are not incriminating. They do not say that the writer is the father of the girl's unborn child. Indeed, one of them says that he received her letter 'with no small surprise.' Neither is it incriminating that the letter-writer made arrangements for a meeting. He might have done this in order to save the peace of himself, his wife and family by making a pecuniary sacrifice—in short, to pay her off, and to silence, in this way, privately, a false charge."

Mr. Howe now put aside his notes and leaned forward, as if about to confide a secret to his listeners.

"It seems to me, very frankly, that the best way to adjudicate this case is by adverting to the testimony which relates to the man's character, to the woman's character, to his former dealings with her, and to her condition at the time of her death. The respondent appears, from the testimony of persons of the highest respectability, for many years to have always sustained a perfectly unblemished reputation, and by the distinguished purity of his moral, Christian, and ministerial character, to have been eminently entitled to it.

"*She*, on the other hand, appears to have been addicted to almost every vice and to have been for years going about from place to place and staying but a little while at any; and variously contriving everywhere to thrust herself upon the religious. She went running about from one mill-town to another, finally alighting at Lowell. Mr. Avery probably tolerated her longer than anyone had ever before done, but finally was obliged to expel her from his church, after trial and proof, for falsehood and fornication. But although she confessed to Miss Barnes, whose testimony you heard, that she had been guilty of the offenses imputed to her, and had even devoted a Sacrament Sabbath to the sensual gratification of a young man, who took her to a country tavern for that purpose, she was angry with Mr. Avery for causing her expulsion and preventing her readmission; and there is reason to suppose that she cherished feelings of enmity and revenge against him ever after. And if anything more were wanting to determine the probability of his abhorrence of her, we have it in the fact that she was notoriously afflicted at Lowell with a disease, which, if no moral or religious principle could be supposed to have restrained the minister, must yet have deterred him from any sexual intercourse with her."

There was now a good deal of buzzing among the spectators,

and opening and closing of doors as the gist of Mr. Howe's remarks was passed to those outside. Mr. Howe had to rap for order.

"In conclusion," he said, "if I could bring myself to believe that the respondent wrote the letters and had indeed met the girl at Durfee's stackyard, I feel sure he would have spoken to her in this vein: 'Sarah, you have given me a great deal of trouble heretofore, and your letters, which I wrote you so much surprised me, have given me a great deal more. You are pursuing me, who never did you an intentional injury, with great malignity. I did not know but it might be in your power to do me and my family an injury and bring a scandal upon my profession, when I solicited this interview and promised you aid. But I have concluded to retract my promise and set you at defiance. If I thought you had any just sense of future accountability, I would warn you of the sin of thus following up one crime with another; and I do warn you of the danger of perjury and I also warn your real paramour, whoever he may be, of the danger of being your accomplice.'

"Such a speech, in my view, might well have driven the young woman to destroy herself, confident that the letters she had forged would avenge her upon Avery. It is therefore my opinion that there is not probable cause to suspect that Ephraim K. Avery has murdered Sarah Maria Cornell."

Mr. Haile then rose and made an anticlimactical speech, fortunately much shorter than his colleague's but arriving at the same conclusion: "There is not probable cause to suspect that Ephraim K. Avery is guilty of the murder of Sarah M. Cornell."

The respondent was discharged.

Ephraim sprang up with an involuntary shout of joy, and his ministerial friends gathered around him to shake his hand. But few others came forward to do so, and the courtroom was curiously silent. People fell back to make way for the ministers, but many of the faces that Ephraim saw out of the corner of his eye were grim and hostile. Outside, it had begun to snow, but the crowd stood about with coats and hats turning white, in order to look at him.

Someone said, "We won't let you get away with it, Avery," and there were shouts of agreement.

The two Merrills each took one of his arms, and in this protective manner they walked him home. But many of the courthouse crowd followed.

"Why did nobody see you at the coal mine, Avery?"

"Because he wasn't there!" someone answered for him.

"How did she hang herself with both hands under her cloak?"

"Who gave her the oil of tansy?"

"You sanctimonious hypocrite! We'll teach you not to meddle with factory-girls!"

"What's the Seventh Commandment, Reverend?"

"Seducer!"

"Murderer!"

Walking fast, the ministers reached Wardwell Street and hurried into the house.

"Sophia!" Ephraim cried, bursting into the kitchen. "It is over! I am exonerated!"

Sophia was at the kitchen table, hearing Edwin's catechism, and she looked at her husband without smiling.

"Well, aren't you happy, woman?" Ephraim said, his brows drawing together. "Can't you say you're glad?"

"Oh, Mr. Avery!" she said, bursting into tears. "Only see what someone has left at our door!"

She showed him a broadside with two poems printed on it. The first, which, according to a footnote, was to be sung to the tune of "The Star-Spangled Banner," began:

Oh! list the sad tale of the poor factory maid,
How cheerful she went when the days work was over,
In cloak and in bonnet all simply array'd
To meet a dark fiend in the shape of a lover. . . .

The other was entitled "The Clove-Hitch Knot," and fitted the tune of "Auld Lang Syne":

> Ye virgins all a warning take.
> Remember Avery's knot;
> Enough to make your hearts to ache,
> Don't let it be forgot.

Each poem had five or six verses, but Ephraim did not read them. He tore the broadside into pieces and threw the pieces into the fire.

"*That*," he said "is what I think of *that*."

"Mrs. Avery," said Abraham Merrill softly. "Mr. Howe and Mr. Haile have exonerated your husband. The people who print such rubbishy verses are very ignorant people. They don't matter. Believe me, your husband is free and we have heard the last of this unpleasantness."

"He is not free," Sophia cried out hysterically. "That girl may be dead, but she will still destroy him!"

III

Sarah Maria

She was born into a failed romance. Ephraim Avery once said to her, when she talked to him about it, that perhaps that was why there was a bittersweet quality to her nature—an underlying sadness, even in happy moments. She seemed to snatch greedily at joy, as if it were a firefly dancing by and she wanted to capture it in a jar. Yes, she had said, yes, she knew she was like that. It was hard for her to be content with a dull lot in life, as other girls were. To her, something always seemed to be missing.

The only way her birth could have given pleasure to her parents was if the midwife had been able to announce a boy. James Cornell, Sarah's young father, needed sons, as all farmers did, and especially in the stubborn hill-country of Vermont. He had one son, little James, but it would be years before the child would be fit to help drive a plow or lay stone walls, and now Lucretia Cornell was saying she had had enough of childbirth and didn't want him pestering her any more.

"You didn't call it pestering, back at your father's house," he shouted at her. "You simpered after me then, right enough; and me just a young fellow, trying to learn a trade."

Lucretia became furious, as she always did when he reminded her, directly or indirectly, that she was older than he. Five years older. She had been twenty-six when they courted—an old maid, a thornback, with two younger sisters married.

"I was a catch and you know it," she would shout back at him, over the new baby's head.

"Much good it did me," James would answer.

Between these raised voices, Sarah Maria passed her first year.

The following summer, 1804, was a dry, hot year in Vermont, and James's crops failed. He had never been much of a farmer, anyway, and didn't like farming. In August, he could think of no solution but to pack his clothes in a bundle and walk away toward the west. His family never saw him again.

When Lucretia realized he had gone, she sat and cried, and let the kitchen fire go out and did nothing for her children. James and Nancy, the two older ones, aged six and four, took hands and walked two miles to the next farm for help.

The neighbors asked Lucretia what she intended to do. She didn't know, and seemed surprised that anyone would expect her to know. To them, however, it was apparent that if she stayed where she was, she and her children would become a burden to the people of Rupert, Vermont. They would have to be put out as bond servants to whoever in the community would keep them at the lowest cost. It was reasoned that Lucretia ought to be the responsibility of the place she *belonged to*. And that was Norwich, Connecticut, where she had been born and raised. Accordingly, the Rupert neighbors stowed Lucretia's household effects, her children, and herself into the old wagon, hitched up the horse, and sent them all off in a southeasterly direction.

Lucretia's father, Colonel Christopher Leffingwell, was one of the important citizens of Norwich, and owned one of the largest houses there. The colonel was one of those splendid products of Revolutionary times, when capable, common-sensical men had appeared when needed from the simple villages of the colonies and won the Revolution. Having done his duty under fire and earned the rank of colonel, he had returned home to become a man of the new age—the industrial revolution. He built, on a small scale, a paper mill, a chocolate factory, a hat factory, a fulling mill, and a dyeing house. He outlived two wives, taking a third, a blooming widow, when he was seventy. He had no complaint of his three sons or of four of his five daughters. But he strongly opposed Lucretia's infatuation with James Cornell, one of his least promising apprentices in the hat factory. When James asked for Lucretia's hand, the colonel refused. Lucretia threw a fit of hysterics and threatened to elope. One warm June evening she went for a walk with her lover, and was found creeping up to bed at four in the morning. The colonel, as canny at home as on the battlefield or in his factories, decided to cut his losses. His four other daughters had married well. If Lucretia was a fool, he decided, she was expendable. The young pair was married within the month, presented with a horse-and-wagon and a few farm tools and advised to try Vermont, a new state with opportunities for pioneer farmers without being as risky as Ohio, where Indians were still to be subdued.

James came from Rhode Island. His father, a seaman, had fallen off a topmast and drowned, somewhere in the West Indies, leaving nothing. James had hoped to remain in Norwich, basking in the prestige of kinship with the Leffingwells, and perhaps even inheriting the hat factory. In Rupert, Vermont, the name of Leffingwell meant nothing.

Lucretia's relations were less than delighted to see her back in Norwich with three children. Fatherless little ones were a liability, especially when the father had behaved badly. There was no feasting and merriment for Lucretia, the prodigal daughter, but only large helpings of humble pie.

"Why did you not listen to me?" asked her father. "In my day, daughters always listened to their fathers."

The sisters, all of whom had nice houses in Norwich and nearby villages, asked her where she was planning to live.

The old Leffingwell house had once been an inn and it had plenty of bedrooms. Lucretia was reluctantly permitted to settle in one of the smallest, with her baby. Little Jamey was taken in by an uncle who lived in New London, and Nancy, just turned five years old, went to live with Cornell cousins in Providence. No one wanted a baby, so Lucretia kept Sarah Maria.

Although Colonel Leffingwell was an up-to-date businessman of the early-nineteenth century, he was a typical eighteenth-century father—authoritarian and remote; and his religion, like that of most Yankee village people, was Calvinistic. Not long after Lucretia came home to live, two of his favorite children died, one right after the other: Daniel, newly graduated from Yale College, died of consumption, and Fanny, the youngest and prettiest girl, who had married at sixteen, in giving birth to her first child. The old man said it was a visitation; that, like Job, he had unwittingly displeased the Lord; perhaps by having allowed Lucretia's marriage. And he became more aloof and severe than ever. When anyone living in his house heard the sound of his cane on the wide floorboards, they got out of his way if they could.

One day, when Sarah Maria was two years old, a peddler of ribbons and laces came to the back door and played a lively Irish tune on a tin whistle. The little girl, in the kitchen with her mother, was observed to be dancing—actually spinning and bobbing in time to the music.

"What's your baby's name?" asked the peddler.

"We call her Sarah. Or Sally. Or Sally Maria," Lucretia answered indifferently. She pronounced Maria "Mar-*eye*-ah," in the usual New England way. It was true that the child was called by several names, or none. Nobody cared much about her.

"Well, Sarah Mar-eye-ah, ye're a wonderful young'un," said the peddler. "Ye're dancin' like the fairies."

At that moment, Colonel Leffingwell appeared in the kitchen. They had not heard his cane because of the music, and the baby, joyful at being admired and encouraged by the peddler, danced into his path.

"What's this?" the old man said angrily, poking her with his cane as if he were turning over an insect. "Lucretia, can you not control your child? What is she doing?"

"Sure, and that's a dancer ye've got there, sir," said the peddler.

The colonel took the peddler's pack from the kitchen floor and heaved it out the door. Then he turned his cold eye upon Lucretia.

"The child's will must be broken, daughter. See to it, or I shall have to do it for you."

Lucretia snatched her child up and fled to the cellar, where she beat the little creature with a narrow, flexible strip of birch traditionally kept there for that purpose. Lucretia did not like to beat children, but more because of the effort involved than from reluctance to give pain.

"You are bad luck, nothing but bad luck," she said, breathless from wielding the birch. "Nothing has come right ever since you were born."

Sarah Maria's will was never broken to the satisfaction of her grandfather. He died when she was seven years old, and when she was escorted to his deathbed, he turned his sunken eyes upon her and did not give her his blessing, as he did the other grandchildren. Instead he said, "Have a care, Sarah." Perhaps he was going to bless her—she dared hope so—but instead, at that instant, the death rattle came into his throat and he spoke no more.

The Leffingwell house was left to the colonel's widow for her lifetime, which turned out to be twelve more years; after which it was to be sold. Lucretia was allowed by her stepmother to stay on. She was in her thirties, and not bad-looking, but neither wife nor widow. A second husband was impossible as long as the fate of the first remained unknown. James had simply vanished. "Gone off," as the village people said. And whether to Ohio, to New Orleans, to Missouri or no farther than Hartford, no one ever knew. The life that Lucretia had dreaded—that of a single woman—was now hers for good.

Lucretia was a languid, moping creature, quite unlike her daughter, Sarah, who was one of those children who charges into everything she does: who slams doors, drops plates, and is always too noisy, even when trying to be quiet; who laughs too loudly and too long; and who is subject to tantrums and to jumping up and down for joy.

"She needs a father," people said of Sarah; not because of a father's love but because of a father's birch rod. At school, her companions teased her because James Cornell had "gone off."

Her cousins were always critical of her, for at home they heard a lot of discussion of the Cornells and their shortcomings. The Lathrop cousins, who lived nearest and were closest to Sarah's age, all underwent religious Conversions at the age of ten or younger, and became exceedingly pious. They played missionary and they played preacher, and sometimes would allow Sarah to join their games as some sort of villain—a Hottentot, perhaps, or a Methodist.

Sarah did not care much for her cousins' games, but she liked the kind of games the boys and girls played at birthday parties and on holidays. "Break the Pope's Neck," for example; also "Button, Button," and "Pack the Stage for Boston." These were all kissing games, involving forfeits and the redemption of forfeits with kisses. The boys and girls exchanged kisses "wheelbarrow-fashion," meaning that they stood back to back, joined hands on each side, and quickly turned through their arms, kissing as their lips came close.

As Sarah grew older, she was one of the girls the boys always wanted a forfeit from. She was tiny, pink-cheeked, and slightly plump. Her mass of dark hair was combed back and held just below the nape of the neck with a hair-clasp, from which it fell in a thick and curling ponytail. But her kind of beauty was not in the prevailing fashion. The most admired girls in the village looked to be on the verge of consumption, if not actually in its grip. They had flat chests and long, slender necks, and faces of an angelic pallor brought about by anemia. Some, indeed, did waste away and then there would be a funeral, and bereaved young friends would write memorial poems and paint tin panels with weeping willows and graveyard vistas. Whether they lived or died, these ethereal girls were doggedly religious. They attended all meetings and lectures of the Congregational Church; they saved their pennies for the missionaries, and some, like Harriet Lathrop, Aunt Lathrop's eldest, determined to go personally to convert the Hindoo. Deeply felt or not, a strong show of religious fervor was the surest route to approval and admiration.

As for Sarah Maria, she went to church every Sunday, like

everyone else, but she was too full of good health and noise to seem at all like a young Puritan saint. And there was another thing about her to which no one offered to put an adjective, because no one could find the right one. It was a way she had of moving that seemed to command the notice of the opposite sex. Something in the sidelong looks she cast had the quality of a sultry summer night with lightning in the distance.

The minister, Dr. Cresswell, a solemn middle aged man, saw it and didn't like it. Conscientiously looking after his flock, he spoke about it to her Aunt Lathrop, who was one of his most devout parishioners.

"If she were not a Norwich maiden of good family," he said, "I might almost be tempted to use the word *wanton*."

"Her mother made a bad marriage," Aunt Lathrop said. "Perhaps there is bad blood in the Cornells. Or—please keep this private between us, Dr. Cresswell—I have to say that our great-great-great-grandmother Leffingwell was a Mohegan Indian. Perhaps Sarah takes after her."

Next time she saw Sarah, she mentioned this possibility to her.

"Her name was Singing Lark," Aunt Lathrop told her.

"What a fine name!"

"It had to be changed, of course, when she became a Christian," Aunt Lathrop said. "They baptized her Prudence. I don't know what she was like, but I know what Indians are like. Wild. Maybe that's where you get your wildness, Sarah."

"But I don't look anything like an Indian," Sarah objected. She did not like to be thought of as being different, because she felt alien enough already. "For one thing, my hair is curly."

"I'm afraid, Sarah Maria, that you have the heart of a wild Indian," said her aunt. "You ought to pray for Grace. Pray just as hard as you can that the Lord will make you quiet and sober."

Sarah prayed, but without visible effect. She still ran about and cavorted, made noise, and generally attracted too much attention.

In school, the boys were thrashed for being too noisy and the girls had their hands birched or were made to kneel on tacks. The schoolmaster had often disciplined Sarah with birching or tacks, but one day, when she was fourteen, he asked her to stay after the others went home. When they were alone in the schoolhouse, he told her he was going to thrash her; that since she behaved like a boy she must be punished like one.

"Lie across my knee," he said, "and pull up your dress."

Like most country girls in 1817, she was not wearing anything beneath her petticoat. Blushing deeply, she told him that.

"But you are sinful," he said, "and I must correct you."

He had a sly, white face, like a mean hound. When he seized her around the waist, she slapped him and fled out of the school-house. After that, she told her mother she had had enough school. She was old enough to stop.

"But you like learning," Lucretia said. "You could stay another year."

"No," Sarah said. "I have had enough."

"Well, then, if you are old enough to leave school, you are too old to behave like a hoyden," said her mother, and Sarah took it to heart. The episode had upset her so much that she trembled when she saw the schoolmaster and hurried out of his way. Was she indeed so much like her ancestor, the Mohegan Indian, that people would not treat her like a proper young lady?

In desperation, she decided to go and see Dr. Cresswell and ask him how she could achieve Grace, or at least become more like other girls. The minister, whose high, bald head was a store-house of Puritan doctrine, begged her to remember that most of humanity is bound for Hell and that only a select few will ever get to Heaven.

"And only the Lord knows which ones they are," he continued. "In His wisdom, He may save sinners and cast the righteous into the flames. Whatever He decides, we must be ready to acquiesce. You must be ready for your own destruction. His will, not yours. You must agree to everlasting torture, if He wishes it."

"God is very hard to understand," Sarah said.

"Ah! If you understand *that*, it is all you will understand of Him," Dr. Cresswell said. "We are no more than fly droppings in His sight. And if He likes, He will sweep us all into the eternal dustbin. We may count on that."

"Then it's hard to see the use of trying."

"Only the truly lost say that," Dr. Cresswell said severely. "You must pray for Grace, you must pray for Conversion, and you must put aside the things of the flesh. Do not take pride in being a pretty girl, because that only moves Him to wrath."

Sarah was surprised to learn that aloof, cold-eyed Dr. Cresswell considered her a pretty girl. She smiled at him gratefully. Dr. Cresswell put out his hand toward her, as if he were about to lay it on her round white arm. Instead, the outstretched hand suddenly became a white-knuckled fist and was withdrawn.

"Go and pray mightily," he said brusquely, and showed her out.

As soon as she turned fifteen, she was apprenticed to a local mantuamaker, Miss Sophronia Sims. Miss Sims, who lived at the other end of Norwich, was a fine seamstress and made dresses and bonnets that were beyond the capabilities of most home-sewers. Most of the wedding dresses in Norwich came from her, as well as Sabbath Day silks and fancy bonnets for the well-to-do. Sarah was very fond of finery, and at first it seemed to her a privilege to sit all day among watered silks and embroidered muslins and clouds of bonnet veiling. But Miss Sophronia was a hard task mistress and a bitter old maid. While frivolous things passed through her fingers, she had grown sallow, plain, and taciturn. It seemed to Sarah that all her share of softness and prettiness had gone into her handiwork. Sarah was frightened of becoming like her. In bad dreams, Sarah sat in a blazing corner of Hell, forever dressed in dingy rags, her lap filled with bright and billowing fabrics that she would never be allowed to wear.

After six months of Miss Sims, Sarah wrote to her sister, Nancy, whom she could scarcely remember, telling her of the plight she was in. She saw no one of her own age, except in the other

pews at church on Sunday. Miss Sims forbade youths to set foot
on her property, and did not hesitate to set her flock of geese on
one who came to the door to leave Sarah a valentine. There was
little spare time in the mantuamaking business. Sarah worked as
long as there was daylight, and sometimes, when there were rush
orders, Sophronia lit the astral lamps and the two of them sat and
sewed all evening. Sarah had headaches most of the time and her
eyes hurt. The only good thing about her situation was that she
learned to sew very well. She wrote Nancy that she would be glad
to make her a dress if only she would rescue her.

Nancy wrote back that their Aunt and Uncle Cornell, with
whom Nancy lived in Providence, invited the little sister to visit
any time she could. In January there was always a lull in the
demand for dresses, and Miss Sims said Sarah might be spared
for a week or two, while she trained a second apprentice. She told
Sarah's mother that Sarah was a deft worker, but "not diligent.
She daydreams." This was true. Sarah daydreamed about escap-
ing from Miss Sims.

Until now, the life Sarah knew consisted only of Norwich: the
ample old frame houses, the Common, the schoolhouse, the Congregational meetinghouse. Beyond, in every direction, like the
edges of the world, were fertile fields and orchards, marked off
from the wild forests beyond by stone walls. Every day, as long as
she could remember, she had seen the stagecoach clatter into the
center of town, change horses at the inn, and clatter away again.
Now, her mother and Aunt Lathrop took her, with a new little
trunk and a bandbox, to the stage-stop and put her aboard the
stagecoach for Providence. She wore a pink muslin dress that she
had made herself, high-waisted, and ruffled in the latest fashion
from Boston; a warm gray cloak, and a gray, velveteen bonnet
trimmed with pink-and-gray ribbon.

"She is certainly pretty," sighed Lucretia, responding languid-
ly to Sarah's spirited waving from the coach window.

"Pretty is as pretty does," Aunt Lathrop said. "I can't help but
be concerned for her. It isn't easy to be poor and pretty, especially
for a girl who's silly and light-minded. I wouldn't have allowed

her to wear pink as a traveling costume, Lucretia, especially in the middle of winter."

"She didn't consult me," Lucretia said. It seemed she was always having to explain and apologize in behalf of Sarah Maria. "She made it at Sophrony Sims's, and I never saw it until this morning."

"I'm concerned for a girl who fails to consult her parent in all things, big and little," Aunt Lathrop said. "My girls would have chosen plain gray, and, of course, no ruffles."

Meantime, the Providence-bound stagecoach was dashing along the turnpike at ten miles an hour. The other passengers were all gentlemen, and they had given Sarah the best seat, so that she could look out of the small, mud-splashed window and watch the landscape rushing by. Except for a few villages, she saw the same view all day: a few farms and an infinity of bare trees with patches of snow beneath. But Sarah did not tire of wondering at it all.

"My dear, what do you see out there that is so interesting?" inquired an old gentleman who sat beside her.

Sarah turned her animated, rosy face toward him, and laughed.

"Oh, I guess it's not so interesting, exactly," she said. "But I never was away from Norwich since I was a baby."

A young man with pomaded hair and an oily complexion took out a packet of barley sugar candy in the shapes of animals. He helped himself to a lion and then held the bag out to Sarah, who declined. She liked barley sugar, but Aunt Lathrop had admonished her to take nothing from anyone.

"May I tender you assistance when we arrive at our destination?" the young man inquired. He spoke in a prim and unctuous manner, studiously avoiding the suspicious gaze of the old gentleman. "I shall be delighted to convey you to wherever you desire to terminate your journey."

"No, thank you, sir," Sarah said. "I am being met."

"Fortunate," murmured the older man.

Toward twilight, they arrived at the outskirts of Providence, but it was such a large town that the stage rolled through street after street before finally coming to the central stopping point. Sarah saw a river, with a cold sunset reflected in it; wharves where large sailing ships were tied up; and a steep hill covered all over with substantial houses and meetinghouses. The house windows were at that moment glowing with sunset light, so that they looked, Sarah thought, as if they were made of jewels. Her mother had a garnet necklace that glowed like that, and Sarah suddenly felt sure that house windows sparkling like garnets were a good omen. From now on, her life would sparkle, too.

Sister Nancy, with Uncle Cornell, was waiting for her. They put her luggage into a barrow and trundled it up the hill to one of the houses, a stylish, dark-red frame one, on Benevolent Street.

Ezekiel Cornell was an older brother of the ill-fated James Cornell. Through his own efforts, he had become owner of a substantial sail-making business. His wife and seven children were well-dressed and robust, and the house was filled with pleasant things. Sarah noted big beds with canopies over them, blue-and-white Canton china, a Turkey carpet, Hepplewhite-style chairs, made in Rhode Island of Honduras mahogany, and a towering grandfather clock, from London, that struck the quarter-hours in a sweet, high chime.

Uncle and Aunt Cornell seemed fond of Nancy. She had a room of her own, and when a certain young man came courting on Friday evenings, she was allowed to receive him in the parlor, while the family sat in the kitchen.

The young man's name was Grindall Rawson, the son of a Providence cabinet-maker. He welcomed his sweetheart's little sister, and she thought him handsome and clever. She was overcome with jealousy of her sister. Why had Nancy been so lucky?

Grindall had recently finished apprenticeship to a tailor and was setting up his own tailor shop.

"I could work for you," Sarah said. "I'm apprenticed to a mantuamaker, and it would be easy as pie for me to learn tailoring."

"We'll think about that," Grindall said gently. "You are very young to go away from home."

"Oh, but I could live *here*," Sarah said optimistically.

She had not realized that Aunt Cornell was not taken by her. When Sarah first arrived, she had been so tired and so overawed that she was quiet and demure, but as soon as she became accustomed to her sister and the houseful of Cornell cousins, she began to talk loudly, rush up and down stairs, and jump for joy if something pleased her. Aunt Cornell preferred the young to be quiet. Another mistake Sarah made was asking questions about her long-gone father. Nancy, a gentle-mannered young person of nineteen, advised her sister to leave that subject alone.

"Uncle and Aunt think of him as dead," she said. "They say, when people behave outrageously, 'tis best to turn your back on them forever and forget they ever were."

One morning, after Sarah had been in the house a week, Aunt Cornell announced at the breakfast table, "Sarah's mother is anxious for her. She had better be going home soon."

The children expressed disappointment. Sarah played games with them and made them laugh.

Sarah exclaimed, "Oh, no, Aunt! My mother won't be in the least anxious."

"I say she will," Aunt Cornell said firmly. "We have enjoyed your visit, Sarah, and we all hope you can come another time. Nancy, here is thirty cents. Take your sister down to Richmond's and buy her a yard of grosgrain ribbon as a farewell present from us all. She may choose whether it is to be black, brown, or gray."

Sarah would have preferred scarlet, but she said nothing. Any present at all was pleasing.

Richmond's Drygoods Emporium, on Weybosset Street, belonged to relations of Aunt Cornell. It was far more exciting than the drygoods store in Norwich, which offered little choice. Here there were laces from France and Belgium, wools from England, taffetas and crepes from Italy, cashmere shawls and Chinese brocades. It was enough to make her think of liking the mantua-making trade, to imagine the lovely clothes to be made from such fabrics. She had to remind herself that she would never wear them.

Besides fabrics, the store had a small selection of jewelry, such as coral beads, mosaic pins, and silver-gilt bracelets.

"Oh, Nancy, let me try the corals," Sarah cried. She put a single strand of matched beads around her neck and admired herself in a square of looking glass.

"Oh, lawzy me!" she whispered to herself. "How elegant."

"Come and pick out the ribbon," Nancy said.

Sarah did not take off the beads. Instead, she closed the collar of her cloak over them and moved to the other side of the shop, where she chose a yard of plain brown grosgrain. It would make nice bonnet-strings.

When they got home again and took off their cloaks in Nancy's room, Nancy suddenly gave a scream. She had glimpsed a flash of red as Sarah adjusted the high-ruffled collar of her dress.

"Sarah, the beads! You are still wearing them!"

Sarah put up her hand, felt the beads round her neck, and colored deeply. She knew quite well that she had hidden them under her cloak and that just now she had pushed them inside her dress-collar. But had she meant to? She was aware that there were serious lacks in her life. But had she really supposed that a string of stolen coral beads would help?

"I didn't *plan* to do it, Nancy," she said. That much, at least, she was sure of. "I guess I forgot I had them on. Oh, Nancy, I just forgot." She took off the beads and handed them to her sister. "You can take them back and say what happened."

Aunt Cornell overheard and came marching in.

"To steal is very bad, to lie and say you didn't is even worse," she told Sarah furiously.

"I didn't."

"Then how did it happen?"

"I don't know. I was only . . ."

"Only stealing, that's what," Aunt said. "Well, I can tell you one thing, straight off. We can't have any thieves in our house. Not with little children, to set a bad example to. Your visit is over."

They packed her belongings and took her to the stagecoach, but not before stopping at Richmond's store, where she handed over the beads. Neither Aunt nor Uncle said good-bye, and certainly not "come again." They gave her a letter to deliver to her mother.

"Thank the Lord, old Colonel Leffingwell is dead," Aunt said, instead of good-bye, "and did not live to see his grandchild a common shoplifter."

Sarah considered destroying or accidentally losing the letter. But, she reflected, Aunt Cornell would certainly write another and send it by post.

Lucretia, upon reading the letter, wept and screamed, and then felt compelled to tell Aunt Lathrop and Miss Sophronia Sims. Aunt Lathrop saw it as her duty to inform her children, and also Dr. Cresswell, so that they might all redouble their prayers on Sarah's behalf. Soon there was no one in Norwich who did not know that Sarah Maria Cornell was a shoplifter.

To everyone's surprise, Miss Sims was willing to keep her, although Sarah knew she was now counting the buttons and spools and keeping track of the needles. Sarah was too miserable to care, and she was grateful to remain secluded from the world and come and go when it was dark. She went no more to play "Break the Pope's Neck," nor to quilting bees nor to sleighing parties with the other young people, and when she went to meeting she kept her eyes resolutely on the psalm book, or on Dr. Cresswell's bald head, or sometimes on the high, clear-paned windows. Never on the curious or disapproving faces around her.

The winter passed, spring came, and the tall elms rising to Heaven outside the meetinghouse were thick with fresh, green leaves. One Sabbath morning a white butterfly came fluttering in, and Sarah thought, if only she could be like it—pure white, blameless, and yet entirely free. She wondered if the butterfly

might be one of those "signs" she was always looking for—
because just as it flew past her, Dr. Cresswell announced that
there would be a Congregationalist Revival throughout the coming week.

"Sinners, come to God," he cried. "We will hew down Satan
with the great battle-ax of the righteous."

This striking phrase did not sound like Dr. Cresswell, who
usually was expounding difficult theology—the true meaning of
Socinianism, for instance, or the mysterious import of Whelpley's
Triangle. Perhaps he had realized that Revivals were effective
drawing-cards among other denominations. The Methodists, in
particular, had been winning people away from the Congrega-
tionalists, and it was time to fight them with their own weapons,
although in a modified and seemly manner. Sarah had heard of
Revivals where sinners crawled up the aisle, but she was confident that Dr. Cresswell would consider that excessive. For him,
contrition should occur inwardly. As he put it, one's heart should
"crack and dissolve with guilt and cry out in humility." But this
had not yet happened to Sarah. She did not feel like a shoplifter,
because she had not *planned* to shoplift. It was as if someone else
had put on coral beads and walked out of Richmond's store.

During the Revival there were sermons every day, and when
the meetinghouse was filled to overflowing, people knelt in the
middle of the Common. At last, a sense of penitence overcame
Sarah. Although she had not planned to take the beads, she had
certainly wanted them. She had coveted them, and so had broken
one of the Ten Commandments. She had set her heart on worldly
things instead of on spiritual ones. Why? Because, as Dr. Cresswell had shouted from the pulpit, we are all born wretched sinners, as filled with Original Sin as rotten meat is filled with mag-
gots. And whose fault is that? Eve's, for listening to the Serpent,
the Devil in disguise. The Devil dwells within sinners, and unless they cast him out he causes them to stray even against their
wills.

Sarah went to see Dr. Cresswell and told him that she at last
understood these matters. She would strive to resist temptations,

she assured him. She longed to be as pure as a little white butterfly. And the tears flowed as she thought of herself as a free and winged white creature. But when she rocked back and forth and began to sob and wail loudly, he was displeased.

"This high state of excited feeling is hazardous to your spiritual well-being," he said. "Perhaps it is natural among young Christians of a choleric temperament, which I would judge yours to be, but it is too agitating. Pray for a constant, intense, but mild and seemly desire for Conversion. Do not ruffle the passions."

Sarah went home and tried to feel intense desire for Conversion without becoming agitated. She prayed for Grace and for a sign that God forgave her.

Miss Sophronia's cottage was beside the river, and when Sarah raised her eyes from her needle and looked out of the window, she saw the blue water, the green rushes, and a flock of swans at rest there. One day, the thought came to her, "I will grow in purity. It cannot happen all at once. From a small and fragile butterfly I will become a beautiful white swan."

Such thoughts were the right ones and sounded like Dr. Cresswell. The idea went through her mind that she could be a preacher herself and lead people to Christ. She wondered why the Bible said that women had to keep silent in church, but when she went back to Dr. Cresswell she did not mention that subject, knowing that he would say that nothing in the Scriptures should be questioned. She quietly told him about the swans, and he made her a Church Member.

After that, she attended church regularly for a time, and people pointed her out as the thief who repented. Some who had not done so before nodded when they met her, but others still snubbed her in the street, or whispered and giggled behind her back. A young man she liked, nice, upright Ezra Stoppard, who had once been first in line for a "wheelbarrow-fashion" kiss, now looked away when he saw her, and went strolling on summer evenings with her cousin, Harriet Lathrop, who intended to become a missionary.

"You had better work hard," Miss Sophronia said when she

daydreamed. "Girls like you need a trade they can depend on. After all, you don't have very much choice, do you?"

Miss Sophronia's choice, if it had been a choice, haunted Sarah. Had she had even one chance to marry? But perhaps bending over needlework all day was better than the hardships of a farmer's wife. Sarah had heard of farm wives who went insane from the unending labor and the loneliness. Suicide was not an unfamiliar word in rural New England. One heard, "She drowned herself," or, "She hanged herself," or, "She took rat poison."

If one couldn't or wouldn't marry, and had no vocation for missionary work, there was one more alternative—a new one—and that was to go to work in a mill. Grandfather Leffingwell's mills still employed a few local people, but now larger mills of all kinds were springing up all over New England, wherever there was a river to provide waterpower.

When, in the summer of 1820, Sarah began to talk about going to a mill, her mother objected strenuously.

"You have been disgraced enough," she said, "without going out into the world like a foundling. You are a Leffingwell."

"Much good it has done me," Sarah said. But it was important to be respectful toward one's parent ("Honor thy mother and father") and she went on in a subdued tone, "Mother, you know that lots of girls go to the mills, just for a year or two. They save money for their dowries."

"Well, the good Lord knows I can't give you a dowry," Lucretia said. "How much could you save in a couple of years?"

"Maybe a hundred and fifty dollars, if I'm careful."

Lucretia began to look interested. "Well, certainly *you* need a husband."

"Why do *I* need one—more than other girls?"

"Take my word for it," Lucretia said mysteriously. "And the sooner the better."

That was all the information about men that Sarah ever got. She wanted to ask more: what was her mother's own romance like? How had James Cornell come courting, and for how long?

But Sarah knew better than to mention the name of her father; it invariably brought on a crying fit. And other questions she had about men could not be asked. But Sarah had said the right thing when she mentioned saving for a dowry, and Lucretia gave her permission to go and work in Jewett City.

Dr. Cresswell was not so easily won over. He was shocked when he heard of it, and asked Sarah to come and see him at the parsonage.

"Employment for women away from their own homes can only lead to serious trouble," he said when she called. "You are sure to fall in with dubious companions."

"Oh, no, sir," Sarah said. "Only other young girls like me."

"And men," he added. "Who knows what sort of men!"

"I can take care of myself."

"Women can never take care of themselves. It is a weakness of the sex," he said. He stood up and walked over to her chair. Although not much more than forty, he was thin and bent, with the unhealthy pallor of one who rarely goes outdoors. "Women need husbands and fathers. You, poor child, cruelly lack a father. But you might have, someday, a husband."

"I hope so."

"You hope so. Have you someone in mind?"

Sarah thought of Grindall Rawson and sighed. "No," she answered.

Dr. Cresswell began to pace up and down, rubbing his scrawny hands together nervously.

"Sarah, I will now tell you what I have been contemplating. As you know, Mrs. Cresswell died in March. I suffered a great loss. I want you to know that I have been giving some thought to your taking her place. As you know I have six motherless little ones and a large house. In spite of your very serious departure from the path, it has been my observation that I am able to wield a great influence upon you and that you have rather beautifully repented. I believe that, with unswerving obedience, you will make a fitting helpmeet for me."

Sarah sat absolutely still, dumbfounded. In her daydreams, she

had had romantic thoughts about Grindall Rawson, Ezra Stoppard, and several others, but never of Dr. Jonah Cresswell. She
tried it now, for half a minute, and knew at once that romantic
thoughts of him were out of the question. He had a small, pursed
mouth full of irregular, yellow teeth. Sarah could not imagine
kissing it.

"I've startled you, I see," he said, coming nearer. "It is quite
becoming that you are speechless. You are perhaps aware that a
clergyman's wife must work from morning to night, and set the
community a good example. Her sole wish is to please her husband."

Something in his expression reminded her of a hungry dinner
guest, waiting for Grace to be said, while eyeing a full plate
before him.

"To please her husband," he repeated, "in every way. Do you
know what I mean when I say, 'in every way'?"

"I . . ."

"Quite proper that you shouldn't. In time, I shall instruct
you." Again, the look of the greedy dinner guest. "I had not
intended to inform you of this matter until more time had passed.
Poor Jane has been gone only a few months. But I must warn
you that if you go to work in a mill, I cannot marry you. It is
something I so entirely disapprove of."

"I see."

"So, Sarah . . ." He came back to her chair and stood above
her so that, tight-lipped and Sunday-solemn, he was looking
down into her low-necked, high-waisted bodice. "Is it understood?"

"Sir," Sarah said. "Sir, I . . ."

"Say nothing to anyone. I am still in mourning. And you, after
all, are only recently saved from sin. Better to allow some time to
elapse. Go back to your needle."

"Yes, sir."

Sarah obeyed the minister in saying nothing to anyone. She
knew better than to tell her mother and aunt that she was turning

down the chance to become an example to the community. The following week, she left Norwich for a nearby village, Jewett City, where there was a new mill that made cotton cloth. The girls worked twenty or thirty in a weaving room, and lived in big frame boardinghouses, four to a room and two to a bed. The work was easier than the complicated dress-making she had done for Miss Sophronia, and, far from being lonely, it was somewhat overwhelmingly gregarious. But the great advantage was that no one there had heard of Sarah Maria Cornell, the shoplifter.

Dr. Cresswell wrote to say that he was shocked and dismayed by her act of rebellion in going away to the mill and that his offer was withdrawn. "I fear," he wrote "that the Devil is still within you."

If he was, he had very little leeway. The mill-girls rose before dawn and worked several hours until breakfast, for which they had thirty minutes. Then they worked again until noon and again from one to seven, and there was a nine o'clock curfew. The girls' morals were of concern to their employers, because if the mills were thought to tolerate loose women, parents would keep their daughters at home. If a young man of the town wanted to court a mill-girl, he had to do it in the communal sitting room of a boardinghouse, with the landlady and some forty other girls looking on.

The mill management required the girls to attend church— any church they liked, as long as they went somewhere. Sarah decided to try the Methodists. Her bedmate, Leafy Fitch, was a recent convert and full of enthusiasm. Besides Sunday meeting, there were Love Feasts, as they called their prayer-meetings, every Tuesday evening. And females could get up and "exhort." Exhorting was not preaching, because St. Paul forbade women to preach, but it did not seem to Sarah to be very dissimilar. At the first Love Feast Sarah attended, she stood up and exhorted, talk-ing about white butterflies and swans. The other girls wept, and one of them fell on her knees and screamed out that she was saved.

In the heat of July and August, the poorly ventilated loom

rooms reached a temperature of over a hundred degrees. It was a punishment like Hell, someone said, and Sarah thought, "Dr. Cresswell would think I'm in the right place and I'm not even dead yet."

The boardinghouses were hot, too. Sarah's bedmate, Leafy, came from northern New Hampshire and wasn't used to heat, and the snores of the two in the other bed kept Sarah awake. Often she and Leafy lay and whispered.

"How is it that you are so sweet and good, Leafy? I wish I could be like you."

Leafy did not deny that she was good. "I just never want to do things I ain't supposed to," she said.

"You never wanted a pretty dress you can't afford? You don't hanker to see how you'd look in pale-blue watered-silk?"

"My Pa wouldn't like it," Leafy said, giggling.

"But why do you care what he'd like?"

"He's a good Pa to us. He buys us white sugar sometimes and then Ma makes a saleratus cake. He pets us. He tells us girls we're good-lookin'. He asks us special to make his shirts, because he thinks of us when he wears them. Things like that."

"Is he handsome?"

"I don't know. I never thought much about that. Is your Pa handsome?"

"I don't know," Sarah said. "My Pa's gone off."

She didn't like being pitied, so she quickly added, "I don't care. I don't miss having a father. They're too strict. Anyway, I've got a sweetheart."

Leafy wanted to hear all about him, and Sarah described Grindall Rawson: of the middle height, with light-brown wavy hair, and a very kind look to him. Sarah put more and more embroidery on the story, seeing that Leafy was impressed. No, she said, they weren't to marry for a while, but they'd promised each other. Her sister was jealous. Sarah had stolen him right out from under her nose.

Leafy was delighted, and became even more admiring of Sarah. She must work hard, Leafy said, and save up for that wedding.

A few months later, a letter came from Nancy, saying that she and Grindall Rawson were to be married. Sarah, clutching the letter, called Leafy into their bedroom after noonday dinner.

"My sister is getting married! Here, read it for yourself."

Leafy was not a great reader. "What's it say?"

"She's marrying my sweetheart. He courted me, and now he's marrying Nancy."

"Oh, the way men are," Leafy said, as if out of profound knowledge.

Sarah wept. Not for Grindall—for she knew she had woven a fairy tale around him—but for her own sense of being un-loved.

"I wish I was at the bottom of the millpond," she said, sob-bing.

"Oh, you mustn't talk so, Sarah. It's wickedness."

"But I am wicked. I am a great sinner," Sarah said, thinking of the coral beads.

"No, you ain't," said loyal Leafy. "Don't you remember how you exhorted us girls, all about the white butterfly? You've re-pented."

Sarah went to the clothes cupboard and took out a white dress she had just finished making. Because it suited the melodrama of being a wronged fiancée, she put it on, and tied white ribbons in her hair.

"How do I look, Leafy? Do I look like a pure white butter-fly?"

"You look real beautiful," said Leafy.

The factory-whistle blew, and as there was no time to change, Sarah went to work in the white dress. No one ever wore white to work and the other girls laughed.

"What are you dressed up like that for?"

Since she did not really know, she gave them no answer. But to Leafy she whispered, "I am a bride today. A bride of sorrow."

IV

A Roving Woman

On Sunday mornings early, a stagecoach came through Jewett City, bound for New London. The Sunday after Sarah heard of her sister's marriage, she told her landlady she was going home to Norwich, and went to New London alone. She craved the impersonality of streets where no one knew her. No one here could say, "There goes the girl who is a little bit off her head—she wore a white dress to work," or, "There goes the girl who steals." Sarah looked at people boldly, and thought, "They see I'm a nice, pretty girl who'll do them no harm." But after a rough-looking man looked straight back at her and asked how she'd like to go to bed with him, she went about with her eyes studying the cobblestones and the herringbone-brick sidewalks.

There was little to do in New London on a Sunday morning except go to church, and this—though she would not have admitted it—Sarah had fled Jewett City to avoid. She went down by the wharves to look at the ships—fishing-boats and whalers and ocean-going three-riggers, and one spanking clipper ship, just setting sail. The blue harbor sparkled, the sun shone, and there were heady smells of salt water, whale oil, fish, and tar. She sat down on a barrel and watched the gulls: the free, white gulls.

Very soon a sailor sat down beside her. He had blue eyes and a handsome, merry Irish face.

"Sure, and you're the pretty thing," he said.

She kept on watching the gulls, and did not reply.

91

"Is it shy ye are, or just unfriendly? Will you take a touch of Irish whiskey?"

"I do not go to barrooms or saloons, sir," she said with particular dignity.

"I've a saloon in me pocket," he said, and brought out a bottle.

"I am a Temperance woman," Sarah told him.

"Ah, Temperance, is it? That's why you're looking so proper. What a shame, now. You don't mind if I take a drop?" And he swigged from the bottle. "Something to eat ye'd like, perhaps?"

"I never accept invitations from strangers."

"If I had that rule, I'd starve to death. Aren't you lonely, sitting here all by yourself? Let's be lonely together, what's the harm? Are you far from home, then?"

"I have no home," Sarah said, and in spite of herself she let him see that her eyes filled with tears.

The young sailor put his hand out and then withdrew it. "I'll not touch you, because you are a lady, I can see that. But I'm sorry. I have a home in County Sligo, but it's four years since I've seen it, and I don't know if my mother is dead or what's become of my sisters. Can't we be lonely together?"

Sarah could not help liking him. He was respectful, no doubt of it, and his eyes, blue as the sea he sailed on, were kind. She thought if she had to choose the best of human traits, it would be kindness.

They walked together all afternoon, eating oysters from a street peddler, and watching the ships in the harbor. There was a traveling animal show in New London—not open on Sundays, but Sarah and the sailor saw a giraffe's head poking out of the top of a wagon. The giraffe surveyed Sarah with its mild, long-lashed eyes. She thought it the most extraordinary thing she had ever seen, and she wondered if seeing it were a sign that her life was about to become strange and wonderful.

The sailor, whose name was Louis O'Malley, had seen giraffes before. He had also seen elephants, lifting great logs of teak. And an evil, black snake in a basket. On a sea like blue glass, off Zanzibar, his ship had passed close to Arab *dhows*, whose decks were packed with manacled slaves; and he had watched while Arabs and slaves alike prostrated themselves toward Mecca. In India, he had been inside temples that were decorated with many-armed, dancing gods. And he told Sarah of a golden Buddha, in Burma, bigger than the First Congregational Church of New London.

"I don't know whether to believe you, Louis," Sarah said. "If 'tis true, 'tis shocking."

"Believe me, darlin'," he said. "The truth is so strange over there, I don't need to lie to you."

He pointed out the ship he'd been sailing in for three years, a schooner whose home port was Liverpool. She would not be leaving for several weeks as she was waiting for cargo. Louis put Sarah on the stagecoach back to Jewett City, and gave her a kiss as he handed her up.

"I will come and see you next week," he said, and he did.

Sarah was afraid the other girls would be scornful of a common sailor, but he came in clean clothes and wearing his strawberry-blond hair in a pigtail. Sarah introduced him as a friend of her brother, James. The ever-watchful landlady happened to be in bed with a toothache that morning, and Sarah was able to slip away after church without having to answer questions. She put gingerbread and cheese for two in her pocket, and she and Louis walked into the woods and found a grassy bank to sit on, by the side of a cool brook.

" 'Tisn't proper, being here just us two," Sarah informed him. "But I'm tired of forty girls all the time."

"I'm glad you didn't invite them along," Louis said. "I'd a fair sight rather be here with just you."

"Yes, well, you mustn't sit so close. Have some gingerbread and cheese."

They shared it and it was soon gone.

"I've been lonesome for you, my darlin'," he said. "How close is all right?"

"Two feet away."

"Is that one of them Sunday Blue Laws I hear about in New

England? Sure and that's pretty strict. Don't the boys and girls here ever hold hands, even?"

Sarah could not help laughing as he pretended to measure off the distance between them.

"Yes, sometimes they hold hands, I think," she said. She felt happy—much happier than she could remember. To laugh and to have no one telling her what to do, and to feel admired and wanted—these were all new and marvelous experiences.

"And do they ever kiss?" he went on. "Two feet apart, of course?"

"Perhaps. It's called sparking."

"Maybe you'd show me how it's done."

"Proper girls don't spark. Much."

"How much?" He reached across the two feet between them, trying to take her hand.

Flirting with him, she jumped to her feet.

"Let's look for wild strawberries. There are lots in these woods." She ran away, through the ferny undergrowth.

Nearby, they found a wealth of tiny sweet strawberries, and spent an hour or so gathering them. Sarah took off her bonnet and lined it with leaves, and when it was full of berries they went back to the brookside and made a little ceremony of eating the berries, one by one, with the bonnet between them. The hot summer day made the sweat run, but Sarah and Louis hardly noticed. Louis picked out the best berries and put them in her mouth.

"So," he said, when the last berry was gone, "in New England, you have to eat a bonnetful of strawberries before you kiss. Is that the way of it?"

"Yes," she said mischievously. "And then only one kiss."

He gave her that one.

"You see? I mind the rules. I'm a man of honor," he said. "My mother named me for a king. Louis of France, that is. The one who lost his head." He winked at Sarah and put his arm around her. "I've a different way of losing my head," he said. "Now, tell me more about this sparking."

They sat in the woods all afternoon, kissing and talking and kissing. Louis was talented at both. When she put a stop to his kisses, he told her about Ireland and the little, gray stone house where his mother lived. In his childhood, he told her, he had looked out over the cliffs at the misty Atlantic and thought that if he could only lift the mist, like a curtain, he would see America. He had always wanted to be a sailor, and had run away and left his brothers to work the little farm.

"Who wants to plant the same potato fields all his life?" he said. "I like variety!"

"Variety in girls?" demanded Sarah.

"Not any more," he said. "Show me why I shouldn't want variety any more, darlin'. You kiss *me.*"

She put her strawberry-stained lips fairly on his, and as she did so, felt an unfamiliar urgency to move very close to him and to put her hand in his hair. But she was too shy, and withdrew, panting a little. This he noticed at once, and tightened his arm around her.

"Now, I'm going to show you how they kiss in France."

"How can there be any other way?" asked Sarah. "A kiss is a kiss."

He tipped her chin up, and kissed her, working his tongue delicately into her mouth. When he released her, he said, "So a kiss is a kiss, is it? I think you like the French way."

Sarah had her eyes closed and opened them slowly. The expression on her face was no longer playful and flirtatious, but troubled.

"Louis," she said. "I think that is too much sparking."

"But why? You're so lovely to love," he whispered, his cheek on hers.

She drew back and looked at him, wide-eyed.

"Do you *love* me?" she asked.

He seemed to perceive how serious she was, for he hesitated. "You're a lovely thing," he said.

Her next question seemed to startle him: "Are you a Methodist?"

"Begorra! What an idea. I'm a Catholic, to be sure."

"A Papist? I never met one before." The memory of "Break the Pope's Neck" flashed into her mind.

"We don't bite," Louis said.

But Sarah, a little rattled by this news, jumped up and tied on her bonnet.

"I must get home. The landlady will be asking me all kinds of questions."

"Give us a farewell kiss," Louis said.

"No, I told you, we've already had too much sparking. People shouldn't spark unless . . ."

"Unless what?"

"Unless there's something coming of it."

At that, he was silent. Both looking rather solemn, they found their way out of the woods and walked down the village street to Sarah's boardinghouse.

At the door, she gave him her hand and he bowed over it.

"Good-bye, Mr. O'Malley," she said.

He turned to go, but almost immediately turned back again.

"Come to New London next Sunday," he said. "I'll take you aboard a ship and we'll eat at a tavern."

"I shouldn't."

"Then I'll come here."

Sarah could see the landlady waiting for her just inside the door.

"Oh, no," she said, "that wouldn't be a good idea."

"Then I'll meet you at the stage, Sunday next," Louis said, and walked off, whistling.

All week long, Sarah thought about Louis, and sometimes planned going to New London and sometimes not. But in her heart of hearts she knew she was going, even though she would have to tell more lies to get away. Most of the girls were willing to submit to the strict rules, but Sarah found it difficult. There were often good-looking young blades hanging around the factory door, looking for a chance to lollygag with a pretty girl. "Walk you home, Miss? Carry your bundle? Carry your um-

brella? Carry *you*?" The girls generally turned up their noses at
such talk, but Sarah sometimes could not help giggling and cast-
ing a young man a sidelong look. But that was as far as it went.
Romance had to come out of novels, and these the girls read with
avidity, passing them around from apron pocket to apron pocket
so that the landlady would not see. A great favorite was *Charlotte
Temple*, a sorrowful tale of a young girl seduced and ruined.

"What do you think about Charlotte?" Sarah asked her bedmate, Leafy. "Why did she run away with that man?"

"Oh, I wouldn't know, I'm sure," Leafy said, blushing.

Sarah did not mention it again, but she thought about it. Was
it love that made Charlotte give in? And if the young man loved
her as much as he said, why did he leave her? And why could he
go gaily on his way, while there was nothing for her to do but lie
down and die? But Sarah knew no one who could answer such
questions.

It was still early in June and the following Sunday was cloudy
and cool. Sarah set off at dawn, wearing a new dress she had just
finished. It was a dress for a hot day, made of flowery chintz,
with short, puffed sleeves and a flounce at the hem. Today she
needed her shawl over it, and this hid the charming lowcut neckline, which she had edged with a frill of narrow lace.

Louis was waiting at the New London stage-stop, his face covered with smiles. As it looked like rain, they went at once to the
tavern. Sarah had been in the tavern at Norwich, but this one
was bigger and more interesting. There was a big stove, and men
sitting around it with mugs of drink. Some were plainly dressed,
like Louis. Others seemed to have gone to considerable trouble
with their clothes and wore well-polished boots, coats with velvet
lapels, and very high collars. These were clerks and peddlers in
their Sunday-best. There were only a few women present and
they seemed to Sarah to have brassy voices and a bedraggled
air.

Everyone stared at Sarah and Louis. Louis escorted her to a
seat by the window and grandly ordered chops and wine for two.

"I didn't know all this would be allowed on the Sabbath,"
Sarah whispered.

"All what? Just a little merriment?"

At that moment, one of the men by the stove produced a banjo and began to play and sing "Rolling Down to Rio."

Louis added, "*And* a little music. In Bantry, we'd think this a highly respectable sort of place."

"Those men keep looking at me."

"Then they are men of good taste, my darlin'."

"Are those women their wives?"

Louis rolled his eyes comically.

"Don't worry about it, love. Open your shawl and let's see your pretty new dress."

"When they're not looking," Sarah said, blushing. She had copied a sketch of a London model, and the bodice of her dress was lower than was customary in New England.

The men went on staring at her all through dinner.

When it was time to call for the bill, a heavy rainstorm began to pelt the street outside. Louis asked the proprietor if he had a room to rent, just until the storm would be over.

"Oh, but I couldn't go to a room," Sarah protested. She had said no more today about religion, but now she suddenly felt sure she ought to tell him that Methodist girls did not go to rooms with young men. But while she was wondering how to say this without spoiling the delight of their being together, he took her by the elbow and led her upstairs.

"It's no different from sitting by a brook," he assured her, "except it's got a roof on it. We were alone there, and we're alone here. How is it different?"

Part of Sarah knew clearly that it was different. The other part wanted to do whatever Louis wanted to do.

"Give us a kiss, then, Sarah love."

"No."

But after he had kissed her once or twice, she kissed him back. The wine they had been drinking made her feel languorous as she had never felt before. Languorous first, and then loving. He looked shrewdly at her.

"Lie back here, my darlin'," he said very softly. "That's better. Take your ease."

The mattress was made of barley straw and the quilt was clean. Over Louis's shoulders, which now leaned above her, she could see a framed lithograph of dreamy young people in a boat. The picture was called *The Golden Age*, and the maidens were playing lutes and dangling their fingers in the water and twining flowers, while two youths in togas paddled them along.

"I feel so happy, Louis," Sarah said.

"You are my darlin' and I want you to be happy," he said. "It makes you beautiful. Now, take off your shawl and show me your new dress."

He admired the way she had put lace at the neckline, and traced it around with his finger. Then, in a gentle, even reverent way, he unfastened the bodice and took first one and then the other nipple in his mouth.

"No," she said, and made a futile effort to rise. "What are you doing?"

"Let me show you what I can do," he said, and pushed her dress up and put his hand on her thighs.

"No, no," she said, gasping.

"No, no, no, no," he said, imitating her, and tickling her a little, so that she had to giggle. His hand went higher, and she gave a little scream.

He got up, as though he were offended.

"As you will, then," he said, and went and stood at the window.

For several moments, neither spoke.

Finally, "I thought you loved me," said he.

She looked at him in confusion. "I don't rightly know what to think about love," she said.

"Don't they say that word here in New England?"

"Not much."

"What do they say, then?"

"I'm not sure," Sarah said. "I guess they say, 'I think a good deal of you,' or maybe, 'I'm real partial to you.' "

"Well, in Ireland we say, 'Darlin', I love you.' And that's what I'm sayin' to you."

"Oh, Louis!"

"And don't you love me, too?"

Cautiously, Sarah walked over to the window where he stood.

"I reckon I do, Louis. Better than anyone else in all the world."

"But not well enough to touch. Or come close to, at all."

At that, she put a timid hand on his chest.

"Couldn't we just spark and nothing more?"

He took her in his arms and began to kiss her, at first gently and then deeper and harder, until she thought there was nothing in the world but him and herself. She wanted it to go on forever, and she let him carry her back to the bed. Then the great sense of contentment and joy was suddenly disrupted. He entered her and made a few vigorous thrusts that caused her pain. Then, in bewilderment, she saw blood on the quilt, and all she could say was, "Oh, look what you've done."

"You've done, my dear," Louis said. He gave her an apologetic look. "I don't feel right about taking a virgin. But ye'll not be rooned if ye only keep your mouth shut. Nobody will be the wiser."

"But *God* knows," she said, watching him finish off the bottle of wine. "Will God forgive us?"

"He'll forgive me, because I'll make it a matter of confession," he said. "And as for you, my dear—all Protestants are damned."

He laughed, but then he noticed how unhappy she looked and he said, "But don't forget, I love you."

Sarah burst into sobs. "Then you must take care of me. We must be married."

Louis drained his glass before replying. Then he said gently but firmly, "No. The one doesn't necessarily mean the other, my dear."

"But it does! In our country, it *does*."

"Yes, well, you see, I'm a stranger here. I'm a sailor, a roving man. I can't bide by your rules." He patted her hand. "Cheer up. You're a beautiful thing, Sarah, and you'll be married in no time."

But her tears made him melancholy, and after finishing the bottle, he took her to the stage-stop.

"And I'll see you next week, darlin'," he said, "if my ship don't sail."

But it must have sailed, for Sarah never saw Louis O'Malley again.

"Hast thou not poured me out as milk, and curdled me like cheese?" Lucretia demanded. She was quoting the *Book of Job*, as she was fond of doing. "What am I to do, Sarah Maria, with a ruined daughter?"

"I must waste away and die, I suppose," Sarah said grimly. "People never say anything bad about dead girls. It wouldn't be proper."

"You are a wretched and wicked young woman and your remarks are not humorous," Aunt Lathrop said.

It was now late in September. The two sisters had called Sarah into the Leffingwell parlor, where only serious events took place. Lucretia had opened the windows, but there was still a shut-up smell, and some lingering whiff of flowers from the last funeral.

"She must go away into the country," Lucretia said. "The deepest country."

"Fortunately, Sarah Maria, I have thought of the right place," Aunt Lathrop said. "You will go to our distant cousin, Miss Fanny Winsor, in Scituate, Massachusetts. She is a maiden lady, very charitable, a true Christian, and since I have done things for her from time to time, she will not refuse."

"But, Joanna," Lucretia said. "Is she not a Methodist?"

"I declare, Lucretia Cornell, you do beat all!" Aunt Lathrop said severely. "A pregnant daughter with no husband and you worry about her being corrupted by Methodists!"

"But, I only meant, suppose this foolish child should take to camp-meetings and praying at the top of her lungs, and all those crazy things they do?"

"We cannot choose," Aunt Lathrop said. "The Cornells won't have her, you can be sure, and she must go well away from Norwich."

Sarah said nothing. She was frightened and miserable, for it was now clear to her that Louis would never be back. She had left Jewett City as soon as she realized that her waist was thickening, but not before others had noticed it and caused talk. She had stared into the cold, dark millpond and considered drowning herself. But even in her distress, she was tenacious of life, and instead she had come home and confided in her mother and aunt, which was only slightly less awful than the millpond. No other alternative existed.

Now, once again, she packed her things and let Lucretia and Joanna see her to the Norwich stage-stop—not so exciting now as it had been that brisk day in January, not three years before, when she had set out for Providence with a heart as high as the stars.

On that day, she had scarcely noticed how the stage rattled her insides. Now, she found the jolting painful, and when they stopped to spend the night at an inn, she had severe cramps. Sharing a room with a stranger, she did not complain, but in the middle of the night she was in such pain that she found her way out to the privy and there had a miscarriage. She did not at once know what had happened. The woman who shared her room, seeing much blood on Sarah's skirt and petticoat, made the diagnosis.

"And a good thing, too," the woman said nastily. "Miss!"

"I'm married," Sarah said defensively.

"Married, is it? Then what's your name?"

"Excuse me," said Sarah quietly, "but I don't believe it is any of your concern."

"What is the world coming to?" said the woman. "Bad women going about just like anyone else and talking disrespectful. You'll be cursing me next, I suppose."

Sarah forebore to do so, although she knew how. Louis had known some rare oaths and curses which he had liked to reel off to make her giggle and put her hand on his mouth.

The woman tied on her bonnet before the looking glass, took up her portmanteau, and left the room, saying as she went,

"When I was young, girls like you were drummed out of town. And if they ever came back they were tarred and feathered. How would you like that, *Miss?*"

When she was gone, Sarah lay on the bed and cried. She cried for her baby, she cried because Louis's arms were not around her, she cried for the physical pain she had been through, and she cried because her life was ruined before it began and there was no way to mend it. Her mother had put it this way: as ruined as a smashed pitcher.

That took a lot of tears, all that were in her. When no more would come, she got up, put on her shawl and calash, and sat in the parlor of the inn—a place that made her feel respectable— and thought about what to do. She could go home again to Norwich, now that there was no baby; but she knew that nothing could distress her mother more than to see her walk in the door again. So she decided to go on to Scituate, to stay a while with her cousin.

Fanny Winsor was a maiden lady of forty-five, very pious and very poor. Once she had been the village belle, but had turned down various marriage offers to remain true to a young man who had gone away to make his fortune. He had written faithfully, but the years went by and he still had acquired no fortune, and then word came that he had been killed in a skirmish with Indians. By that time, Fanny was over thirty and not many men would take on so old a woman. Besides, Fanny was particular. She wouldn't look at the others who'd look at her, the middle-aged widowers who needed a housekeeper and readymade mother for their children. Fanny prized her independence. She preferred to keep her own house, inherited from her parents, and teach the village children in the dame school.

Single women in Fanny's position justified their existence by acting as nurses, mother's helps, and funeral directors, all on an unpaid basis. Another thing they were sometimes called upon to do was to give asylum to erring female relations, although if they did that they expected a fairly handsome present. Sarah brought one with her, which her mother and aunt had paid for: enough black silk for a dress, and some real lace to trim it with. But even before she saw the presents, Fanny kissed her young cousin and made her feel welcome.

The old Winsor house was at the end of the village, standing alone among farms that had been abandoned by westward-faring owners. When Fanny died, hers would be abandoned, too, for she had no heirs. Meantime, owning it gave her more status than most spinsters had, even though it was too much for her to keep up. The fields were growing up in sumac and blueberry bushes and maple saplings. The grass in the yard flourished unchecked, and overgrown lilac bushes scratched against the gray-shingled house.

Every weekday morning, Fanny walked two miles to the opposite end of the village, where she helped conduct a dame school. She was glad to have Sarah mind the house all day. She never mentioned the subject of why such a young, pretty girl had been sent to this dull spot, but on the first day she saw Sarah washing her bloody clothes, and Sarah's woebegone face made Fanny pat her kindly. Any comment would have struck her as superfluous and even improper. A minimum of communication was her rule.

The loneliness of life here was relieved on Sundays, when they went to meeting, and on Tuesday evenings, when there was a Methodist "class." The minister, Mr. Beach, was kind, and the parishioners welcomed Sarah because she was Fanny Winsor's relation.

"Fanny is a saint," one of the women said to Sarah. Her name was Mrs. Babcock and she came visiting one afternoon, bringing a seed-cake she had just made.

Sarah invited her in and made her some tea. It was clear she had something to impart.

"Fanny Winsor has been sorely tried," she began.

"In what way?"

"Well, I don't mind if I tell you the whole story."

Mrs. Babcock, a portly old soul, settled down to her tea and a good slice of her own cake. "*She*'d never tell you, I know. She's above all pettiness. Well, there was a minister here last year. A young feller. Newly ordained. Ephraim Avery was his name, and he was real handsome, too. But bad-tempered. One day Fanny heard him speak unkindly of a man here who had just lost his wife. 'That one will soon drown his sorrow,' says Avery. Well, it was true, the man liked his glass of rum, but that didn't mean he had no feelings for his wife. In fact, he'd set great store by her, and Miss Fanny spoke up and told Mr. Avery so."

"That sounds like her," Sarah said. "She's kind and she's spunky."

"Yes, indeed. Well, kind and spunky didn't cut any ice with that young Avery. He never rested until he arranged a trial for Fanny, a Methodist Church trial, accusing her of lying. Of course, he just ended by making a fool of himself. Nobody here would say a word against her, and in the end she was acquitted. But it was an ugly thing for her and made her powerful unhappy for months."

"What happened to the minister?"

"They relocated him. I heard he married, so let's hope that improved his disposition. Last I heard, he was down on Cape Cod somewhere. But our ministers are always moving, you know. It's part of being a Methodist. Our true home is Heaven and we want no other. The love of the Lord is better than jewels and ermine and we don't want none of such things."

Sarah thought she could be happy as a Methodist, but there was one serious impediment. To become a Church member, you had to make a public confession. If you held anything back and it was later discovered, you must be tried and might easily be expelled. On the other hand, certain sins—such as her own— were considered beyond the pale. If she publicly confessed to stealing a coral necklace in Providence or to fornicating with a sailor in a tavern, she would never be accepted, and, even worse, her shame and ruin would become common knowledge.

She went to meetings, but she sat quietly while others became converted, confessing modest faults with great drama. There was not a shoplifter or a fornicator among them. And, as everyone said, Cousin Fanny was as without sin as a human being can get. Sarah was afraid to open her mouth in such virtuous surroundings.

In Scituate, people sometimes referred to the trouble with Reverend Avery as an example to show Fanny's strength of character.

"Folks had a lot of confidence in Fanny," one of the churchwomen told Sarah, "and Avery said he would see she wasn't made a goddess of. Nobody was making a goddess of her, of course—it was just that the whole village thought a lot of her. She'd walk through a blizzard if someone was sick and needed nursing, and she'd sew and darn for the widowers that had holes in their clothes, and knit for all the babies. And she laid out bodies and made shrouds, and knew how to close their eyes and fix them a nice, peaceful smile. People love a woman like that, but just because she didn't faint with delight when Avery was in the room, or in the pulpit, he resented her."

"What was that Mr. Avery like, Cousin Fanny?" Sarah dared ask her one evening. To her surprise, Fanny answered with unusual volubility.

"I'd say he was a pretty good-looking fellow," she said. "And with a voice that would charm a snake. The young girls here, they thought he was the likeliest thing that ever came down the pike. And wasn't he anxious about the Conversion of all the pretty ones! Somehow the plain ones didn't concern him so much. Well, I feel sorry for the girl who married him. Must have been a silly young thing is all I can say."

"But why was he so unkind to you?"

"The truth of it was, he didn't like an independent woman," Fanny said. "He wanted them all to fawn on him—young and old, handsome or homely."

"What did he look like?"

"Oh, I dunno—something like a pirate or a gypsy, I guess. Dark-complected. But there, I don't want to talk about him. I've said all I want to say, ever again."

No other subject ever aroused Miss Fanny to say even that

much. She never questioned Sarah about why she had been ban-
ished from Norwich, nor inquired how long she intended to stay.
And for some time, Sarah was so happy to be away from people
who pried into her life and who talked behind her back and made
her feel her deficiencies and her transgressions, that she felt no
loneliness.

Autumn was late and warm that year. Ragged, brilliant gold-
englow made a sunshiny pool of color outside the kitchen window, and Fanny's cabbages and pumpkins kept on growing well
into November. There were no sounds all day, except of birds
and little wild things; but they, and Fanny's cats, kept Sarah
company.

The villagers, she knew, were suspicious of a young girl who
came to stay with a distant relation in a retired part of the country. It amused Sarah to sit at meeting with her cloak around her,
and then, as she stood up, to let it fall back and reveal her slender
body. By Thanksgivingtime, people were much more friendly,
but they let her know that they still wondered about her. Any
normal young girl would live at home with her family, or perhaps go into the mills for a year or two.

When the first snow fell, Sarah began to feel lonely. She
remembered the tavern, that rainy Sunday, with the jolly sailors
and traveling men singing and playing cards; Louis holding her
hand, and other men glancing at her continually with that special
look in their eyes that she both feared and wanted. And now that
she had discovered exactly what it meant, she both feared and
wanted it even more.

There was only one looking glass in Miss Fanny's house, and
it had a big crack diagonally across it. Fanny kept it by the kitch-
en door, only to see if her bonnet were on straight when she left
the house. But that was all one could expect to learn from it. It
could not tell a girl she was beautiful, and a better answer could
be obtained from the brook back of the house. In the late fall, the
water flowed very clear and very slowly, and Sarah could lean
above its pebbly bottom and find her black curls, her high tortoise-shell comb, her pink cheeks, and her parted red lips. She

smiled at herself and thought of those days with Louis. *"Sure, and you're the pretty thing!"* As she thought how she missed him, her smile disappeared, and a tear fell into the brook.

One day in early December, Fanny came home at twilight to find the lamps unlit and Sarah sitting by a dying fire, weeping. Fanny simply laid her strong hand on Sarah's shoulder.

"A fine sunset tonight," she said, going to hang up her bonnet. "It means a fine day tomorrow. 'Red sky at night, sailor's delight.' "

But at mention of a sailor, Sarah sobbed aloud. Fanny poked up the fire and threw two logs on it.

"You know, Sarah Maria, this ain't no life here for a lively young girl. It just is not the right thing for you."

Sarah gave a little moan.

"Don't you want to go back to work in the mills?"

"I don't rightly know what I want," Sarah said faintly.

"If I were you," said Fanny, "I'd join the Methodist Church and then I'd go into one of the mills. That way, being a Member, you'd be sure to be with the right sort of friends."

Sarah began to cry harder. "I can't join," she said. "I can't confess, Cousin Fanny. You see . . ."

Fanny interrupted quickly. "I don't have to hear any more'n I know now. And neither do the folks at meeting. You confess *some* and God'll understand the rest. You need the Church and the Church needs you." She put her hand briefly on Sarah's hair. "Do it tomorrow," she said. "You can have a good life, Sarah, if you just hold your head up. Now, run down cellar and fetch us some currant jelly for our tea."

After Sarah joined the Church (admitting to covetousness and lust, but not mentioning theft or fornication) she packed her trunk and bandbox, hugged her cousin tightly but silently, and departed for the cotton mills of Dedham. Fanny had given her new hope, and it was like an oar held out for a drowning person to catch hold of. Seeing her Church Member's certificate, the Methodists of Dedham welcomed her. Among them, holding hands and singing, "I shall depart from flesh and sense," she felt as if at last she belonged somewhere. Not in Dedham, Norwich, Scituate, or Jewett City, but in a Safe Somewhere that belonged to God.

The Methodists had their own world. Most of them were poorer and humbler people than Leffingwells, Lathrops, and Cornells, and less well-spoken or well-read; but most seemed truly fervent in their desire to be good Christians. Their propensity to shout and sing, weep with joy and faint with the strong emotion of their love of the Lord astonished Sarah at first, but she soon began to show emotion, too. Unlike her taciturn family, it was her nature to be demonstrative, and she welcomed the opportunity. Religion, she thought, would be her whole consolation, as it was Fanny's. Maybe, like that admirable woman, she could earn everyone's respect and love—everyone's except that of the strange young minister, Mr. Avery. What could such a person have been like? Sarah felt thankful that the minister in Dedham was a gentle, elderly man, kindly and peaceable, although not an inspiring preacher.

Remembering her cousin, Sarah began to volunteer to sit with the sick. She was quick and deft and she made a point of subduing her naturally loud voice and laughter. Moreover, she was entirely willing to perform unpleasant chores. "This you do for Me," Jesus said, and she found, remembering this, that the most heavy task was lightened.

One February day, Sarah was sitting with one of her co-workers, Ada Peck, who had terrible, sudden pains in the abdomen. The doctor diagnosed constipation, which was common among the mill-girls. The unrelenting winter diet of bread and cornmeal, potatoes and pork, with perhaps a very few turnips and cabbage leaves if the autumn supply held out, hit some constitutions in a near-fatal manner. In winter, privies were like icehouses, and a chamber pot at night in an unheated room a species of torture. At the mills, the girls were embarrassed to ask the overseer for permission to leave the looms, because, of course, he would know why. To most of the girls, constipation seemed preferable to indelicacy.

The doctor administered a purge. Next day early, the stomach cramps worsened, and Ada—a girl of eighteen who looked as virginal as any girl in the mill—miscarried a half-formed infant boy. Sarah helped her, solaced her, cleaned her up, and made her as comfortable as possible, hoping that the doctor, who rarely went so far as to turn back a patient's bedcovers, would not know what had happened. But he came in before she had finished.

He was a hearty, bluff young man, debonair and cocky. His first reaction was to laugh.

"My girl, why didn't you tell me what kind of stomachache you had?"

Ada, white-faced, turned her head away from him.

"That kind of stomachache cures itself. You'll be back at work in a day or two. Mind you don't catch it again, though!" He winked. "Here, I'll give you a piece of advice that'll prevent it for good. Keep your knees together!"

But there must have been something more seriously wrong with Ada, because in a few days she died.

The boardinghouse-keeper notified Ada's parents, and her father came from Maine to get the body.

"Don't tell him what happened," Sarah begged the doctor.

"But he'll want to know what his daughter died of."

"Why darken Ada's memory? Why cause her father great unhappiness?"

The young man laughed. "Girls who let things like this happen to them must take the consequences."

"She is no longer here to take the consequences," Sarah said intensely. "It is her poor father who will take them. Instead, it should be the man who caused this grief."

The doctor stopped smiling and looked at Sarah coldly. "For an unmarried girl, you take a surprising interest in unsavory matters. But at any rate, I must do my duty."

And, on the death certificate, he wrote "miscarriage" as the cause of death.

When Ada's father saw it, he refused to accept his daughter's body, and she was buried in a plot for paupers, near the mills, with only a wooden marker.

Sarah was deeply distressed by her friend's death. All that

spring, on Sundays, when the other girls were walking or chat-
ting together, she would go and sit by Ada Peck's grave, morbidly
thinking that it might be her own. Of course, Ada had sinned;
and so had she. But what of Louis, and what of whoever it was
who had fathered Ada's child? Why was the world so unfair?
She asked God to tell her, over and over, but the bleak wind blew
and the bare branches shook and the snow and sleet battered
Ada's wooden marker until the newly carved name on it grew
faint. Sarah remembered the pretty graveyard at home in Norwich, where the Leffingwells lay. Each grave had a solid granite
stone, and there was a stone wall around the entire burying
ground, grown over with wild roses. For the second time in her
life, Sarah briefly thought of suicide. *But*, she thought, *I suppose
if I commit suicide they will not allow me there, in consecrated
ground.* For that would be the ultimate sin. There had been a
Norwich woman, a neighbor, who had killed herself by jumping
into a well, and her grave had been made all alone at a cross-
roads. Anyway, Sarah, although wretched, did not want to die.

The only answer she got from God—and she did perceive it to
be some kind of answer—was that spring came and the wind
grew softer, and one day she came to Ada's grave and found that
it was grown over with green grass and yellow buttercups.

She could not, of course, discuss either the question or the
answer with her fellow Methodists or with the minister. She
decided that when summer came she would go to a camp-meeting, and there, among strangers, perhaps she could find someone
to talk to, someone she would never see again.

That spring, Sarah heard of a very strange event in Norwich.
The Methodist meetinghouse had been lifted off its foundations
by a sudden freshet, and, with lamps still burning in its windows,
had floated away down the Thames River, all the way to New
London, where it had finally gone aground on a rocky island.
Surely, Sarah thought, this was a sign. Although the symbolism
was hazy, she was sure that it could not be a mere coincidence
that both she and the Norwich meetinghouse were travelers.

Other mill-girls did not move about as often as she. She
remembered that Dr. Cresswell had told her it was "a baneful

habit" to rove from place to place, especially for a woman. Most people lived and died in the village of their birth. Why should they move? It was generally assumed that the reason could only be a bad one. Good people, with nothing to hide, had no reason to go anywhere.

"Our ancestors moved," Sarah said once to a girl who was questioning her in a spiteful way. "If they had not moved from England, none of us would be here at all."

"But that was in the olden times, when there was religious persecution," said the girl. "The Pope and that. Nowadays, you don't have to move on account of your religion."

"Methodists move," Sarah pointed out. "The ministers only stay a year or so in each place. They have no earthly home, only a heavenly one."

"Oh, well," the girl said. "Who would want to be a Methodist?"

In July there was a camp-meeting at Eastham, on Cape Cod, and the faithful went there by ship from Boston. Sarah was among them. She hoped at last to get her conscience straightened out, and, anyway, ten days at the seashore sounded pleasant. Also, she was curious to see one of the four ministers who were to take charge of the meeting: he was Ephraim K. Avery, Cousin Fanny's persecutor.

On the shores of Cape Cod Bay arose a little city of tents. Between religious exercises, the assemblage rambled on the beach and on the sandy, bayberry-covered dunes. Sarah and some of the young people took off their shoes, hitched up their clothes and waded, feeling for clams with their bare toes. An inland girl, Sarah found this a new and delightful experience. She ran on the beach and laughed and frolicked as she had as a child. She was popular with the others. They found her warm and friendly, if a little odd in her lack of restraint. Some of the older women turned up their noses.

"Indecorous," they said. "Too free."

But she was careful not to be alone with any young men, or to joke with them too much. There were girls there who weren't careful enough, and they were asked to leave. No one, however, could say anything specific against Sarah. But when the time came for public confessions, she could not bring herself to do it, and her sins remained heavy on her heart.

She looked at the preachers who were leading the revival. Which one would she be able to confess to? Certainly not Mr. Avery: he was handsome, to be sure, but good looks were not what one looked for in a confessor. She thought she would like a fatherly sort, and there was one, gray-haired and about fifty years old. But when she went to him one day, he said, "How fine it is that our Church attracts the innocent and pure, like you, Sister." And she went away again, saying nothing.

On the last evening of the camp-meeting, Sarah walked out to the dunes with the others, where the service was to be held. Some evenings there were clouds of mosquitoes and gnats, but tonight a strong, warm breeze off the water carried them away.

The tents of the campers were like an Indian village on the dunes, crowded with people who were Sarah's kind in the sense of being Anglo-Saxon New Englanders, but not the sort who would have been welcome at the Leffingwells'. They did not speak well. They were poorly dressed, not just in the sense of Methodist plainness, but wearing clothes so worn as to be almost in rags. Some were barefoot. These were the sort whom Sarah, all her life, had seen going in and out of almshouses or wandering like lost dogs along the turnpikes. Tonight they had come first and had taken the best places.

There was a strong fragrance of crushed bayberries. (You had to know where to sit—in bayberries, not poison ivy.) There were fireflies everywhere in the salt-breezed evening, and the bright stars overhead were like fireflies fixed in place. Sarah thought, *They are like the lights in the meetinghouse that floated away.*

The preacher was Ephraim Avery. In spite of herself, she liked his sermon; though she was willing to admit that it was greatly helped by a beautiful speaking voice. "Let the Spirit enter into you and change your life," was the gist of his message, and, of course, that was what she had been longing to do.

"Leave the world and all its glittering toys," he declaimed.

"And devote the rest of your life to the service of God. You will search this world for happiness, but, alas, you will search in vain."

He spoke as if he could understand anything, forgive anything. Sarah almost forgot about Fanny, and was thinking how she might approach him after the service. But when he had finished, others flocked about him, and she heard him say, "Sorry, I haven't time tonight."

She stood at the side of the path by way of which he was walking toward the village, surrounded by the other ministers. He carried a torch, and as he came toward her, its fire shone on both their faces. She saw that he had dark-blue eyes, under heavy brows. He looked directly at her and she parted her lips as if to say something, but she could not speak. If she had, she would have said, "I need to feel forgiven."

He seemed to hesitate for an instant. She felt that he had truly noticed her, that she was not just another figure there, among the many. But he was silent; she was silent; the moment of contact passed. He went on into the village.

Next day, she wrote to her mother, "I have resolved to leave the world and all its glittering toys."

As the boat sailed back to Boston, a gale came up. Some of the people were frightened, many were seasick, but Sarah stayed on deck, a little figure standing at the base of the mast, wrapped in a big, coarse shawl. The wind made her cheeks pinker and tossed her dark hair, which curled tightly in the damp.

"Aren't you scared?" a sailor asked her, and she shook her head.

"You must be a seafarin' gal. Your father a sailor?"

She knew that her father's father had been a sailor and had died falling from the mast. She looked up at the high crow's nest and shuddered to think of that fall, but did not move away.

"Yes," she said, "I'm a seafarer." And she thought once more of the meetinghouse on the waters.

The Reverend Mr. Avery was also on board the little schooner, but Sarah did not see him until they had docked in Boston. Then she glimpsed him, going down the gangplank, looking white and wan.

"That one may be a pilot of souls," the young sailor said, "but he wouldn't do for no sea pilot."

One of the Methodist women said to Sarah, "You're a very independent young woman—so familiarlike with the crew."

"Why shouldn't I be?" Sarah answered sharply. "He's as good as we are."

"Hoity toity! And you're the one was runnin' barefooted on the beach. Seems you're pretty free for a respectable mill-girl."

Unfortunately, the woman turned out to be the wife of one of the foremen at the Dedham mill. It wasn't long before he called Sarah in and told her she didn't work hard enough, and since they were laying girls off, she would be among them.

And so she took to the road again. This time she went to Slatersville, Rhode Island, and learned to run a water-loom. She stayed there nineteen months—"the happiest of my life," she wrote her mother. "I am done with the trifling vanities of this world. They have almost been my ruin."

Not long after, the Slatersville mill burned down, and Sarah moved to Dorchester. And then to Waltham. And then to Taunton. Sometimes she moved because she was restless and tired. (From Dorchester she wrote to her sister, "I have got almost beat out. I have been weaving on four looms at the rate of 120 or 130 yards per day, a half-cent per yard.") Another time she moved because of "talk." ("Much has been said. I have suffered very much from false reports.") Her reputation had caught up with her again. A Jewett City girl recognized her and talked about Louis.

In Waltham, she even tried a different name—Maria Snow. She liked the sound of it and she thought perhaps it might bring her some peace and anonymity. But about that time her brother, James, whom she had not seen for years, came looking for her, and let it be known that her real name was Sarah Maria Cornell. Her landlady, declaring it very dubious for a girl to live under a false name, asked her to leave.

And all this time she was a Member of the Methodist Church under false pretenses, for she had never made a full confession. On the other hand, all this time she had led a blameless life. Since society decreed that a ruined girl was not marriageable, she avoided men who might have approached her as honest suitors; and the others terrified her. Since New London, she had not had a glass of wine, nor visited a tavern, nor even been alone with a man. And this had not been easy, because men often asked her to do all manner of things—from walking out with them on Sunday to spending a few minutes alone with them in a locked storeroom. It seemed to her that she was as good as any girl in any mill and that surely the Lord must have forgiven her. And yet she longed to hear that from a minister and to become a Member of the Church with nothing to hide.

In the spring of 1830, she met some girls who had been working in Lowell, the most up-and-coming of the mill-towns. It was a thriving and exciting place, they told her. It had fine shops and a bathing-house, fifteen churches, and lots of work. And on days off, one could get aboard a canal boat and travel down to Boston along the Middlesex Canal. Moreover, Lowell had a fine congregation of Methodists, who had lately received a new pastor. People said he was eloquent and inspiring and easy to listen to. His name was Ephraim K. Avery.

V

Lowell

In Lowell, the Methodist Church rented a house for the minister and his family, which they shared with its owner, Mr. Hoskins. In this way, the Church kept the rent as low as possible, and enabled its minister to live in a very plain manner, with a remarkable lack of comfort and convenience, thereby setting an example for his flock.

Mr. Hoskins was a widower, disabled by rheumatism, and he lived chiefly from the rent he charged. His house was something of an old rattletrap; it had been an isolated farmhouse before the village of Lowell had sprouted up around it. The minister's family had the lower floor. Two small children slept in the back parlor, which was also the dining room, and Mr. and Mrs. Avery and their new baby occupied a room off the kitchen, which had been intended for a storeroom and was therefore cold and dark. Mr. Avery had a large front room on the second floor, which he used as a study. It had a bed in it, where he often slept. Visitors could enter by the front door and go directly upstairs without bothering Mrs. Avery.

Israel Hoskins watched over his property like a mother bird watching her nest, and called his tenants' attention to every dent, scuff, or chip. If in wet weather, callers left mud on the stairs, Hoskins would stand glaring, and follow them with a scrubbing brush and bucket.

A garret room was also available to the Averys, and here Mrs.

Avery's niece, Betsey Hills, stayed when she was with them. Soon after they moved to Lowell, they decided to let this room to a mill-girl until Betsey joined them in late summer. In return for a very low rent, the girl would help Sophia Avery with some of her housework. Ephraim put up a notice at the meetinghouse, and the first to apply was a newcomer in the parish, Sarah Maria Cornell.

She called one evening, on her way from the mill. Sophia answered her knock.

"Is Mr. Avery at home?" Sarah asked.

"Yes, but he's in his study. Is it about Church business?"

"At the meetinghouse I saw a notice that he wants a household help. I've come about that."

There was certainly nothing wrong with what she said, but Sophia disliked the way Sarah looked directly at her. It seemed to her that a girl applying as household help ought to be timid and humble.

"Then it's me you want to see, isn't it?" Sophia said.

"If you do the hiring."

Sophia's impulse was to tell the girl that they had already found someone, but she knew that Ephraim would quiz her. He thought people ought always to have reasons for their actions. Impulses, he said, nearly always came from the Devil.

"I'll let you know," she said, looking a little more closely at the girl. She noted that Sarah was good-looking and wore a better-fitting dress than most factory girls—two points that were not in her favor.

"You don't want me?" Sarah asked, in her direct way.

"It isn't that, but you're not the only one to apply," Sophia said, frowning still more as she heard herself telling a lie. "I'll let you know."

She closed the door firmly, but, with a vague sense of alarm, realized that the girl continued to stand there for another minute or two. Then footsteps sounded, going away down the path.

Ephraim called from his study, "Who was that, Sophia?"

"Only someone for the spare room."

Ephraim appeared at the head of the stairs. "Then send her up," he said.

"Oh, but Mr. Avery, I sent her away. I didn't care for her."

"*You* didn't care for her?" He hurried down the stairs, and she spontaneously shrank back. "It is not for you, Mrs. Avery, to make these decisions. Call her back."

"She's gone. She'll be far away by now."

"What was her name?"

"I didn't ask her."

"You are a stupid, incompetent, pitiful woman. If this is how you behave, I won't get you a household help. What did she look like?"

"Black hair. Pert. Too independent."

"A pretty girl, would you say?"

"I wouldn't say, but you might."

"Now who is pert?" Ephraim said. "I ask because I was told that there is a new young Methodist woman in town, who is looking for a room. It would be good to have a Methodist."

"I doubt this one is a Methodist."

"You know nothing at all about it," Ephraim said, and retired to his study, banging the door.

Later that evening, there was a Love Feast, and Ephraim, after leading prayers, asked that whoever had applied for the room and employment at his house should return, because his wife had made a mistake in sending her away.

Sarah, accordingly, called again after work the following day. She was living at a boardinghouse where six girls shared one room, and was anxious to get out of it, even though she had not cared much for her glimpse of Mrs. Avery. In her experience, thin, timid women always turned out to be complainers.

The day had been very humid, with intermittent rain and a sultry thunderstorm that had failed to clear the air. Sarah came from the mill after work, still in her sweat-soaked working-dress, and wearing pattens to keep her shoes out of the mud.

Israel Hoskins stood in the doorway, glaring, as she came up the walk.

"Is Mr. Avery at home, sir?" she asked.

"He's upstairs. I guess you can go up," Hoskins said. "They all do." He stared at her muddy pattens.

"Shall I take these off?"

"It would save my stairs. Your shoes wet, too?"

"Yes. I'll take them off. I don't mind."

And she went upstairs barefoot.

"First door to the left," Hoskins called after her.

She knocked and Avery opened the door. It was already deep twilight, and he had a lamp in his hand, holding it high to see who was there.

She saw a tall, black-haired man in a loose homespun shirt, such as farmers wore. The lamplight illumined his dark-blue eyes, and she was reminded of that other summer evening, on Cape Cod, when he had passed her on the dunes, with a torch in his hand. She had known, of course, that this was the same man, but actually seeing him again in the same sort of flickering light made her catch her breath.

"I saw you at a camp-meeting last year," she said.

He peered down at her, and held the lamp to her face.

"You won't remember me," she said. "I was only . . ."

"But I do," he said. "It was at Eastham. On the dunes."

"Yes," she said, startled. "But we did not meet."

"No. But I saw you. Please come in." He stood aside for her to pass. "What is your name?"

She hesitated. Sarah? Or Maria?

"Cornell. Sarah Maria Cornell."

"Please sit down. What can I do for you, Sarah Maria Cornell?"

The room, from what she could see of it, was very bare. It had no rug or curtains, and contained only two rush-seated chairs, a pine desk, some books piled on the floor, and a bed. It was the study she would expect of a Methodist minister—except for the bed.

"I've come to see about the room you have, and the extra-help situation. I am the one who was here yesterday. But your wife sent me away."

"Yes, yes," he said. He had set the lamp down on the desk, and now moved it so that it shone directly on her face. "It seems she did not fancy you. Perhaps you had better tell me about yourself. And your faults."

She looked apprehensive, and he added, somewhat sharply, "What, have you no faults?"

She dropped her eyes. "Yes, sir, I do."

"Then you are human, like the rest of us," he said. "What would you say is your worst sin?"

There was a pause, and Sarah blushed.

"I am—too light of mind," she said in a low voice. "I do not always remember what God has in store for those who are frivolous and silly. Especially when they are women."

Avery seemed to take note of a slight catch in her voice, and he looked at her sharply as if wondering what caused it.

"But you are a Church Member, are you not?"

"Yes, sir."

"Then you must already have confessed your sins, and shown true repentance. I see no reason why we should not employ you here. Mrs. Avery is usually a keen judge of character, but I shall tell her that she has made a mistake this time. Come tomorrow after work, and bring your belongings."

As he rose to bid her good-bye, he looked down at her bare feet, and asked, with a slight smile, what she had done with her shoes.

"They were muddy," she said simply, as if anyone with muddy shoes would be willing to go barefoot.

"You are very obliging, I see," he said. His eyes traveled slowly up her body. "It will be well for you to be near your pastor. If what you say is true and you are tempted by sins of light-mindedness. I hope you and I will be good friends in Jesus."

"Thank you, Mr. Avery," Sarah said, and took the hand he extended.

Speaking so suddenly and roughly that Sarah jumped, he said, "The Devil is here in Lowell, so be very careful. Yes, very careful. Good evening, Sister."

She dropped him a curtsy, and pattered down the stairs in her

bare feet, sitting on the lowest step to put on her shoes and pattens. As she went out of the front door, she had an odd feeling
that he was at the top of the stairs, gazing down at her.

Outside, she looked back at the parlor windows, which were
uncurtained and lit by a single candle. Sophia Avery was standing alone there, gazing rigidly at the door through which her
husband would come if he were intending to spend the night with
her. But he did not come.

When Sarah got back to her boardinghouse, the landlady,
Mrs. Porter, had moved her into a larger room with only three
other girls in it—the nicest room in the house.

"I seen you wasn't happy," Mrs. Porter said. "You're an older
girl, so you need a little more peace and quiet than the young
'uns."

Sarah's heart sank at the term "older girl." She was now twenty-seven, but most people took her for several years younger. But
at least, she told herself, privilege was one advantage of growing
older. She liked the big, light room and the three "older"—nearly
as old as she—girls who shared it with her. One was a widow
and the other two were engaged. She decided to forego the
arrangement at Mr. Avery's; partly because of the extra work she
would have to do; partly because of Mrs. Avery, who was certainly not at all welcoming; but mostly because of a vague apprehension she was experiencing in regard to Mr. Avery. Whether,
remembering Cousin Fanny, she feared him, or whether she
feared the feelings she had when she was in his presence she was
uncertain. But next day when she was sure he would be at the
meetinghouse, she went to his door and left a note to say she had
found other accommodations.

At Sunday meeting, he called her aside.

"I am displeased with you, Sister Sarah," he said. "You told
me that your besetting sin is frivolity and lightness of mind, and I
must say that I find it both frivolous and light-minded in you to
have said you would take our room and then to disappoint
us."

"I'm sorry, sir."

"Sister, I must talk to you about this thoughtlessness of yours. Be so good as to come to my study after tea today."

To be ordered about, even by a minister, did not suit Sarah. It aroused her innate sense of independence. She did as he commanded, but she arrived at his study in a self-protective frame of mind, and said to him at once, "Before we talk about my faults, I wish to put a question to you, sir. What was your quarrel with Miss Fanny Winsor, of Scituate?"

He looked startled, but then said, in a way that sounded open and sincere, "I am happy to tell you. She was a meddlesome woman, and I tried, as her pastor, to induce a needful humility in her, for the good of her soul. Perhaps I was too hard on her, but she was interfering and giving opinions in matters that were not her affair. Why do you ask?"

"She is a distant relation. I think a great deal of her, as most people do."

"But there are always two sides to a story, not so?"

"I suppose so."

"Then, if you trust me, you'll believe there were two sides to this one."

They were sitting opposite each other on the two rush-bottomed chairs. He leaned forward and touched her lightly on the knee.

"Do you trust me?"

"Yes, sir, I think so."

"You *think* so!" He looked amused. In contrast to his usual grave, ministerial demeanor, a smile made him look boyish and somewhat rascally. His smile came slowly around his heavy lips, revealing even, white teeth. Sly little lines appeared around his eyes.

Sarah said demurely, "Of course, I trust you. You are my pastor."

"Good," he said, falling back into that role. "Then, as far as Miss Winsor is concerned, you will trust me when I say that I may have been sorely tried in this matter. We will leave it at that.

I do not wish to speak ill of her. Now, tell me, Sister—do you enjoy yourself here in Lowell?"

This seemed to Sarah like a foolish question. As well ask, do you enjoy working twelve hours a day in a place full of noise, heat, dust, and monotony; do you enjoy having no privacy and functioning as rigidly as a clock; not living, but enduring. Other girls endured, too, but only for a few years. Sarah knew no one else who had, like herself, endured eight years in the mills.

"I do not enjoy myself at all," Sarah said, looking Mr. Avery in the eye.

"Then why do you stay?"

"Because I must live. I must have money."

"But other girls go home again after a while, and marry. Why not you?" And he looked her up and down, again with that slow smile, and she blushed and stared at the floor.

"I haven't found the—the right one," she said.

"I hope you are not telling me an untruth, Sister Sarah," he said. "I will not tell you one. I cannot believe that a girl as pleasing in aspect as you has no chance to marry."

"There is no one I could say yes to," she said. It was not an untruth, but it was certainly an avoidance of the truth. She dreaded more questions.

"And what sort of man could you say yes to?"

She looked away from him, out of the window, where the sun was just setting. She wished it would set and let the room grow dim.

"A loving one," she said in a low voice. "A kind and reasonable one. A man who would—would take me as I am."

"In what way do you mean 'as you are'? You say you are frivolous. Do you wish to be encouraged in this? Is it that you are seeking to escape the ordinary duties of woman?"

"Sir, I think I would welcome them—in behalf of someone I could—could be in love with."

Ephraim began to walk up and down the room. When he reached the corner that was in shadow, she could not see his face. His voice sounded hard when he said, "And what, pray, do you know of love?"

She was silent.

"Come, why don't you answer? It is an awesome word, but you brought it up, not I. What do you know of—love?"

Sarah, trembling, said, "I don't know why you ask these things. Do you ask as a minister of God, for my soul's sake?"

"But, of course," he said. "That is my relation to you. My only purpose in this world is to relieve sinners of their burden of sin and bring them to Christ. You said a moment ago that you trusted me."

"Then, if I must answer," she said, "I know about love with men, and it is all cruel and hurting. They say they love you, but—"

"But what?"

"They only want—something else."

He went and stood at the window with his back to her. He said, "They only want to satisfy their lust, is that it?"

"Yes," she said faintly.

"And—" he said, "and have you let them satisfy it?"

She was silent. He came and stood over her.

In a voice gentle but commanding, he said, "You must answer. Now and at once."

She gave a moan and fell on her knees at his feet.

"Alas, it is true," she said. "I have so been longing to confess. I have asked God to forgive me and I think he has. What do you think?"

Avery remained silent. When she put a timid hand out toward his foot, he drew away, and said, "Get up, Miss Cornell. You must leave me now. You understand, of course, that the Church does not certify fornicators as Members of the Meeting. You must have lied. I will have to consider what is to be done."

"I have repented long ago. Oh, truly, sir."

"I must see evidence of that. I must, in fact, consider this whole serious matter. Leave me now."

She picked herself up and went away down the stairs. Her feelings were in a turmoil. Something deep within her told her that this was a matter between herself and God. Nevertheless, she longed to be told, from the lips of a Methodist clergyman, that her sins were forgiven and she was as good as new. Mr. Avery seemed to like her, and perhaps he would do this for her, relieving her at last of her burden of guilt.

When she got back to the boardinghouse and crept into bed beside one of her roommates, she went to sleep thinking of his slow smile and his sensuous lips and the way he had touched her knee.

Ephraim Avery also thought about touching her. He went to a nearby stable, where people could rent riding horses—for Methodist ministers were too poor to own any—and rode over to the neighboring village of Belvedere, where there was a tavern. He left his black clerical hat and coat at home, and sat a couple of hours by himself in a corner, drinking rum. When he returned, it was after eleven o'clock, and Israel Hoskins had locked the door. Ephraim flew into a rage and beat on it with his feet and fists until Hoskins came down and let him in.

"That's no way for a man of God to act," Israel said. "Out until all hours and then raising a ruckus. The whole town of Lowell has heard you, trying to stave in my front door."

"Nobody locks my door on me," Ephraim shouted. "I shan't stay here, sir, if you wish to insult me."

"Go elsewhere," Israel said, "and take your women with you."

Sophia heard this, in her cubby by the kitchen, having been awakened out of a deep, exhausted sleep. She both feared and hoped that Ephraim would come to her, but instead he ascended the stairs at an unsteady pace and more or less fell into his study, slamming the door behind him.

VI

Ephraim

That summer of 1830, Ephraim Kingsbury Avery was thirty years old. He was born on December 18, 1799, two weeks before the end of the eighteenth century and six days after the death of George Washington. His father, Amos Avery, had a small farm in Coventry, Connecticut. For Amos and for his father and grandfather before him, there had been no question of what to do in life. They would farm the land staked out in the late-seventeenth century by an earlier Avery. They lived in a world of farmers and of people who did things closely related to the agricultural life—blacksmithing, woodcutting, harness-making, and such.

By the time Ephraim was a small boy, there were new choices. His older brother went west. A cousin went to Boston and prospered as a lawyer. Other cousins became merchants and made so much money that they moved into another social sphere and forgot that they were related to plain country people. Those who stayed in their placid villages and did the same things their fathers did were not choosing the forward-leading path.

Ephraim grew up learning how to farm, but he began early to ponder on what else he might do. From babyhood he was handsome and strong, beguiling when he was happy and extremely disagreeable when he was not. He had five older sisters, who doted on him and spoiled him. He was quick to learn the advantage this gave him, and that it was for him to take, them to give.

127

Men took, women gave. The sisters demonstrated this lesson
again and again, especially since it was no hardship for five vigorous girls to indulge the whims of one small boy.

The mother of this family died when Ephraim was six years
old, during the birth of one last child. Ephraim always remembered her screams and the helplessness of everyone in the house,
and he then and there conceived the idea of becoming a doctor.
He knew clearly, when he heard her screams, that he loved her
and wanted very much to help her. However, as the memory
faded, he felt resentful of his mother for leaving him. And very
soon he did not really miss her because of the attentions of his
many sisters.

When he turned sixteen and announced that he would study
medicine, it was less for his mother than because of living in a
houseful of women. He had a strong desire to invade the forbidden precincts of women, and control them. More than once he
had been whipped for peeking through knotholes in the outhouse,
or for lingering by the kitchen window on Saturday evenings
when the girls were having baths in front of the great fire-
place.

But when he went to Hartford and signed up with an established physician for the requisite three years apprenticeship, he
found out that for every glimpse of female secrets, he had to deal
with a great many sore throats, infected toes, and cases of the
bloody flux. He found bodily ailments boring and often revolting;
and after an unfortunate error, when he applied too many leeches
to an anemic old woman and literally bled her to death, he
decided to become a merchant instead.

For a year, the young man worked in a general store in the
prosperous village of East Hartford. The drawback was that the
work, though clean and simple, lacked prestige. Also, Ephraim
had no talent for salesmanship. The customers were mostly
women. The older ones had the money, but he took pains only for
the young and pretty girls. When a middle-aged matron asked for
an India muslin that was a little brighter or paler, he scowled and
shrugged his shoulders. "We don't have anything else," he would
say, rather than go to the trouble of climbing up a ladder and

taking down the heavy bolts. The idea of waiting on women at all did not sit well with him.

He decided to become a schoolteacher. Being of an inquisitive turn of mind, he was better versed in the three *R*s than most farmers' sons, and had even taught himself a little Latin, geography, and botany. He could also rattle off the Westminster Catechism faster than most young people, and sing psalms in a very pleasing baritone.

But his heart was not in teaching. A one-room schoolhouse, smelling of insufficiently washed children, made him claustrophobic. He was meant (he kept thinking) for something better than the boredom of the *ABC*s. Day after day, it was either, "With Adam's fall/We sinn'd all," the old Puritan *ABC*, or the newer "*A*s for man, his days are as grass. . . . *B*e just before you are generous." Sometimes he would lose his temper and beat the mischievous or the dull-witted, leaving welts on their cringing palms or bottoms. Even this did not relieve him of tedium and increasing desperation. He was by this time twenty years old: a well-favored, likely fellow, people said. The kind who ought to leave his mark on the world (and all he was leaving it on was doltish children). Having abandoned the dream of being an eminent physician or a rich merchant, he hardly knew what else to picture. And he hesitated to change again. Most twenty-year-olds were already well settled in their life's work.

One day in summer a Methodist circuit rider, Leander Lamb, came to the Connecticut village where Ephraim was schoolmaster. He wore a broad-brimmed, black hat, and he rode a tired and bony mare. He was a middle-aged man with missing teeth and an expression between exaltation and ferocity, and he looked as tired and ill-fed as his horse.

Ephraim was just closing the schoolhouse, where he had been sitting alone, making red-ink slashes on his students' papers, and fuming over his fate.

The Methodist hallooed to him. "Brother, do you know where a Man of God might get supper and a place to sleep this night?"

"I am not a Methodist," Ephraim said in a surly way.

"But you are a Christian, my friend, I can see that. A man who loves his Brother, am I right, sir?"

"I suppose I do," Ephraim said. Something came over him (afterward, he said it was a visitation of the Holy Spirit) and he invited the man to his own house, where he gave him part of his own supper, and a quilt on the floor. Ephraim lived in a disused house, abandoned by its former owner and acquired by the school board. It was a bleak place, and lacked a woman to make it tolerable.

Next day being Sunday, Leander Lamb rode through the streets, ringing a bell.

"Come, sinners, come to the Lord, who waits for you," he cried. "Come and hear the comfortable words of God."

In Ephraim's yard, Brother Lamb set up a makeshift pulpit by piling two chicken coops one on top of the other. Four housewives, half a dozen children, one old man, and Ephraim stood around him while he preached. The next day he did the same, and again the following day. Each day, the listeners became more numerous. Leander Lamb alternately shouted and ranted and spoke gently, in a voice that trembled with emotion. At last, he wore out his voice so that he scarcely had one left.

"Ah, I am sorry, my dear Brethren," he said, barely above a whisper. "But perhaps Brother Avery would speak in my place."

"But I am not qualified," Ephraim said. "I am a schoolmaster, not a minister."

"In our religion, everyone is qualified to exhort his Brethren. Even women. Even little children. Try, Brother."

"But I am unprepared," Ephraim protested. He was frantically trying to remember a good text to get him started.

"Simply speak, Brother, and the Lord will give you utterance," said Brother Lamb.

Ephraim mounted the chicken coops and began with the verse, "I am good for nothing but to be cast out and be trodden under foot by men."

But this Calvinist-sounding idea was not the message of the Methodists; this he had already learned from listening to Brother

Lamb. Therefore, he quickly added, "Unless, my friends—oh, *unless* you will come to God and cast your sins upon His mercy. His mercy, my brothers and sisters—do you not realize that God's mercy is great and infinite and that anyone who truly repents may go to Heaven? Anyone! Yes, ALL of you!"

Realizing that he had now gained the full attention of the little crowd, Ephraim warmed to his work. "Like you, I am a sinner, and I have lived in deadly fear of eternal damnation. But Jesus Christ will put out His hand and help us to our feet. Yes, oh, yes, He will, but you must confess your sins to Him." He glanced at Brother Lamb and received an approving smile and nod.

The people drew closer, and one woman cried out, "Jesus, forgive me!"

Brother Lamb seized her by the hand and led her forward.

"Stand here where the Lord can see you, Sister."

The workworn and frail-looking woman stood before them with tears streaming down her face. Ephraim continued to exhort. In a short time, word swept around the village that the schoolmaster was preaching, and nearly everyone came to hear. Curiosity brought them, and some jeered, but Ephraim ignored that. He was amazed by the mellifluous sound of his own voice, previously wasted on farm children. As he spoke, he had a strange feeling that he was, at this moment, two men: one inspired by God, earnestly and devotedly delivering His word; and the other, an onlooker, an observer; dispassionate, even sceptical of what was going on here. This second man was not a religious person at all, but one who shrewdly controlled the first one, judging when he should raise his voice and when to lower it, when he should shout and when he should weep.

The people began asking him about the Methodist faith. All he knew was what Brother Lamb had told him in the evenings and had preached during the past days. Ephraim looked anxiously toward the Brother, who said, "It's a simple faith and you have already understood it. It's all about God's pure love, and that's all you have to know. We don't teach nothing more complicated than that."

"You teach a lot of lies!" shouted one of the bystanders. "The

Bible says, 'Many are called, but few are chosen.' That means most of us are bound for Hell and there ain't nothin' you or anybody else can do about it, Mr. Methodist."

Immediately a chorus of voices was raised in protest. "Be still, Rufus. Let's hear from Mr. Avery."

Ephraim began again in a throbbing voice, "It's all about love! It's all about God's love, it's all about salvation, it's all about confessing our sins, it's all about repenting . . ."

He had caught the repetitious chant of Brother Lamb's technique. It had a hypnotic effect, he began to observe, like the many-times-repeated rocking of a cradle, or the ticking of a clock. Ephraim thought of things in nature, too, that had the power to soothe and lull and comfort: birdsong, brooks running, rain falling. And for the climactic moment of a sermon or an exhortation, when the preacher's voice rose and he shouted and ranted, he thought of the ecstatic moments of sex.

As he talked on, he was filled with exhilaration. He felt powerful. He knew he could go on and on like this and that he was no longer an ordinary young schoolteacher, but a Man of God. At this moment, he could have mounted Brother Lamb's bony mare and ridden off to save souls in every town and village in New England. He imagined himself invited to supper, given the best bed, admired and consulted by pretty women. To be a man of the cloth suddenly seemed the most natural thing for him in the world, and as he continued to exhort, and as the people kept coming forward to confess their sins, the watching man within him said to the preaching man, "You have been called."

After the preaching, Ephraim told Brother Lamb that he thought he would go to Boston and talk to the Methodist elders about becoming a minister.

To Ephraim's surprise, Brother Lamb did not appear overjoyed.

"Have you thought and prayed about it?" he asked.

"Of course."

"You are an effective preacher," Brother Lamb said, gazing at him critically. "But I wonder if you truly believe all you preach."

Ephraim, rather put out, bid the circuit rider a cool good-bye. That afternoon, without even expressing his regrets to the school board, he packed his few belongings, and departed for Boston.

Sarah was at meeting the Sunday following their talk in his study, but hurried away immediately afterward, and Ephraim did not detain her. She, on her part, feared that if she spoke to him he might be reminded that she ought to be expelled from the Church. And as for him, though he was well aware of her presence, he did not speak to her because of some fear that he could not define, even to himself.

Since his evening of drinking rum, with its subsequent noisy dispute with Mr. Hoskins—which had not gone unnoticed by the neighbors—he had been melancholy. He reflected that he had been a minister for ten years now, forgiving sins and bringing souls to the Lord, but how had his own soul fared? He had a bad temper, he liked to drink, and he was often tantalized by pretty women. He was also prone to act on impulse, which perhaps was one reason why some of his best sermons attacked that failing as a mortal sin. He hated and feared it in himself.

Meanwhile, Sarah was finding that, as mill-towns went, Lowell was pleasanter than most. Unlike others, where the mills were superimposed on existing villages which more or less resented them, Lowell was new. Less than ten years before, only a few farms had stood there beside the clear, rushing falls of the Merrimack, with woods and fields all around. Now, the falls and the river bore away refuse from the stone factories beside them. To the sound of the water was added the cacophony of factory-wheels, big drays carrying loads of finished goods, and, at regular intervals, the strident bells that announced opening and closing times, as well as the breaks for breakfast and noonday dinner. The town was raw-boned and growing, like an adolescent, and as full of verve and energy. Most of the inhabitants were new to town life and industrial life. The overseers and clerks looked like farmers, awkward in their fitted coats, high stocks, and waistcoats. The girls who kept the looms clacking were nearly all fresh from the country. There were several thousand there already, and a few more arrived every day in stagecoaches, recruited from all over New England.

Sarah enjoyed Lowell in the evenings. Until the nine o'clock curfew, she could stroll about with other girls, laughing and chattering and going in and out of the shops, while men watched them circumspectly. (No rude remarks, no admiring whistles, no jostling, or the offender's job would be in peril.) The piazzas of the two hotels were always thronged, and music floated from the little bandstand on the green. Here and there on street corners, auctioneers bawled loudly in praise of mill seconds and slightly damaged peddlers' wares. A brand-new theater presented plays of a strictly moral nature, but few of the girls attended, most of them having been strictly forbidden by Puritan parents to set foot inside a theater. Acceptable alternatives were organ concerts in one or another of the fifteen churches; or visiting the public baths, where, in private, carpeted dressing-rooms built over the flowing river, patrons removed their clothing and bounced up and down directly in the cold, refreshing Merrimack.

The shop windows, in warm weather, were open to the street, so that their well-lighted contents could easily be seen by passersby on the brick sidewalks. Sarah's advice was often sought by her friends as to what fabrics to buy and how to make dresses and bonnets. There were drygoods stores, shoe stores, milliners, and tailors. A confectionery and a pastry shop were always crowded, and an apothecary sold a lot of remedies for stomachache and constipation.

There were periodic epidemics of sickness among the girls— flu in winter, bouts of diarrhea and mysterious fevers in summer. Sarah, usually among the healthiest, fell victim to a fever toward the middle of July, and for a time her life was thought to be in danger. Mrs. Porter, her boardinghouse-keeper, without asking her, sent for Mr. Avery to pray at her bedside.

He came at once. Sarah had been put into a single room, reserved for girls who became as ill as she was. When he saw how small she looked in the white bed, and how alarmed she seemed at sight of him, he was genuinely moved by pity and sympathy.

"I have come to pray God to make you well," he said gently.

She said in a low tone, "I have been so afraid that I would die and go to Hell."

"No, no," he said. "The Lord has forgiven you and I forgive you. Dear Sister, you will get well and you will take your place in the Church."

"Oh, Mr. Avery!" she said. "You have made me very happy."

He took her hand, glancing toward the door, which Mrs. Porter had left open. But there was no one about.

"Be easy," he said. "You must not tire yourself."

For a quarter of an hour, he sat by the bed, praying aloud and reciting psalms. And when Sarah opened her eyes, he gave her a sip from a tumbler of water, supporting her head from the pillow.

"I will get better quickly now," she said with great emotion.

"I have wanted to see you," he said, "so very much." Scarcely aware of what he was going to say next, he went on, "I wanted to ask you to forgive me."

"I? Forgive you?" Sarah, astonished, tried to sit up, but could not.

"I made you unhappy. I made you cry and I am sorry," he said. He was almost as surprised as she to hear himself say this, but he felt it to be true.

"Oh . . ." She gave the hint of a smile. "Men always make women cry. Even ministers."

"It shouldn't be so. You have had too much of that. I was imprudent and I ask you to forgive me."

"Yes, I will."

"When they told me how sick you were, I blamed myself."

She scanned his face wonderingly. "You seem so different," she said.

"I hope I am," he said virtuously. His contrition was real, but at the same time, as usual, the watcher within him was looking on and admiring him for it. What a fine fellow! What admirable self-abnegation!

Sarah smiled, but tears came into her eyes.

"I have a friend at last," she said.

As he rose to go, he took a little volume from his pocket and laid it on the bed.

"When you are better, read these poems of Sir Walter Scott," he said. "A fine and morally admirable poet. Let me know which poems are your favorites. I will come again in a day or two."

After he had left, Sarah leafed through the book. Four lines were underscored in pencil:

> Where shall the lover rest,
> Whom the fates sever
> From his true maiden's breast
> Parted for ever?

Sarah felt much solaced by Mr. Avery's visit. She could not but wonder if these lines of the morally admirable Sir Walter Scott were meant for her.

In fact, Ephraim had underlined this bit of Scott some years before, when he had taken a strong fancy to one of his parishioners in Eastham. But something had made him remember the lines today and bring the volume to Sarah.

He walked down the street in a state of exaltation. *I have done right,* he thought. *I have shown that the Devil does not rule me.* Before doing anything he might have regretted, he had behaved properly and decently to Sarah Maria, and with great consideration for her feelings. More than once he had done rash and regrettable things with girls. One of the girls had been Sophia, but he had made amends by marrying her. That kind of amends, however, could be made only once.

Not anxious to encounter his wife at this moment, Ephraim went for a long ramble in the forest back of Lowell. He sat for a time on a sunny, flat boulder beside a brook; then suddenly flung off his black ministerial coat and trousers, his shirt—in his haste, tearing off a button—and his underlinen, and plunged naked into the cold, clear stream. To dry himself afterwards, he lay in the sunshine. He had not been naked out-of-doors since his boyhood, and it made him want to shout and sing. At this moment, the two persons within himself—the watcher and the doer—drew close together and almost joined. The watcher pointed out his temper, pride, and lust, and the doer, for once, fully agreed and was flooded with remorse. Ephraim meant it all, but the difficulty was, he much preferred not to strive or suffer. He wanted this sinner called Ephraim Avery to be purified of sin as easily as the cold, clear brook had washed over him. And he remembered what Leander Lamb had said to him: "*I wonder if you truly believe what you preach.*"

On the flat, sunny rock, Ephraim came to a sitting position and looked curiously at his body. He seldom saw it entirely naked. Only in the bath on Saturday nights, and that was always hurried, before the water turned tepid. It seemed astonishing that this strong, white, well-formed male body was part and parcel of the black-clothed minister to whom the flesh was enemy. *This is a man*, he thought, *a human being as he really is. All the rest, walking about in frock coats and beaver hats, that is not the truth at all. None of us know ourselves. We are all pretense.*

Someone had told him that in Europe there were many marble statues of naked men and naked women, and that these were to be seen in public places. Sometimes there would be a leaf or a bit of drapery over the most private areas, but not always. Ephraim wondered if it were really true, and, if so, whether the presence of such statues would have an effect on people. Would it make them more carnal? Or simply less self-deceptive?

Ephraim's own body pleased him. He felt almost as if he had just met someone new. That idea made him chuckle and then laugh aloud, and he also liked the sound of his laughter, which startled a chipmunk off the rock and a flock of wood doves out of a pine tree.

When he arrived home, late for supper, and looked at Sophia's martyred face, he thought that perhaps he could start over with many segments of his life. He kissed her. He kissed the children.

His little daughter was so unaccustomed to affection from her father that she burst into tears.

"Stop that at once, Katharine," said her mother in anxiety. "You must embrace your father when he has shown you that he desires it."

"Never mind, Sophia," Ephraim said. "It is my fault."

Sophia cast him a look of total astonishment.

Next day, when she was doing the laundry, Sophia noticed that a button was dangling from his shirt, and she imagined that he must have torn it off impetuously, as he had done on their wedding night. A dizzy feeling came over her, and a pain in the abdomen, as if there were small, fierce animals biting her there. She knew the feeling well: it was jealousy. She tried to put it away from her, because it was a sin. But the sharp little teeth went on attacking her all day, and when the children lay down for a nap, she went to her bed and curled herself into a ball and lay with open, staring eyes, clutching her abdomen.

The minister called on his sick parishioner four more times that week, and her health improved dramatically. By the end of the week, she was sitting up in bed, reading Sir Walter Scott. When Ephraim walked in, she gave a little cry of joy and stretched out her hand to him.

"You seem much better, Sister," he said, holding her hand for a few seconds longer than it took to shake it.

"Oh, yes, I am nearly well. I think tomorrow I shall go back to the mill."

"You *look* very well. As handsome as ever. Tell me, what do you think of the poems?"

"They are very fine. And very—romantic."

He looked at her keenly and noted that she was blushing. " 'She look'd down to blush, and she look'd up to sigh/With a smile on her lips, and a tear in her eye,' " he quoted. "Yes, Scott's poetry is romantic, but why not? Romance is a part of life. Did you like 'Young Lochinvar'?"

"Oh, indeed," she said. "I *loved* it."

And, he thought, *it is clear she loves me, too.*

He sat down by her bedside, crossed his legs, and took out his Bible. He read a few psalms, but kept looking up from the page, and at her, as if his heart were not in the reading. The sixth or seventh time he did this, she smiled, and he, smiling back, stopped reading.

"I'm afraid my mind is not on the psalms," he said.

"Nor mine neither," she said softly.

"Perhaps you would prefer just to chat." She looked a little startled, and he added, "Yes, ministers do chat, you know. They're human, too."

They chatted. Ephraim asked where she had spent her childhood, and she described Norwich, the old Leffingwell house, and her pious cousins.

"Harriet went to Ceylon and died," she said. "She laid down her life for the Hindoo."

"Most missionaries, alas, die young," he said. "I considered going myself, but my wife preferred not. 'Save the souls in Massachusetts first,' she said."

"Oh, yes! Please don't go away, so far off. That is—I mean— you are so good to everyone right *here*."

"Not to everyone, I fear. But I hope I am to you." He leaned forward, took her hand, and gazed into her eyes.

"Oh, yes! You have so kindly come to see me." Sarah became confused by his gaze and dropped her eyes.

Presently, Ephraim, still holding her hand, said gently, "Was he very cruel to you?"

She was puzzled for a moment, but then realized he must mean Louis. She hesitated, and then answered in a low voice, "More thoughtless than cruel."

"Where is he now?"

"I don't know."

"Do you miss him?"

"No. It was a great while ago. Ten years."

"Did you love him?"

"For a little while."

He was still holding her hand, and now he stroked the palm. "It would be fine," he said softly, "to be loved by you."

It was so quiet that they could hear the tick of a grandfather clock on the stairs and a bee buzzing in and out of the open window. In the village street outside, a cart rattled by.

Finally, Ephraim broke their silence by rising to his feet and picking up his hat.

"You must not go back to the mill tomorrow," he said. "You must have a day up and about, but not working. I can offer you a ride in the Methodist carryall. It would do you good to take some country air."

"How kind!"

"It would be best, perhaps, if you meet me at the stables. Come to the side door—not the front, where there are always idle men standing about—and you will find me there."

"I will, sir."

He leaned over the bed and kissed her lightly on the forehead, and she reached up and touched, very timidly, the lapel of his black coat.

To be a convalescent invalid and to be taken to ride was delightful to Sarah, who had never had any kind of special treatment. If she felt any misgivings about the intent of the handholding and the kiss on the forehead, she did not allow herself to entertain them. She could not imagine—at least, not in her conscious mind—that a minister would ever behave other than ministerially. Still, some kind of discretion made her refrain from mentioning this rendezvous to the other girls. She told them that she was going out to do errands and get her strength back, and would be at the mill the following morning.

Ephraim was waiting at the back of the stable in a covered cart—the Methodist carryall—hitched up to an old chestnut mare.

"She won't go at any great pace," Ephraim called out cheerily when he saw Sarah. "But an invalid needs a quiet ride. Here's a hand up."

He pulled her up beside him, shook the reins, and moved off. At this time of the day, two o'clock, there were not many people on the street.

"I wish we might meet someone I know," she said.

"Why?" he asked. He seemed anxious to leave the town behind, and drove the mare forward at her best trot.

"So that folks will know how good you are to me."

"Folks often get a wrong idea about something like this, my dear," Ephraim said. "It is as well if we meet no one and if you mention it to no one."

They rode in silence until they were out of the town. It was a perfect midsummer day: hot but breezy; a sky of unclouded blue; tiger lilies in bloom along the wayside, and a subtle fragrance of blueberries ripening in the sun.

"So let us go on with yesterday's chat," Ephraim said, turning to smile at her. "Tell me more about Norwich."

To counteract a strange feeling of combined anxiety and anticipation that was rising within her, she talked on and on, like a child, telling him about the mantuamaking business, and the stagecoach rides, and the Congregationalist Revival.

Ephraim tugged the left-hand rein and turned the mare into a narrow woodland road. They drove more slowly than before, under arching forest trees.

"I didn't tell you about the Methodist meetinghouse, did I?" Sarah went on. "It came away from its foundations in a freshet and floated away down the river. Did you ever hear of such a thing?"

"Extraordinary! Was anyone in it?"

"No, but they say the lamps were lighted for an evening meeting. They were still burning halfway to New London. I always wondered what God thought about it. It seemed almost like an offering to him, a beautiful, amazing gift."

He laughed. "I like that notion. A gift for God. I think you must be a very generous young woman. Is that true? Do you like to give presents?"

"Yes—if I like the person I'm giving to."

"I wonder if you like me well enough to give me something."

He stopped the horse, laid aside the reins, and looked at her meaningfully.

She knew what must be in his mind, but she was silent, searching wildly for a prudent answer.

Suddenly, he took her in his arms. "Be generous," he said. "Be generous to me."

She buried her face in his coat. "I think you know I—I like you. But I must not."

"Must not what?"

Again, she could not find words. What if she had misjudged the situation?

But he took her face in his hands and said, "You have not understood me—or you are pretending not to. You know what I want. And if I'm not very mistaken, you want the same. Admit it."

She was weak from her illness and weak with love for him. Pushing him away was impossible, particularly since she did not want to. Instead, she threw her arms around his neck.

Ephraim took her inside the carryall, where there were some cushions. And Sarah soon found that this was an entirely different matter from the meager moments with Louis. Ephraim seemed to have quite another idea of how to proceed—a much better one. And when, after the first lovemaking, she started to get up, he told her to lie still a while, and whispered to her what a beautiful and bewitching woman she was and that she had made him happier than he had ever been before.

"How do you know all these . . . these things to do?" Sarah murmured in his ear.

"I make them up as I go along," he said, laughing. "You can make some up, too, if you like. It's a game for two players."

"I never knew it was a *game*," she said. "That doesn't sound . . . well . . ."

"Doesn't sound proper? Oh, it's very improper, lovely Sarah. Show me how totally improper you can be."

The second time was even more of a revelation to Sarah, and she told him so. And, as before, he lay and held her and talked to her tenderly.

Neither of them had a watch, but when they looked out from the canvas cover of the carryall, the sun was low in the trees.

"When will you come to me in my study?" he asked.

"I don't know. I can't think at all right now."

"But you love me?"

"Oh, yes, yes,"

"Then you will come."

For the next few weeks, they lived heightened lives. Sarah tended her loom mechanically, her thoughts far away. Ephraim relied on old sermons to see him through his Sabbath obligations, although he delivered them with a new intensity. Several newcomers joined the Church and said Mr. Avery had saved their souls.

The lovers contrived to meet often. Ephraim told Mrs. Porter that Sarah had made great spiritual progress during her illness and would benefit by more instruction. Mrs. Porter, a great admirer of the handsome clergyman, showed them to an empty room off the barn. It had once been a dairy and was now only used for drying vegetables in autumn and for storing things.

"You won't be disturbed here," she said.

Fortunately, there were sacks of goose feathers stored in the room, waiting to be made into featherbeds.

They found other places, too. One day, Sarah took an afternoon off from the mill and went with Ephraim into the forest to see the brook and the flat rock where he had been before. Until now, being as reticent as other born-and-bred New Englanders, they had not been naked before each other. But today they took off all their clothes and made love in the brook.

It was Sarah's idea. Ephraim was delighted.

"Now you are making up better games than I am," he told her.

The one place where Sarah did not want to go was to his study.

The idea of making love with sad Mrs. Avery downstairs and glaring Mr. Hoskins somewhere near, was, she said, intolerable. And this led to a quarrel.

Ephraim said, one day, "When fall comes, Mrs. Porter's barn will be chilly. I shall have a fire in my study."

They were riding in the carryall, another of their safe retreats. Sarah looked at him with sudden seriousness.

"You know, Ephraim," she said slowly, "we must realize that we will have to stop sooner or later."

"Don't say that."

"But it is true. Neither of us thinks of consequences or duties. Neither of us has thought of anything sensible since . . . we began."

Ephraim's thick eyebrows drew together. Sarah had never seen his bad temper, but now she sensed that it was rising, like thunder in the distance on a still-sunny day.

"I must be the judge of that," he said.

"Why not I, too?"

"Because," he said, tensely, "women don't decide things for me. I decide them."

Sarah said quietly, "Well, perhaps this will decide you." And she showed him a drawing that she had found pinned to her loom. It showed a minister, black hat and all, in bed with a girl who looked remarkably like Sarah.

Ephraim tore it up. "Nobody can offer proof of any kind," he said angrily. "And even if they could, nobody would believe it of me."

Sarah said nothing more, but she felt deeply hurt. It was the first time he had referred, even indirectly, to her status as a fallen woman.

Until now, her happiness with Ephraim had been flawed by her dread of becoming pregnant. That morning the blood had finally flowed, a week late. And she had told herself that now was a time for new resolves.

On recent Sundays, Ephraim had let her know, by a note or a

whispered word, where to meet him in the afternoon. This Sunday, she did not wait; she had made an engagement to ride out in a buggy with one of the overseers at the Appleton mill. He was Enos Bliss, a quiet bachelor, who often asked the girls for buggy-rides. Those who had accepted had found him pleasant, rather boring, and a perfect gentleman.

"He seems almost like a woman," one girl told Sarah. "Interested in dress fabrics and flowers—things like that. He lives with his mother."

With Sarah he discussed the new dyes they were using in the mill, and, in the pain she felt at not being with Ephraim, she found it as acceptable a subject as any.

Sarah's other new resolve was to go to see a doctor about what women usually called "a female complaint," meaning anything unusual in the genital area. Sarah's complaint was an itch, and so she described it to Dr. Graves, a medical man whose sign she had seen in a house near the mills. Sarah had seldom been to a doctor, but she knew from listening to other women that they usually asked a few decorous questions, examined the tongue, and took the pulse. Therefore, when Dr. Graves asked her to take off all her clothes, she declined.

"You'd better do as I say," Dr. Graves said. He looked her up and down, more like a tavern tout than a physician. "Suppose you have a certain disease?"

"What certain disease?"

"You must have heard of vile diseases—even if you aren't married," said the doctor, coming closer. "I have to examine you, to see if you have it."

Sarah had heard of such diseases, and she turned a little pale.

"Can it be cured?" she asked.

"Yes, but it is an expensive treatment. It might be as much as ten dollars."

Sarah gave a little moan. "Nearly a month's salary," she exclaimed.

The doctor moved closer still, and stroked her arm. "Perhaps it wouldn't cost you anything," he said. "Take off your clothes and we'll see."

In a rage, Sarah slapped him, and ran all the way back to Mrs. Porter's, determined to tell everyone what had happened. But by the time she got there, she realized how impossible that was. In ruining his reputation, she would certainly cause speculation about herself. And suppose she really did have the foul disease? In the end, she said nothing, but discreetly inquired for the name of another doctor.

A few days later, a very hot morning in August, Ephraim was driving along an outlying road in the carryall, with Edwin, his four-year-old son, beside him, when they came upon Sarah, walking in the same direction.

Ephraim switched up the horse, and when the carryall was abreast of Sarah, he leaned out and said, "Would you care for a ride with us?"

Sarah was both delighted and startled. He had just been in her thoughts, as he nearly always was. She was also apprehensive, for she knew he must be angry with her.

"Thank you, sir," she said, after hesitating, and climbed up beside him.

"Get in the back of the wagon, Edwin," Ephraim said. "Sit right at the back and look at the road behind, to make sure nothing falls out."

"Why should it?" Edwin said.

"Do as I say," said his father.

With the child out of earshot, Ephraim said in a commanding way, "And where have you been?"

"For a walk," she said. She had already observed that he was not in good humor, and she dreaded what might follow in the way of questions.

"On such a hot day?"

"Yes."

"You are lying," he said. "I am afraid it is a habit with you."

She said nothing, but when he looked at her he saw two tears advancing down her cheeks.

"Why do you cry?" he asked, more gently.

She could not speak for a moment. Then, controlling herself, she said, "Because you are cruel."

"Tell me where you have been, then."

"I have been to see Dr. Farnum."

"Why?"

"A female complaint."

Ephraim scowled, and he had to control himself, not to become angry.

"Perhaps I should tell you, Sister Sarah Maria, that I know you have already been to see another doctor. Dr. Graves. He told me."

"He should not have done that," Sarah said. "He had no right. What did he tell you?"

"He told me, Sarah, something that shocked me very much. He told me that you have a vile disease."

Sarah turned toward him indignantly. "He is a liar, and Dr. Farnum says so. I have something not serious at all, that many women have, and easy to cure. Dr. Graves told you that because I would not behave improperly with him."

Ephraim heard this with great relief, but he continued to scowl. "How am I to believe you, Sarah? Dr. Graves came to me and said he thought I should know this about one of my Church Members. So that I might take steps to expel you."

"He is a great liar," Sarah said, and began to sob, burying her face in her hands. "And you! I thought I had a friend in you."

At that, he put his arm around her.

"Sarah," he said hoarsely. "I am more than your friend. I want to do all I can for you."

The dusty road was deserted and no one was near, except for little Edwin at the back of the carryall. Ephraim kissed her.

"You offended me very much last Sunday," he said. "How could you disappear as you did, without a word?"

"It was hard for me, too. But it is better so, Ephraim. For us both."

His arm tightened around her waist and then his hand moved to her breast and he kissed her again, very much longer.

"Have mercy!" she finally said, drawing away. "You *must* not."

"No one says must to me," he said. And he dropped the reins, to free his other hand. "You must come and see me," he whispered. "Come tonight."

Edwin suddenly popped his head through the carryall curtains.

"There's a cart in back of us, wants to pass," he said. But the wondering look on his small face made them both know he had seen.

Ephraim whipped the poor old horse and pulled it roughly to one side while a cart clattered past. After that he sat very upright and said nothing. Nor did she. At the outskirts of the village, he broke the silence.

"You had better get down."

She got down and walked away without a word. He called after her, "I shall expect you this evening."

She did not answer. He could see that she was wiping her eyes fiercely with the backs of her clenched fists.

Ephraim felt that he was a sorely tried man. Perhaps the Devil himself had placed Sarah on the road just when he came along; and perhaps the Devil in Sarah had made her so violently attractive to him. It was also the Devil in Sophia Avery that had made her urge him to take Edwin along on this trip; and finally, the Devil in Edwin that had made him spy upon his father. Ephraim's religion had taught him that he ought to take these afflictions humbly and with patience. Instead, he lost his temper.

"Get up there, you devil," he said to the horse, and lashed him so that he went into a stumbling canter.

Sarah was determined not to go to Ephraim's study, and, furthermore, she was determined to stop crying on his account. She loved him, she adored him, she thought of him constantly. But the undeniable truth was that he was a married man and that she herself was all but unmarriageable. She had done too much crying over men, she thought; and anyway, she was aware that her tears, though partly for hopeless love, were also because of great resentment. Men might behave impulsively and independently whenever they pleased, and if they were not always admired for it, they were, at least, forgiven. If a woman did the same, even once, she could be sure of a bitter dose for the rest of her life.

After church meeting on the following Sunday, Mr. Avery asked that Miss Cornell wait for him in the vestry. She did not do so. On Tuesday, she stayed away from class meeting. On Wednesday, after supper had been served at the boardinghouse and Sarah was about to go out with three of the girls, she saw him standing under an elm in the street. She turned back inside, but he knocked at the door and told Mrs. Porter that he had to speak privately with Sister Cornell.

Mrs. Porter obligingly called Sarah and said they might use her sitting room while she ran down-street on an errand.

"Why have you disobeyed me?" Ephraim began. "I sent for you and you did not come."

"You know very well," Sarah said.

He took a step toward her.

"Please, don't touch me," she said.

"You were eager for my touch, if I'm not mistaken, the other day on the road. Do you deny it?"

"No."

"You said I was cruel. It is you who are cruel," he said. He was trembling, but managed to smile. "You kissed me as if you found it quite agreeable."

"That's true," she said in a low voice.

"Then, Sarah . . . my sweet . . . " He advanced again and she retreated to the other side of the table.

Ephraim folded his arms and gave her a look full of barely controlled anger.

"Very well, Sarah," he said. "The reason I have been wishing to speak to you is that word has reached me of your misconducting yourself. You have been seen in the company of a man, riding out alone with him on the Sabbath."

"I have not misconducted myself, Ephraim," Sarah said indignantly.

"I am told you frequent taverns. Do you deny that you went in a carriage to Belvedere with a fashionable young man?"

"Mr. Bliss is not what you'd call fashionable, but I did go to Belvedere with him in his buggy. That is not misconduct."

"And what did you do in Belvedere? As your pastor, who expects you at meeting on Sunday, I demand to know."

When he spoke so coldly, it was difficult for Sarah to remember that she had ever been in his arms. She set her own face to look as cold as his.

"I was determined to stay away from you last Sunday," she said. "Mr. Bliss invited me to ride out with him. We stopped at a tavern for refreshments, but certainly for nothing more. Mr. Bliss is not fast—if that's what you imply—or, at least, not fast with me. He talked about the new dyes at the mill and about the problems he has keeping the looms in good repair. He did not at all speak of what you are imagining."

"I do not wish you to see this person again. It is entirely unsuitable. I presume he is unaware of your . . . your history."

Sarah, becoming suddenly very angry, clenched her fists and resolved not to cry. She said passionately, "You use my history, as you call it, as a weapon against me, and you never try to understand how hard my life is. I am older than the other girls. They will be going home, sooner or later. As for me, my home is a boardinghouse. Because of my *history*, I probably won't marry. I can never go home—my family does not want me. I will grow old in the mills and the boardinghouses and I will die among strangers."

She succeeded in remaining dry-eyed. It was as if she had accepted these bleak facts, as one accepts bleak weather.

She went on. "I do not *frequent* taverns, but it's true that I went to one with Mr. Bliss and, yes, I drank some wine. He brought me home a little after the curfew, but not much after. Nothing happened that you think."

"You have lied before and I cannot trust you."

Now she fought back tears. "I have never given you cause for mistrust," she said. Then she looked him full in the face. "I have never told anyone that you committed adultery with me and would like to go on doing so."

He scowled heavily at this word.

"It's not easy to attack the reputation of a minister," he said. "Especially for a ruined girl like you. Which of us would be believed?"

"Why do you say such hurting things to me?"

"Because you behave badly."

"Well, I think you say them because you are jealous. Yes, you are jealous of poor Mr. Bliss. You would like to be free to go about in a buggy as he does. And you do drink. I've been told so, and in that very tavern at Belvedere, too. But you would like to do it with me. And you imagine all kinds of licentiousness and you are jealous of that, too!"

Ephraim looked so furious that Sarah thought he was going to strike her.

"The Devil is in you, girl," he said, his voice shaking.

"Do you think so?" Sarah said. "Well, *I* think that when you leave this room, the Devil will no longer be here."

Ephraim stormed out of the house, but during the next few days it seemed to him that Sarah might have spoken the truth. The Devil had got into him, and made him love a ruined woman.

His next sermon was as fiery as he had ever preached, the text taken from *Ecclesiastes*: " 'Do not surrender yourself to a woman and let her trample down your strength. Do not go near a loose woman, for fear of falling into her snares.' "

But still the Devil followed him home and made him push Sophia roughly out of his way when she came to meet him at the door.

"Leave me alone, in the Lord's name. You are a confounded nuisance."

As for Sarah, she told herself that she was finished for life with carnality. Never again would she give in to blandishments, never again abandon herself to sensation. She would spend the rest of her life good, and, like Mary Magdalene, hope to gain Heaven. But such resolutions did not keep her from remembering. As she tended her loom, she thought of her lover: his mouth, greedily seeking hers, and his hands so knowingly on her body. In the necessary-room, where there were mirrors and the girls crowded round to tidy their curls and reposition their tortoise-shell combs, Sarah stared at her own lips, reflected in the smudgy glass, and imagined them covered, probed, tasted, consumed, by his.

And at the same time she hated him for his heartless references to her "history," and for depriving her of the comfort and consolation of the Methodist meetings—for now she was afraid to go.

At last, after staying away for several weeks, she attended a Sunday service, and was relieved to find that Mr. Avery did not speak to her. His sermon was based on the text: " 'He rescued us from the domain of darkness. . . .' " But when he saw Sarah in the congregation, he paused for a moment, and shortly thereafter his sermon went off at a tangent, enumerating the various kinds of darkness that a person might need rescuing from. And somehow this brought him to the second chapter of *Peter*: "Above all, he will punish those who follow their abominable lusts. . . . To carouse in broad daylight is their idea of pleasure. . . . For them, the proverb has proved true. . . . 'The sow after a wash rolls in the mud again.' "

When he had finished, the girls who sat with Sarah were thrilled and awestruck. But Sarah said, as they all filed out, "He can preach as easy as a canary can trill."

"Sarah, that don't sound respectful," one of the girls said.

"Mr. Avery is like a father to us."

"I could preach as well as he," Sarah said.

"Girls can't be preachers, Sarah. It wouldn't be seemly."

"It isn't fair. Women could be very good ministers."

"Then why don't you get up at the Tuesday class meeting and exhort. That's allowed, so why don't you, Sarah?"

On the following Tuesday, Sarah stood up in class meeting and gave an impassioned exhortation.

" 'An enemy has honey on his lips,' " she began, quoting from *Ecclesiastes*, " 'but in his heart he plans to trip you into the ditch. . . . If disaster overtakes you, you will find him there ahead of you, ready, with a pretense of help, to pull your feet out from under you. Then he will nod his head and rub his hands and spread gossip, showing his true colors.' "

On Sunday, Mr. Avery announced from the pulpit that he wished to see, in his study after tea that evening, Sister Sarah Maria Cornell. He added, looking blindly over her head, "If she is not here, I ask that someone convey this message to her. Please say that if she does not come, I shall be obliged to say publicly what I would much prefer to tell her privately."

It was now late in summer, and the after-tea hour was after-sunset. Sarah found herself back at the Avery house in just the same degree of twilight that she remembered from her first meeting with Ephraim.

Sophia Avery passed her in the hallway.

"Mr. Avery has sent for me," Sarah said.

"I know," Sophia said in an icy way. "You may go upstairs."

When Sarah was halfway up, Sophia called after her, "Mind you do not tarry long. He has a headache."

"I do not wish to tarry at all," Sarah replied.

She knocked at his door and heard him say, "Enter." She stood in the doorway and he remained seated at his desk.

"Miss Cornell," he said. "I wish you to know that I have been obliged to call for a Church trial. The information I hear of you from Dr. Graves and others leaves me no choice. You are to be

tried for lying and fornication, and, if convicted, expelled from
the Methodist Church."

Sarah leaned against the door. She felt faint.

"I would advise you not to attend, since the matter is of such a
delicate nature," Ephraim went on. "It would be very unpleasant
for you. I would advise you to go to your friends . . ." he
paused ". . . if you have any."

Still she said nothing.

"I regret this very much, Miss Cornell, but you have left me no
alternative."

In a low voice, she said, "Is there any way I can avoid
this?"

He said, "Come in and close the door."

"No," she said, and turned around and left.

Sophia was still lingering in the hallway below, and looked at
her questioningly.

"Poor Mrs. Avery," Sarah said. "I pity you."

VII

Camp-Meeting

Sarah quit Lowell the next day and went to Summers-worth, New Hampshire, about thirty miles away, where she had no trouble finding a job as a supervisor of apprentices. She had so much experience now that almost any mill was glad to have her. She went at once to the Methodist meeting, bringing the certificate that Avery had given her when she was sick in bed; but the minister, Mr. Storrs, had already had a letter about her from Avery.

"Alas, alas, alas," he had written. "I am obliged to tell you that this unhappy woman, who has no husband and probably never has had, has confessed to carnal knowledge of two or more."

Mr. Storrs asked her if this were true, and Sarah pointed out that whatever she might tell him, he would certainly take Mr. Avery's word before her own.

"Of course," Mr. Storrs said reasonably. "But if you wish to make an issue of it, you may stand trial and defend yourself before your peers. We will send for Mr. Avery."

"No, thank you," Sarah said.

In despair, she wrote to her sister, Nancy: "I am not insensible that I have erred, that I have been and fear that I am still a great sinner, a very great sinner! But it is my heart's desire to reform—and believe that if I pray in sincerity to God He will forgive me—yes, I have His promise that if I sincerely repent, He will forgive me—but my earthly enemies will not forgive me! O,

155

no, they seem determined to pursue me and to persecute me wherever I go, and with their slanderous tongues impute to me crimes of which I have never been guilty! Many false charges have been brought against me—and for peace sake I have been obliged to exchange my place of residence when I should have preferred remaining had it been otherwise—and this is the principal cause, as I have before told you, why I have made so many removes and sought employ in so many different factories."

Nancy and Grindall Rawson had settled in Woodstock, Connecticut, where Grindall had a prosperous tailoring business. Nancy wrote to her sister by the next mail, urging her to come and live with them and work for Grindall in his shop.

Ever since her downfall, Sarah had dreaded coming to this—living as a spinster, on sufferance, in a sister's family. But she now saw that she could not remain in the mills. Avery was apparently anxious to entrap her in any mill-town, and she would have to remove herself from his orbit. Besides that, her eyesight was weakening, and in order to see the threads in the looms she had to wear spectacles. Every evening, her head ached. Summersworth was a very small place, with none of the diversions of Lowell, and after work, since she was unable to read, there was nothing to do but go to bed. Winter was coming on, and New Hampshire had long ones.

She wrote to Ephraim several times, furious letters, asking why he wished to deprive her of her very livelihood, to say nothing of any poor scraps of happiness left to her. He did not reply.

She took a Saturday off and went to Lowell and approached his house. The children were playing in the yard, and the crippled relative, Betsey Hills, was sitting by the front door, mending stockings. The window was open in the study above, and Sarah could see the back of Ephraim's head as he sat at his desk. She asked Betsey Hills to tell the minister that Miss Cornell was waiting to see him.

"I can't run up and down stairs," Betsey said.

"Perhaps, then, you could send one of the children."

Betsey went on with her darning. "He don't like to be disturbed," she said, after a moment.

Then Ephraim came to the window and looked down at Sarah. He looked directly into her eyes.

"What do you wish, Miss Cornell?" he asked in his most formal way.

"To speak with you, sir."

"Then you may come upstairs."

"Please, sir, come down."

"Certainly not. I will wait for you to come up."

"No, I cannot," she said and burst into tears.

"Of course you can," he said, and shut the window.

Sarah stood in the yard, hoping he would change his mind, until Betsey Hills asked what she was waiting for.

"Mrs. Avery is feeling poorly," Betsey said. "She don't need any commotion out here."

With her handkerchief to her eyes, Sarah departed. She went back to Summersworth and wrote to Ephraim once more.

"I came to say good-bye to you, hoping we could part as friends. But there is no end to your cruelty."

She moved to another town, Dover, but people there soon heard the gossip about her, and she feared that in any mill-town now it would be the same. She did not want to go to Cousin Fanny and face again the awesome loneliness of that secluded old house. And she knew she would be unwelcome in either Norwich or Providence. So, in November, 1830, she was once more aboard a stagecoach, this time traveling from Dover to Woodstock.

It was not so bad. Nancy was a good-natured young woman, Grindall was a kindly employer, and their rosy, friendly children welcomed a new aunt and caretaker. Sarah had a room to herself over the kitchen of the Rawsons' small Greek Revival house, which stood near the turnpike in South Woodstock. From her window she could see the few buggies and carts and ox-wagons that passed that way.

She thought, *I shan't move again. I shall grow old and die here.* She attended the Congregationalist church with the Rawsons, and every Sunday saw from its windows the neat gravestones in the burying-ground just outside. *There we will all lie in a row*, she thought. *People will say, "This was the Rawson family. And who is this beside them? Sarah Maria Cornell? Who was she?"*

She said this one day to her sister, trying to make light of it, but Nancy replied, with concern, "Oh, fie, Sally Maria, for being so morbid. We will put on the stone, 'Beloved Sister.' I promise."

There were widowers and bachelors in Woodstock who began to take note of the pretty sister of Mrs. Rawson. The situation became awkward. The kind-hearted Rawsons, of course, did not wish to announce that their close relative had been ruined, and yet it was morally impossible to allow a man to come courting unless he was aware of it. Nancy therefore confided to a neighbor, who told the town, that Sarah Maria was waiting for a sweetheart who had gone to New Orleans, and she had vowed never to look at anyone else. After that, people treated her with consideration, and the widowers and bachelors turned their attentions to other girls.

To be ignored by men was a new and depressing experience for Sarah, but at least nobody pointed her out on the streets of Woodstock as the ruined girl, the fallen woman. She was Miss Cornell, or Miss Sarah Maria, sister of the Rawsons. There was standing in that. She missed her old independence, but began to think that this kind of secure comfort was worth its loss. She would eat well and sleep soundly in her little room and grow old and resignedly cheerful.

After she had been in Woodstock more than a year—it was June, 1832—Grindall one day brought home from the post office a letter addressed to her. She took it up to her room and opened it fearfully. It was unsigned, and written in a cramped, disguised hand.

"My Love, My Only Love," it began. "I know now that I cannot live without you. You are in my thoughts night and day. Now, I have finally succeeded in finding out where you are.

Have no fear. I will never again hurt you or your reputation. I only desire your forgiveness. When can you come to Lowell and talk with me? Address your reply to Betsey Hills, Lowell, and I will get it."

After a great deal of soul-searching, Sarah replied: "I forgive you, but we must not meet."

Must. The very word that had caused their rift. But she did not change it, because she believed in her right to say it.

Within a week, there was another letter:

"I have a plan, concerning opportunities in the West. We can be happy yet. Be sure to attend the camp-meeting at Thompson at the end of August. I am now moving to Bristol, Rhode Island, so do not write. But *be there.*"

And, in August: "I must see you at the Thompson camp-meeting. Trust me."

Sarah burned the letters and did not speak of them to her sister. Her tranquility was shattered, but so was the apathy she had lived in, the passionless, numbed existence of one who has despaired and yet survives. She began to wonder whether she had been right to hate Ephraim. Perhaps he had only been carrying out God's wish that she be punished, and now that he had done it, he would be her friend and guide. Over her tailoring, day after day, she thought of him. She hardly ever stopped thinking of him. She wondered whether to go to the Thompson camp-meeting, and decided to go only if she saw a "sign" that she was meant to.

But no sign evinced itself, so when the week of the meeting came round, she said very casually to her brother-in-law, "There don't seem to be much tailoring for me to do this week. And if there isn't any, I was thinking to go over to Thompson, to the Methodist camp-meeting."

"Sally Maria, ain't you had enough of the Methodists?" Nancy asked.

"Well, mostly, but it would be something for me to do. But only if you can spare me, Brother Grindall."

The truth was, the Rawsons dreaded to have her on her own.
They loved her, but they were not quite sure she had good sense,
even yet.

"Maybe I could go with you," Nancy said.

"Oh, don't bother. I know you don't care about it. Let's say I'll
just go for a day or two, if I can get a ride."

Thompson campground was not far from South Woodstock—
about six miles—but too far for a girl to walk on a hot summer
day. To herself, she said she would leave it at that: if chance
found her a ride, it would be a sign she should go.

Chance found her one. A neighbor, John Paine, happened to
be driving a wagonload of hay to Thompson on the second day of
the meeting and would pass right by the campground. Grindall
asked him if he'd take Sarah, and John said he'd be glad of company.

John Paine was a taciturn, young married man, the father of
seven children and not the sort who broke Commandments, even
by look or thought. He invited Sarah to sit on the hay, and drove
her to the campground outside the village of Thompson without
exchanging two sentences with her. At the entrance, he let her
slide down off the hay unassisted, set her luggage beside her, and
drove off.

The campground occupied several acres, with a meetingplace
in the center on a small rise. Tall, old pines shaded this outdoor
church, where benches had been set up in rows. The pines
shielded the congregation from the sun. In the evenings, there
were meetings by the light of whale-oil lamps, tied to the trees.
Each Methodist community from many miles around had its own
little encampment of tents. The one from the vicinity of Woodstock was called Muddy Brook, and Sarah took her little carpet-
bag and the rolled-up pallet she had brought with her and headed
for the Muddy Brook tents. Each tent held eight or ten men or
women, and there was also a communal tent for cooking. Some of
the faithful had even brought their bedsteads, as well as trundle-
beds for small children. Experience had demonstrated that the

living quarters had better be well removed from the latrines; also, that four days was as long as several thousand people could happily remain in this manner. Already—and this was only the second day—the location of the latrines was obvious.

Sarah found the womens' tents at the Muddy Brook encampment. They were nearly filled, but she spotted an empty corner and put her pallet and belongings there. Then she changed into a claret-colored calico dress that had a bit of white crochet-work at the throat. It was in the style now replacing the high-waisted silhouette of the last three decades: full-skirted, with a natural waistline and dropped sleeves. Ephraim had once admired it.

Sarah went out to stroll around the campground. Someone was preaching in the meetingplace, but at midday the plank benches were a hot place to be, and the preacher droned on, persistent as a fly. Sarah saw several black-coated ministers, but not Mr. Avery. She overheard two girls, giggling, say that "the tall, good-looking one" would be preaching after supper and that if any preacher could save them they thought that one could. Overcome with melancholy, Sarah did not mingle with the other women, though she recognized a few from Jewett City, Slatersville, Dedham, and Lowell. She walked about alone. Once, she stopped at a tent where there was a small crowd. Inside, a hysterical young girl was lying on a pallet, alternately screaming and moaning, "Lord, I want to die! Lord, I am ready, Lord I am fit, Lord, I want to die in the arms of Jesus!"

"Ah, she is saved, she is saved," cried a young man who was kneeling at her side. "For a certainty, we shall have the Holy Ghost here among us tonight."

Sarah sighed, reflecting that even if the Holy Ghost did decide to join them, He would ignore her, for she felt not a trace of the religious fervor she had once known.

She walked on. Sarah's walk was always sensuous, and the calico dress, with its full, swinging skirt, accentuated it. Furthermore, the dress was a little tight now that she had been eating good country food at her sister's table, and sitting all day at her tailoring. But the dress would have attracted notice anyway, for most of the women present were still wearing the old high-waisted style.

A married couple from New Bedford, Reverend Henry Mayo and his wife, fell in behind Sarah on the path to the meeting-ground. Lydia Mayo, observing the direction of her husband's gaze, said crossly, "What you looking at?"

Mayo lowered his eyes from Sarah's rear to the pine needles in the path.

"Ain't looking at nothin', Liddy."

"Oh, ain't you!" said his wife. "You're looking where you oughtn't. That girl's got a tight dress if I ever did see one. It's fair to bursting open." She took Henry's arm in a proprietary manner. "If that girl ain't married, she'd better be."

"The world needs you, Liddy, to tell 'em what to do," Henry said drily.

"Let's take another path," Lydia said, and they turned off.

Sarah had overheard them. In earlier years, she might have been tempted to turn around and stick out her tongue. But now, even the impulse did not come to her. Instead, she felt almost amused. She thought, *I'll warrant he's a sly dog when his wife's not around. I could almost* feel *his eyes.*

She was wearing her glasses, which had green lenses and were not at all becoming. Few girls wore glasses, and those who did looked like grannies. No girl who wanted to attract men—and they all did—would dream of defacing her looks with these green monstrosities, the color of a dirty pool. In wearing them, Sarah wished to announce to every man, Ephraim Avery included, that she had not the slightest interest in their attentions. However, there remained her hip-swaying walk, her red lips, her curling black hair. Others on the campground besides Henry Mayo followed her—most of them with their eyes only, but some literally.

That evening, as the Muddy Brook people assembled for the evening preaching, a hulking blond farmer addressed Sarah.

"Sister, ain't I seen you at a class meeting up Worcester way?"

"I have never been up Worcester way," Sarah replied, and went to sit beside two very old women.

"Only asking," the farmer called after her, in an aggrieved tone. She ignored him, but she heard an older man say to him, "Don't bother with that kind of woman, Abel. She ought not to be allowed here. She's the one they expelled from the Lowell Meeting."

Sarah was glad of her glasses, which helped disguise both her looks and her feelings. She turned resolutely toward her two elderly seatmates, and offered them some peppermints she had in her pocket.

The sun set, the mosquitoes began to buzz, someone blew loudly on a ram's horn, and the preaching began. Those who had already felt intimations of repentance sat down in front on the bench called "the anxious seat." They were all quiet for the time being. At one side of the pulpit was a large tent with straw strewn thickly over its floor. Young girls were kneeling in the straw on one side of the tent, young boys on the other. Some prayed aloud, others sang—there were several tunes in the air at once—and there was a crescendo of excitement as more young people joined them.

"The Devil is after me! Oh pray, let me go!"

"Lord, lift me up or I fall into the fire and brimstone!"

As Sarah watched, she beheld a tall figure walking in among the young people, holding a lantern. She saw at once that it was Ephraim Avery.

"Oh, Lord!" he prayed loudly in his most eloquent tones. "Receive these repentant sinners, receive them into the fold!"

He walked among the boys and girls, putting his hands on their bowed heads.

"Save your children, Oh, Lord, for they are truly repentant."

There were groans and wild screams. Some threw themselves prostrate in the straw and contorted their bodies.

"I am saved, I die, I die, oh, glory. . . ."

"Cry aloud unto the Lord!" shouted Avery. "Don't hold back! Confess aloud your most terrible sins!"

"I am full of the Spirit! Oh, sweet Jesus, oh, Mr. Avery, I am safe at last!" cried a girl with long, tangled red hair. She gave a blood-curdling scream and fell, apparently senseless, on the ground. A friend pulled her dress down, but otherwise she was left where she fell. She was still there at the end of the meeting, and Sarah saw Avery hovering about her and asking some of her companions to remain with her. He took a sponge and bathed her pretty little insensate face.

To see Ephraim Avery touching another woman like this put Sarah into a turmoil. She hated him, she loved him, he was a cruel, unfeeling man, he was her lover, he was her minister, he was the only person in her meager life that mattered to her. But whatever she felt about him, she did not want to confront him now, while he was attending to the young people who were getting saved. Before he saw her, she fled, back to the tent.

It was deserted, except for a middle-aged woman named Patty Bacon, who was feeling indisposed. She told Sarah that one of the ministers had been there, inquiring for Sarah Cornell.

"His name's Avery," Mrs. Bacon said. "Said he comes from Bristol. *You* don't come from Bristol, so how do you know him?"

"I met him once," Sarah said briefly. She knew better than to tell too much to strangers.

But the woman persisted. "You married?"

"No."

To be good-looking, single, and older than the early twenties was a suspicion-rousing condition, and Mrs. Bacon looked her up and down thoughtfully.

"How come you left the meeting so early? Ain't you feeling good?"

"I am quite well, thank you."

"You don't look good. Something about the eyes."

Sarah was silent.

"Widowed?"

"No. And now, if you don't mind, I am going to pray silently."

Mrs. Bacon stayed quiet, but watched while Sarah undressed.
She spoke once more as Sarah lay down on her pallet.

"I suppose you mind having such a full bosom," she said. "Unmarried women are generally flatter."

Next morning, Sarah awoke to smells of cornmeal mush and
frying bacon and brewed coffee. The girls on the pallets around
her were gossiping.

"They say," one of them was saying, "that there are bad wom-
en on the campground, and they are to be turned out."

Sarah thought she would like to see what these women looked
like, since she had sometimes been accused of being one. She
dressed and wandered about and finally spotted them, sauntering
arm-in-arm near the men's tents. One had hair the color of a gold
coin, very frizzled. The other had oily, straight black hair and
high cheekbones, like an Indian. Their dresses were finer than
most campers wore, but rather dirty, and one of them had dirty
silver shoes. They wore no jewelry—*After all*, Sarah thought,
they are masquerading as Methodists—but Sarah was sure that
anyone would know them for what they were. *And*, she thought,
I do not look like them. Not at all. And in sudden revulsion, she
felt her old longing to be utterly pure and clean, and she sought
out the oldest and kindest-looking of the ministers and asked to be
forgiven.

"I see that whatever your sins were, you have repented of
them," he said. "I freely forgive you and I assure you, Jesus has
already done so."

"Oh, thank you, thank you, sir!"

The old man looked at her with concern.

"Mind you sin no more," he said. "God does not forgive so
easily the second time."

"Truly, I mean not to ever sin again, sir," Sarah said fervently.
And, more running than walking, she started back toward the

tent. She had the sudden plan of packing her things and leaving at once for Woodstock, even if she had to walk.

But as she turned into the path that led to her tent, she met Ephraim, coming away from it.

"Sarah," he said. "I have been looking for you."

She stopped, still, in the middle of the path. She was so small that her eyes were level with his chest, but she slowly raised them to meet his. He smiled.

"Ah, Sarah," he said gently. "I am so very glad to see you."

"And I!" she said, her voice catching. "I am glad to see you."

"Sarah, I should like you to name a time and place when we might talk." He spoke in a low, caressing tone. "Will you do that for me?"

Sarah answered helplessly, "As you like."

"I am to preach now, but I shall be free at suppertime. When the horn blows for preaching, directly after supper, will you meet me at the house where I am staying?"

There were two or three houses on the campground where the clergymen were accommodated. Ephraim gave her directions to the one he was in.

"Do not fail to be there," he said, and took her hand for an instant. "I feared you would not come."

"I had to come," she said in a sad way.

"You must be cheerful," he said. "Believe me, you are not to suffer any more. I meant what I said in my letters."

Sarah plucked up courage and said, "And I meant what I told you in mine—the ones you didn't answer, over a year ago. I told you that you persecuted me."

"We will settle these difficulties, believe me, my dear Sarah. You will come after supper?"

"Yes," she said, but she dreaded it.

She spent the whole day dreading it, but at the appointed time, washed and tidied, she knocked at the house where Ephraim had told her to come. There were a lot of people about, coming and going. Ephraim opened the door and stepped out.

"There is no room free here where we can be private," he said.

"Please walk along toward the woods and I will overtake you."

She took the path he indicated and in a few minutes he appeared at her side, arriving by way of a side-path. He offered her his arm, and they walked on, away from the tents and the meeting-ground. Everyone else was hurrying in the opposite direction, and very soon they were alone.

Although he did not show it, Ephraim was fully as nervous as she. Ever since Sarah's Church trial *in absentia*, and after his rage against her had cooled, he had deeply regretted allowing such a thing to come about. Dr. Graves, who swore Sarah had a venereal disease, had not inspired Ephraim with any confidence in his truthfulness. Even Sophia had said her friends avoided him because of his unsavory reputation. Nobody who testified at the Church trial seemed to have had first-hand information about Sarah. It was all hearsay. And Ephraim had learned that his own intense jealousy of Enos Bliss was a waste of energy; Bliss was as proper as a little old maid. Ephraim, therefore, was forced to face the fact that his own jealousy and vindictiveness had driven Sarah away and destroyed their love affair.

It had taken him more than a year to ferret out her address, which he finally managed to do through some of the girls at Mrs. Porter's. By that time, the thought of Sarah had become an obsession with him. And now, her presence at his side, moving trustingly along with one hand on his arm, flooded him with happiness, and he thought, *I am indeed truly in love with this woman.*

Their path led across a rough field, over a stile, and on into a forest. Here the trees were very tall, nearly shutting out the late sunlight. The forest floor was covered with cool, feathery grass. With a courtly gesture, Ephraim offered Sarah a low, flat boulder to sit on, and seated himself beside her.

"You don't need your glasses here," he said, and reached over and took them off. "I need to see your eyes. I have thought of them—I have thought of *you,* so very much. Have you thought of me?"

"Yes, of course!"

"I am afraid," he said, taking her hand. "I am very much afraid that I am still in love with you."

Sarah's heart beat faster, but still she wanted to say the thing that had been making her very unhappy: "You think of me as a bad woman. You love me, perhaps, but you believe the devil makes you do it."

"No," said Ephraim. "I have told you before, nobody makes me do anything. Even the devil. I knew, Sarah, that you were not a bad woman when you wrote me those letters after you left Lowell last year. You convinced me that, although you had been a sinner, you had truly repented, and that you had been greatly sinned against. They were wonderful letters of confession and showed me your fine soul."

"I hope you destroyed them. I would not want anyone else to read those confessions."

"I did not, because I treasured them," he said, with his slow smile. "But I promise I will if you do something for me now." And he took her in his arms.

"Ephraim, we ended it. Let it stay ended."

But he was accustomed to commanding and she to submitting.

"You don't mean that," he whispered, and he was quite right. He began to kiss her. "Oh, my darling," he said. "I have so dreamed of this!"

"And I, Ephraim! But . . ."

"Don't talk," he commanded, beginning to open her dress. "We will talk later. I promise. I have plans to tell you. But don't spoil this now. Let us lie here in the grass."

"Oh, my dear, please, no."

"Then why did you come?" he asked, in a less gentle tone.

"You said we would talk, and . . ."

"You knew what we would do," he said. "Now be quiet."

And she was, until she cried out in pure joy.

He held her tightly. "It had to be, did it not?" he said. "You knew it had to be."

"Yes," she answered. "I didn't want to know, but I knew."

He had thought that having her just once again might bring him back to his senses, but now he could see that this was not going to be the case.

"We will go away together," he said.

"How would that be possible?"

"We will go to the West. There are immense wild places there. People live far apart, and circuit riders are needed. Who would know we are not man and wife?"

Across Sarah's mind came wonderful pictures of the little house they would have, her house and his and no one else's. Never again would she be a boarder or a poor relation. She would keep this house and love it and fill it with children and at night she would lie by Ephraim.

She caught hold of his hand and kissed it passionately. He ruffled her hair as if he owned it and everything about her.

"You love me, Sarah, don't you." It was more of a statement than a question.

"So much!" she said. "Oh, Ephraim, the West! How perfect it will be!"

"Of course, we must expect many hardships," he said. "But we are both strong."

She lay looking up through giant treetops at the sky. "I imagine that everything is bigger there," she said. "Bigger trees, bigger sky—and bigger storms, I suppose."

"And bigger love," he said, stroking her cheek.

But suddenly she sat up and her smile faded.

"It's only daydreams, isn't it, Ephraim?" she said.

"Why do you say that?"

"Because you couldn't leave your children."

He disliked being reminded of this. "I'll send money back for them."

Sarah shook her head sadly. "I was a deserted child," she said. "The cruelest thing a man can do is to desert his children."

"Do not tell me what I can do," he said roughly.

He did not want to admit that he had been talking of daydreams. Certainly, he did not want her to tamper with them.

"Come," he said, standing up and brushing off his clothes. "They will be looking for me at the campground."

Sarah sighed deeply and blinked back tears.

"It was a good daydream," she said.

Hand in hand, they walked out of the forest. The sun had set and a light mist was rising about them. The air was filled with abundant and overabundant odors of late summer: pungent goldenrod and asters, wild herbs, and blackberries and purple wild grapes beginning to rot on the vine.

Sarah trembled, perhaps because of a slight chill in the air.

"Ephraim, suppose—," she said. "What if—if there should be a baby—."

"Nonsense." He did not wish to hear this, for the idea had already crossed his mind. "You did not conceive before. Certainly it wouldn't happen from just once."

Sarah remembered Louis; but said nothing.

"I desire that you come to Rhode Island," Ephraim said. "You can get work there and we will be able to meet."

"Where would I work?"

"Fall River is not far from Bristol. They have big new factories and employ hundreds of girls."

The dread that had pursued her all day began to return. Now she knew that it was a dread of loving him so much that she would do anything he asked. She was silent.

"Will you come?" he asked.

"Maybe."

Now they were back on the pathway into the camp, and there were people not far away. They could not kiss good-bye.

"Never say *maybe* to me," he said. "I shall expect you."

VIII

Fall River

"Oh, no, no, Sally Maria! Surely it cannot be!" "Alas, Nancy! I am afraid it is."

"But a clergyman! I never heard of such a thing in all my born days. What a disgusting man he must be."

"No," Sarah said sadly, for she could not bear to hear him criticized. "He didn't mean to. He forgot himself."

On this Sabbath evening in late September, after the family had gone to bed, Nancy Rawson had heard a sound of muffled weeping. She came downstairs and found Sarah sitting at the kitchen table with her head on her arms. With great reluctance, Sarah had recounted the story—or part of the story—of her encounter with Avery at the camp-meeting.

"He forgot himself, did he?" Nancy exclaimed. "He'd better not forget himself when he's asked to pay support."

"Oh, Nancy, Methodists are very poor, and he has three children of his own."

"He should have remembered that—before he forgot himself," Nancy said grimly. "I'm going to wake Grindall."

"Don't. I'm ashamed for him to know."

"He will have to know," Nancy said, and went upstairs to call him.

Both Grindall and Nancy were kindly, sympathetic people, but they could not keep wondering about Sarah. How could she let this happen *twice?*

171

"Was there nothing you could do?" they asked her.

"I tried to get away, but I could not," Sarah said. Was that exactly true? He had used no physical restraint, but she knew that she could no more have run away from him than the mouse escapes the swooping owl.

Next day, Grindall took her to see Mr. McLean, a lawyer in Woodstock. He advised that she ought to go to Rhode Island, where Avery was now living, and as soon as she was certain of her pregnancy, demand help from him.

"Tell him," said Mr. McLean, "that you will keep the matter secret, but he must help you. Three hundred dollars would be a reasonable sum."

"He has no money at all," Sarah said. "And certainly not that amount."

"Then he will have to find it," the lawyer said.

On the second of October, Grindall escorted Sarah as far as Providence and put her and her belongings into the Fall River stagecoach.

"Write to us," he said, and kissed her on the forehead. But, in truth, he was relieved to see her go.

Sarah, of course, was quite aware of that. People had no patience with unmarried girls who became pregnant. No matter how it happened, in the end they were blamed; and she knew that it would be a long time before she would be welcomed back to Woodstock. *Never mind,* she thought, winking back tears. Very soon she would see Ephraim Avery, who loved her and would help her.

It took most of the day to get from Providence to Fall River, which turned out to be a pretty little village overlooking Narragansett Bay. Its only commercial aspect was a complex of new stone factories. Sarah had no difficulty finding work at the top wage of $3.50 a week, and she went to board with a Mr. Cole, who had a daughter, Betsy, in the mills.

Sarah at once sent a note to Ephraim, at Bristol, discreetly worded: "I have arrived in Fall River, and am boarding at Mr. Cole's. *S. M. C.*"

A week passed and there was no answer. Sarah decided that the next step must be to consult a doctor, and Betsy Cole told her that all the girls liked a nice old Quaker gentleman, Dr. Wilbur.

Dr. Wilbur was nothing like Dr. Graves. He received Sarah in a courtly manner and scarcely touched her at all. When she said she feared she was in a certain situation, he asked how long she had had this fear.

"For about six weeks," she said.

"And the author of the situation? Is he prepared to help thee?"

"I don't know," Sarah said.

"Well, if he isn't, thee had better tell me his name. It is not right for thee to suffer. He must marry thee."

Sarah bent her head. "He cannot," she said.

"Ah, my child! Is he married? How could thee have been so foolish?"

"He loves me," Sarah said in a low voice.

Dr. Wilbur sighed deeply. "Well, come back in two weeks," he said. "If he loves thee, he had better prove it and not let thee starve."

"A lawyer told me he ought to give me three hundred dollars."

"At least," Dr. Wilbur said.

After nearly another week had passed, a note came from Bristol. Ephraim wrote that his wife was very poorly, but that he hoped to see Sarah "sometime after the New Year." For the first time, Sarah felt deeply frightened, but then she learned that there was to be a Methodist meeting in Fall River on October 19, 20, and 21, and that the minister from Bristol was expected. On the evening of October 19, she went to the house where the meeting was being held and waited until she saw Ephraim come out. He was with two other ministers.

Going up to him, she said, "Mr. Avery!"

He started at the sound of her voice, but then collected himself.

"What can I do for you, Miss?" he asked coolly.

"I must speak with you, sir."

"I'm afraid I am too busy."

Sarah held her ground. "Then," she said, "I shall have to come to see you in Bristol."

He stepped away from his colleagues and took her a little aside.

"Sarah, as I told you, my dear, I cannot see you for some time. For some reason, my wife has become quite crazy with suspicions. And I must be indulgent of her. She is poorly and expecting a child."

The truth was that when Ephraim had returned from the Thompson camp-meeting, Sophia had found several long, curly black hairs clinging to his linen. She had had a hysterical fit that had culminated in a frightening convulsion. When she at last recovered, she told Ephraim very convincingly that if anything of this nature ever happened again, she would stand up during church service while he was in the pulpit, and denounce him.

This threat alarmed and sobered Ephraim. He did not doubt that Sophia would carry it out. It seemed to him that he could cope with an intelligent mind and a strong will, like Sarah's, because he was confident that he knew better and had an even stronger will. But Sophia was stupid and hysterical, and that he did not know how to combat. A woman in hysterics terrified him.

The other ministers were waiting for Ephraim, and he started to walk away from Sarah. She put her hand on his arm and said rapidly, "But I have something to tell you."

"I'm sorry. I will get in touch with you next winter."

"Ephraim, I must tell you that I am in a certain situation."

At that, she felt him recoil from her, drawing his arm away. He made a move as if to return to his companions, but then turned back to her.

"Are you sure?" he asked in a tight voice.

"Alas, yes."

"Then come to the meetinghouse about nine o'clock tomorrow evening and I will talk with you in private."

Ephraim spent a sleepless night. Until now, he had worried only about Sophia and the scene she had promised to make if he gave her the slightest cause for suspicion. He had put out of his mind the possibility of fathering an illegitimate child. Since the camp-meeting, his thoughts had alternated between contriving how he might continue his love affair and a sober conviction that he had better watch his step. He had also asked himself whether he seriously wanted to leave his respectable and safe position, desert his wife and children, and start over in strange surroundings. And he had reached the conclusion that he was not quite uncaring enough and also not quite brave enough.

The Methodist circuit rider, Leander Lamb, had asked him whether he really believed what he preached; and Ephraim was well aware that he did not. Still, in very sober, soul-searching moments, he believed in Hellfire and feared he was already in mortal danger of it. To run away with Sarah would seal his doom. He also believed, at the bottom of his heart, that there were no excuses for fallen women. And when this mood was upon him, he would take out his Bible and read, " 'Lust not after her beauty in thine heart; neither let her take thee with her eyelids. For by means of a whorish woman a man is brought to a piece of bread. . . . Can a man take fire in his bosom, and his clothes not be burned?' "

All night long, on October 19, he tossed and turned, sometimes planning how he might help Sarah, sometimes convincing himself that since she was a ruined woman and a liar as well, she might well have become pregnant by another man.

Next day, he hit upon a solution. He went to an apothecary in the neighboring village of Tiverton, where no one knew him, and bought a bottle of oil of tansy. He remembered, from his time as a physician's apprentice, that oil of tansy would cause abortion, but unfortunately he could not remember the dosage. There was no one of whom to ask such a delicate question. Finally, he decided that thirty drops should be enough.

Sarah was waiting for him the next evening outside the meetinghouse door. He cut his sermon as short as he dared, and ended the meeting just before nine o'clock. He was first out the door, came up to her at once, and said, "Quickly. We must find a private place."

And they walked off together.

In the street they passed a young couple, and Sarah recognized the woman as a co-worker at the mill, Mary Borden.

"Damnation," Ephraim said, when the couple passed out of hearing. "We must not be seen together."

No moon shone, but there were countless bright stars. On the outskirts of the village, Ephraim and Sarah came to an orchard of large, old pear trees, which cast deep shadows. Ephraim helped Sarah over a stone wall and they went into the orchard and stood close in beneath a tree.

"Sarah," Ephraim began, looking away from her. "If you are in a certain situation, how can I be certain that the matter has to do with me?"

The coldness in his voice was felt by Sarah as if it were icy water. After a pause, she answered, "I suppose I should not be surprised that you say something as cruel as that. You have been cruel before. But we both know what happened at Thompson and it is only right that you should help me. My brother, Rawson, says . . ."

He turned quickly. "You have told him?"

"I am not without friends or protectors," she said. "I remember your saying in Lowell, 'Go to your friends, if you have any.' Well, I do, and I have been advised that you have to help me. It is the law and a lawyer told me so."

"A lawyer! Who else knows about this?"

To her consternation, he began to weep. He leaned against the rough trunk of the pear tree and sobbed for some minutes. Sarah put her arms around him and tried to comfort him, though the thought crossed her mind that it really ought to be the other way around.

"Dear Ephraim," she said, "I will never tell that it is yours. I will never expose you, but I need your help."

"But how? How can I help in any way that would make you happy? I am a married man. I cannot marry you. If you were to have this child, you would be obliged to say it belonged to a man who is dead, for certainly I am dead to you."

"What do you mean, *if* I have it? I *am* having it."

"My dear," he said, "if you are willing to finish the whole business, I have a way of helping you."

And he took from his pocket the bottle of oil of tansy.

"You must take thirty drops of this," he told her.

"What is it?"

"A certain cure for what you have."

"Would it be very painful?"

"A few cramps and you might miss half a day's work. Have no fears. You may remember that I was trained as a physician. I know this is a never-fail remedy."

"Well," she said doubtfully. "I will ask my doctor."

"No, no," Ephraim said in alarm. "A doctor would have to advise you against it. And you didn't tell me your had consulted a doctor. It seems the whole world knows about this."

"Believe me, he does not know your name," Sarah said. "I have no wish to injure you."

Her gentleness quieted him, and he took her hand and pressed it. He thought, *How strange it is: she is a fallen woman and perhaps a bad one, and yet I feel so very tenderly toward her.* He thought of the child within her, and of how glad he would be, under other circumstances, to have a child by a woman he loved.

"My dear, dear Sarah," he said impetuously, "I do believe you when you say the child is mine. I do not doubt you."

"I could not bear it if you doubted me."

He leaned down and kissed her. "Only do as I told you and all this will be behind you, dearest," he said. "And then, perhaps next winter . . . "

"No, no, Ephraim," she said sadly, but very firmly. "As you have said, you must be dead to me."

Dr. Wilbur told Sarah that thirty drops of oil of tansy would be enough to kill her.

"Even four drops would make thee very sick," he added. "Does this man want to murder thee?"

"Of course not! He must have made a mistake."

"I would be very careful of him," Dr. Wilbur said seriously. "Did thee tell him thee must have three hundred dollars?"

"No, I . . . I forgot."

"Then thee must tell him at once. And throw this bottle away."

"Are you sure I am pregnant?"

"It is now nearly the end of October, and thee says thee has not been sick as women are since the third week in August. I think we may conclude that thy situation is as thee feared."

Sarah waited nearly two more weeks, hoping the doctor was mistaken. Then she wrote to Ephraim to say she had been advised not to take the medicine, because it would kill her. "I pledge my word of honor not to swear the child on you, only you must settle it. My lawyer tells me three hundred dollars."

The mail service between Fall River and Bristol was fast and efficient. On November 14, Sarah had an answer—a letter written on straw-colored paper, which began, "Miss Cornell: I have just received your letter with no small surprise, and will say in reply, I will do all you ask, only keep your secret. I wish you to write me as soon as you get this, naming some time and place where I can see you. . . ."

Sarah did not answer until November 19. She told him it was difficult for her to get time off from work, but that if he would tell her where to meet him, she would try to do so.

In response came a letter (on pink paper) written in Providence on November 29. Ephraim suggested that she come to

Bristol on December 18 or 20 and meet him after dark. But he added, "If you cannot come, you might meet me . . . just over the ferry. . . . Or, if you cannot do either, I will come to Fall River one of the above evenings, back of the same meetinghouse where I once saw you, at any hour you say, when there will be the least passing. . . . Direct your letters to Miss Betsey Hills, Bristol. Remember this. Your last letter I am afraid was broken open."

Ephraim was right about that, although Sophia had never said anything to him about steaming a letter open. He had been unusually pleasant ever since she had had her hysterical fit, and she did not wish to press her luck.

Sarah wrote back at once, saying she would meet Ephraim after dark on Thursday, December 20—if the weather permitted—and suggesting they meet back of the meetinghouse, and then walk to Durfee's farm, where they could be private. On December 1 she moved to Mrs. Hathaway's. Her situation would soon become apparent, and as Mrs. Hathaway and Lucy seemed to like her, she hoped they would let her stay on with them, despite her disgrace. The Coles, a dour Puritan family, would surely have asked her to leave.

On December 8, Sarah received a letter on white paper, posted in Fall River: "I will be here on the 20th, if pleasant, at the place named, at six o'clock; if not pleasant, the Monday evening. Say nothing."

For the next twelve days, Sarah lived in fantasy. Nothing had changed, and yet she felt optimistic. She had heard of a girl in Fall River who had had an illegitimate child and who had gone back to work in the factory six weeks later and boarded the baby for fifty cents a week. She thought, *I can do that, too. Or maybe Mrs. Hathaway would keep it, and I could take care of it at night. Or perhaps Sister Nancy would take care of it, and they could say it was a foundling, left on the doorstep.*

But whatever happened, she was sure of one thing: she would have the baby. The idea of a human being that belonged to her alone seemed altogether wonderful. At last she would have someone to love, and someone to love her. After Ephraim brought her the three hundred dollars, perhaps she and the baby could go west. She could pretend to be a widow. She pictured herself running a boardinghouse for miners or trappers or whoever there might be in the West.

Ticking off the days until December 20, and watching the weather anxiously, she felt an unaccountable happiness. She pressed her belly lovingly, and brought home skeins of waste yarn from the mill, preparing to knit a wardrobe for the baby.

At last it was Thursday, December 20: cold, blustering, but not stormy. Sarah got off early from the mill and went home for tea and to change her plain mill-dress for a better one. Not that Ephraim would be able to see what dress she had on, in the dark, but *she* would know. Before she left the house, she put the three letters in her trunk, and, as she did so, saw the bottle of oil of tansy lying there. Seeing it gave her an uneasy feeling, and on an impulse she scribbled a note and put it in her bandbox: "If I should be missing, inquire of the Reverend Mr. Avery. He will know where I am gone."

At candlelight, she left Mrs. Hathaway's and walked through the village streets to the meetinghouse.

Ephraim was there ahead of her, pacing up and down and stamping his feet to keep them warm.

"Ah, Sarah! How are you? What a cold night!" he said, almost jovially. He had made up his mind that he must be calm and friendly; must, above all, stay in control, both of himself and of her. That would make it easier to accomplish what he had come to do.

She looked up at him in the old, loving way. Her face was rosy with cold.

"You are looking well, my dear," he said.

"I am quite well, thank you, Ephraim."

Unlike Sophia, she had no hesitation about using his first name. In the past, he had thought this agreeable, but now it suddenly struck him as an example of her independent and self-assertive nature. A man would not want a wife like that.

"I was sorry to learn, Sarah, that you did not take the medicine I gave you. I know best. Did you imagine that I would give you anything harmful?"

"No, but you did want to kill the baby, and I don't."

"We must talk about that," he said. "But let us find a more private place."

He offered her his arm. She put her little gloved hand on it and they passed through the dark village streets. As they walked, he considered carefully what he should say to her. For the past weeks, he had weighed all his feelings and worried and spent sleepless nights, and now he believed he had arrived at the right answer. It was true that Sophia was much less attractive to him than Sarah, and it was true that his children interested him hardly at all. Nevertheless, his life as a minister was not a bad one. It brought him prestige, respect, honor, and, if not riches, security. His decision now was to bring order into his life, at all costs. He would put passion, and all the chaos it entailed, firmly behind him. From now on, he would *be* the man he had been pretending to be.

Now that he had reached this decision, he felt like a person who has been rock-climbing; who has been a daredevil, has attempted too dangerous an ascent, and has scared himself badly; but who now knows how he may scramble to safety. His only obstacle now might be Sarah's strong will, but he was ready for that, too.

He began the speech he had been rehearsing.

"Sarah, I am older and wiser than you, and have a great deal more common sense. You have been far too independent all your life and that is why you have got into so much trouble. Obey me . . . obey me just this once and you will thank me for it forever."

"How shall I obey you, Ephraim?"

"I am going to give you a flat belly again. You have only to do as I tell you and it will be over in no time."

She looked up at him in alarm and instinctively pressed one hand to her abdomen.

"What are you going to do?" she asked.

"I told you I would help you, Sarah, and although it is extremely unpleasant for me I will keep my promise. I must prevent you from ruining your life."

"But I am only asking you for money."

"Three hundred dollars!" He laughed, not at all humorously. "Don't you know that I have never had three hundred dollars all at once in my life, and never will have? And do you imagine, if I ever had such a sum, that I would neglect my family and give it to you?"

Dark as it was, she could see that his face was set in rigid lines and looked so cold that it chilled her heart.

"Very well," she said. "But this is my baby and I mean to have it."

"And I mean you not to have it, Sarah."

At that moment, they encountered Mrs. Zeruiah Hambley, on her way to visit Mrs. Owens. Sarah vaguely considered calling out to her, but before she could make up her mind, Zeruiah was gone in the darkness.

They walked through the lane that went past Mrs. Owens's house and turned into a path that led toward Durfee's stack-yard.

Ephraim's right hand was in his coat pocket. He had a piece of string there, which he had taken that afternoon from a sack of blasting powder, thinking it might be useful in some way. His fingers now closed tightly over it. It was a light but strong string, and he knew he could easily tie her hands with it, should that become necessary. Also in his pocket was a long knitting needle.

"Now, Sarah," he said, as they walked on, away from the lights of the village. "I can see you have not really thought this out. There is nothing worse for a woman than the life of an unwed mother. And nothing worse for a child than illegitimacy. As for me, I have determined to live a regular life from now on, and I cannot do so, thinking of two such unhappy creatures."

"We will be all right," Sarah said. "It is not as bad as you think. There is a girl in Fall River who works and boards her child. After all, there are no scarlet letters any more."

"The scarlet letter still exists in people's minds," he said. "Wherever you go, you will be branded."

"I don't care."

"Then I care *for* you. And for the child as well."

"It seems to me," said Sarah, "that I am the one to decide."

"Not so," Ephraim said sternly. "And I must now tell you quite plainly: since you have not had the sense to end this situation, I intend to do it for you."

Sarah stopped short in the path.

"You *must not,*" she said.

The word *must* grated on his nerves, but he still kept control of himself.

"How many times have I told you, my dear," he said cajolingly, "no one says *must* to me. If you do exactly as I say, it will all be quickly over. There may be some pain, so perhaps I should put a handkerchief in your mouth."

"No, no, no!" cried Sarah in fright, and she dropped to her knees in the grass. "Please, Ephraim! Have mercy!"

"Sarah, be quiet. Damnation, I don't want to use force, but you will make me! Give me your hands, I must tie them."

At that, Sarah began to scream. She jumped up and started to run back down the path, but he caught her and pushed her down, beating her about the abdomen. When he put one hand over her mouth, she bit it, and blood flowed.

He let out a roar of pain.

"Now we'll see who says *must,*" he said, and he took from his pocket the long knitting-needle.

But he had not counted on her struggles. He could not have imagined so much strength in such a little creature, and it took all of his own strength to flatten her to the ground. She put one arm up, to ward him off, and continued to scream. He wound the string around her neck and pulled it tight in a clove-hitch knot.

IX

Trial

Newport courthouse, Monday, May 6, 1833. A bright spring morning. For the first time in the United States, a clergyman was to be tried for murder; and because of this and also because of the lurid circumstances of the case, no American murder trial had ever attracted so much interest. Those who were to have a part in it—the judge of the Supreme Judicial Court, the lawyers, and the prospective jurors—were hard put to it to elbow their way through the crowds that jammed the Newport streets and Common. Adding to the congestion were at least a score of reporters, some from as far away as New York City.

In the county jail, the central figure of all this commotion arose early and prepared himself to face the world. Since late-February, he had been in the jail, a stark, deadly cold building not far from the wharves; it seemed to have absorbed all the wind and fog of the wintry Atlantic, as well as various overpowering odors from the fishing-boats anchored nearby.

Ephraim had a solitary cell, but exercised daily in the company of vagrants and thieves. The only gentlemanly prisoner besides himself was a slave-ship owner, whose loaded ship, direct from the slave pens of Lomboko, had been overtaken by a Coast Guard patrol. He was a member of a well-known Newport family, wore a diamond stickpin and a gold watch and chain, and had a servant come in to shave him daily. When he and Ephraim met, he did not seem at all grateful to have a Man of God as his

185

companion. He stared at Ephraim's threadbare clothes, and turned his back in a righteous sort of way when he heard what Ephraim was accused of. As for the vagrants and thieves, they were even more censorious.

"Get that preaching scum out of my sight," one of them said loudly to the jailer. "I'll flatten him if he don't look out."

The ignominy of being reviled by low and evil persons, combined with the terrible restraint, the indignity, the cold and damp, and the boredom, all were appalling. But worst of all were the long nights and the dreams.

So often did he dream of Sarah's dying face that he dreaded sleep. But waking fantasies were as bad. Over and over, he remembered how he had seized the comb from her head, broken it, and then frantically pushed her mass of curling hair—that lovely hair that he had touched so gently once—over her staring eyes, her swollen lips, her frown. He could not recall at what point he had done this. Was she already quite dead? Or was she silent only because he had made a ball of her handkerchief and stuffed it into her mouth?

After weeks in Newport jail, he could scarcely differentiate between nightmare and memory. Sometimes he felt sure it was all nightmare, especially when fellow clergymen came to visit him in his cell, commiserating with him on his undeserved predicament and calling him blameless, fine, upstanding, and a Christian martyr. He could almost believe them; almost thrust away the memory of the stackyard as if it were nothing but an aberration.

At other times, unable to tolerate his conscience, he thought of confessing. Then he would remember Sarah saying, "the cruelest thing a father can do is to desert his children." And, in fancy, he would tell her, "No, it is even crueler for a father to be hanged for murder."

He had been closest to confession after the Bristol hearing, when he found himself continually harassed. But Sophia, about to give birth, seemed so pathetic and miserable that he thought, *I don't want another woman's life on my conscience—and another child's*. The two Merrill brothers offered to help him slip away and go into hiding. They spirited him off to a quiet Methodist household outside of Boston, just the day before the sheriff arrived with a warrant for Ephraim's arrest.

But they hadn't reckoned with the zeal of the Fall River Citizens' Vigilance Committee and of its leader, Colonel Harnden. With several helpers, Harnden was soon in hot pursuit. Ephraim spent the next six weeks skulking from one safe house to another, finally ending in the remote village of Rindge, New Hampshire. There, with a family called Mayo, he enjoyed a fortnight's respite—long enough to try to disguise himself by growing some chin whiskers.

Then, one evening after he had gone to bed, his host burst into the room with the news that the Harnden party was on the doorstep with a warrant to search the house. Ephraim slipped downstairs and stood behind the door of the sitting room, and that was where they found him.

"Ah, there you are, Avery," Harnden said affably, and held out his hand. "How are you?"

Ephraim was so agitated that he could not speak: deprived, in this moment of anguish, of his most prized possession, eloquence. What distressed him most was the extreme ignominy of being trapped behind a door, like a common criminal, or, worse still, like a bad child. Where now was the dignifed and imperturbable clergyman?

Harnden said later that he seemed like a man who wholly lacked the power of speech.

"Come into the entry, Reverend," he said kindly. "You need a breath of air."

In a few minutes, Ephraim recovered sufficiently to inquire whether Harnden was acting legally. Mr. Bullock, the lawyer in Bristol, had told Ephraim that he could not be taken from any state without application to the governor. Harnden told him that this was not true in New Hampshire. Ephraim said, in that case he would start for Rhode Island without delay, but would like first to shave. And Harnden took him back to the tavern in

Rindge, and stood beside him while he removed the unbecoming chin whiskers.

The discomforts of Newport jail were somewhat alleviated by baskets of food from local Methodist housewives and by continual visits from fellow clergymen. The latter assured him that the Lord would make sure he was acquitted, especially since the Church had engaged a famous lawyer to defend him. He was Jeremiah Mason, Daniel Webster's law partner. Although the firm of Webster and Mason did not ordinarily handle murder cases, Mason had nevertheless found time during his long career to defend six other alleged murderers, and he had won acquittals for all of them. His fee, though extremely high (fifteen hundred dollars, plus separate fees for five assistant lawyers), was not as high as the cost to the Church's reputation should one of its ministers be hanged for murder. Already, on the mere suspicion of Avery's guilt, Methodist congregations all over New England had dropped off in size. The Methodist meetinghouse in Newport, which was on the Common not far from the courthouse, was now missing two-thirds of its usual Sabbath Day congregation. Some of the parishioners, unwilling to be ridiculed by their neighbors, were holding private prayer-meetings in their homes behind closed shutters.

Of the numerous clergymen who visited Ephraim in his cell, the only one to ask an awkward question was Mr. Dow, the minister at Dover, New Hampshire.

"Brother Avery, are you guilty?" Mr. Dow asked.

The question seemed quite outrageous to Ephraim, and he glowered and drew his black brows together.

"If I were guilty, sir, I would have said so. Surely you cannot suppose that I would lie to my brothers in religion."

Mr. Dow was not to be intimidated by truculence.

"I hope not, indeed, Brother Avery, yet I put the question to you directly, both of us being quite aware that in Hell a burning lake of brimstone awaits liars. Are you guilty?"

"I am not guilty!" Avery shouted, and got up and paced about the room. He was just as much in awe of the horrible fate of liars as Brother Dow, and for this reason he sometimes almost convinced himself that he was *not* lying and that he was *not* guilty. According to this line of reasoning, he had been obliged to strangle Sarah because she was screaming too much and because the abortion was not working. These things were not his fault.

Mr. Dow had more reason than the other ministers to nurture suspicions of Ephraim. His parish was near enough to Lowell so that people had come to him, after Sarah's death, with stories about Mr. Avery—how he had seemed a little free with millgirls, especially Sarah, but with others, too, driving them about in his carryall and paying pastoral visits to their rooms. His little son, Edwin, was reported to have said, "Pa kissed Sarah on the road." Avery was also said to have shown, on occasion, a violent temper, and to have beaten a horse until its hide was raw.

Mr. Dow was a canny Yankee. He prided himself on keeping his eyes open and making independent judgments. Nevertheless, he had no wish to burden his Church with the stigma of a murderous and adulterous minister.

"Very well, Brother. You would not lie, knowing, as you do, that it is far better to repent and suffer in this short life than to spend eternity in Hellfire. I shall help you anyway I can."

"Find witnesses," Ephraim said. "Find all the people you can who will testify to the vileness of that girl. Mr. Mason believes our case depends on demonstrating her vileness."

"Vileness?" Dow said. "Do you not exaggerate? When she came to my meeting in Dover, I thought her a bit lacking in good sense, but I never heard she was vile—except from you."

"Everyone who knew her said so. She was expelled from the Church. She was a liar and a fornicator. She had a disease."

"*You* expelled her, *you* said she was a liar and a fornicator, and Dr. Graves said she had a disease, but others tell me that Dr. Graves himself has a dubious reputation and is avoided by the mill-girls in Lowell. One of them told me she would rather die than consult such a man."

Ephraim frowned again. "Are you planning to tell the court that?"

Mr. Dow signaled the guard that he was ready to depart.

"It is probable that I shall not tell the court anything," he said. "My work is very heavy now and is sure to prevent me from appearing as a witness."

Desperate with anxiety about his defense, Ephraim hoped for long consultations with his lawyer. But Mr. Mason called on him only once, and asked him very few questions—of which "Are you guilty?" was not one. He advised Ephraim to conduct himself, while before the court, with aloof dignity.

"And do not allow your wife to attend the trial," he added. "Women can be a bother and express emotion indiscreetly."

"I kept her home in Bristol and I shall do so now," Ephraim said.

Then he remembered being told that he had conducted himself very well in court in Bristol, and wanted Mr. Mason to know it.

"What questions will you put to me," he asked "when I take the witness stand?"

"There will be no questions," said Mr. Mason, as he rose to leave. "I do not plan to call you to the stand."

On the morning of May 6, the reporters at the courthouse were generally agreed as to the prisoner's remarkable self-possession. Reactions to his personal appearance varied. "A tolerable good-looking man," or, "Looked like no fool," or, "Looked as though he knew more than he told for." He had a "face that might have passed for good-looking, had not it been for a certain iron look, a pair of very thick lips, and a most unpleasant stare of the eyes."

Ephraim stood erect and easy before the court, with one hand in the breast of his dark coat. His left hand rested on the back of a chair—perhaps more for the graceful and striking effect of this stance (as one reporter suggested) than for support. He did not tremble or even move, beyond a slight rapid movement of the lip, as if chewing it. His eyes, behind steel-rimmed spectacles, were fixed without emotion on the clerk, who read the charges.

The prisoner, Ephraim K. Avery, was indicted on three counts of murder: "for choking and strangling the deceased"; "for tying her to a stake"; and "for inflicting various wounds and bruises . . . to cause death."

The clerk asked Ephraim how he pleaded.

"Not guilty."

"How will you be tried?" This was a prescribed question, as was the prisoner's reply:

"By God and my country."

"God send you a good deliverance," was the clerk's response.

The first task was to empanel the jury. Because it was clear that choosing jurors would be difficult, more than a hundred citizens had been called—all plain country Yankees of Puritan background, neither rich nor very poor; in short, very much like the prisoner. Three questions were put to each venireman: Are you related to the prisoner or to the deceased? Have you any conscientious scruples against finding a man guilty of a crime punishable with death? Have you formed any opinion of the guilt or innocence of the prisoner?

The first man called said yes to the second question, and was excused. The next, Charles Lawton, said he had formed an opinion, but could give an impartial verdict. Lawton and the prisoner were asked to stand, and the Clerk said, "Juror, look upon the prisoner. Prisoner, look upon the juror. What say you, prisoner, will you be tried by this juror? If not make your objection and you will be heard." The prisoner was entitled to twenty objections. In Lawton's case, Ephraim made no objection, and both sides accepted him.

The next venireman, George W. Tilley, said he had an opinion, but "not a settled one." Mr. Mason asked him whether his bias was in favor of the prisoner or against him.

"Against him," said Tilley.

"But after hearing evidence, could you render an impartial verdict?" inquired Mason.

Tilley said he could, and the prisoner, responding to discreet signals from his lawyer, accepted him.

The next four men all said they had strong opinions against the prisoner, and they were set aside. Gideon Peckham answered no to all the questions, and was accepted. Jethro Philbrick and Charles Hambley said they'd heard much talk of the case and had formed opinions. They were set aside. Edward Way was set aside because he was opposed to capital punishment. Pardon Almy was set aside for having an opinion, even though he said he was "superior to all bias."

And so it went. The prisoner, each time glancing at Mason for a nod or a frown, used most of his twenty objections. It took all day to seat twelve jurors and two alternates who were acceptable to both sides. There were five farmers, an innkeeper, a blacksmith, a retired ship's captain, a master carpenter, two traveling salesmen, a shipyard owner, and two fishermen.

The trial began next morning with a two-hour opening statement by the assistant attorney general, Dutee Pierce. He began by saying how sorry he was to have to prosecute a member of a religious society "extensive, pious, respectable," but that it should be remembered that the defendant was being tried not as a minister, not as a Methodist, but solely for his own individual acts.

"I say to you, gentlemen, that the government expects you to convict this man, *though* he be a Methodist minister, on the same evidence—no less and no more—than would be sufficient to convict any other individual of fair character.

"We intend to show that the barbarous circumstances of the death of Sarah Maria Cornell could not have been caused by herself; that she was not suicidal, and that even if suicide had been her intent, she would hardly have picked a cold night in December to go to an open field, a mile from her lodging, and tie herself to a short stake in a stackyard. The post of her own bedstead, the hook in the cellar, the beams of the garret or the barn—many things—offered a more convenient mode of death than the one she is said to have resorted to. And not only these facts, which relate to the mind of the deceased, but the physical evidence, too, proves to a moral certainty and beyond all reasonable doubt that this was a case of homicide."

Mr. Pierce described the physical evidence in such graphic detail that, as several of the reporters wrote, "the judge wept." Then the prosecution began to call its witnesses, including many who had testified at the Bristol hearing. First came those who had seen a tall stranger on the afternoon of December 20, and the three persons who had heard screams after dark. They were followed by John Durfee and the others who had taken the body down; the three old Borden women; Elihu Hicks, the coroner; and Benjamin Manchester, finder of the broken comb.

Thus far, Mr. Mason and his five assistants had little to say, except for an occasional objection. Mason was an elderly man, and a very large one—six feet seven inches tall and weighing about two hundred and fifty pounds. There was something hypnotizing about his very presence, even when he said or did nothing except sit there, with hooded eyes, leaning one cheek on his hand. He seemed like some sort of reptilian creature—an alligator or large lizard—prompting caution and respect even when quiescent.

When Dr. Wilbur was called to the stand, testifying about the post-mortem examinations, Mr. Mason suddenly struck, objecting that the attorney general, Mr. Greene, was trying to get the witness to swear that there had been an abortion attempt.

"The witness has said *probably*," Mason insisted. "That is not the same as *certainly*. Is the prisoner to be tricked out of his life by getting in illegal testimony in this manner?"

Mr. Greene was a small, earnest, dry man, with none of his opponent's charismatic qualities. Perhaps he was a little afraid of Mason and his impressive reputation.

"Surely," Greene said plaintively, "it is unnecessary for me to disclaim the design of attempting to trick any man out of his life. But if the distinguished gentleman is disposed to think so, I will make no further allusion to this matter."

And he excused Dr. Wilbur, neglecting to ask about Sarah's office visits to him, or about the oil of tansy.

Mason gave young Dr. Hooper a hard time in cross-examination.

"Can you tell the precise age of a fetus from its length?" he demanded.

"I do not know that I can," admitted Dr. Hooper. "Even the authorities disagree on this matter."

"Step down," Mason said scornfully. "You were brought here as a scientific witness, and I should think you ought to know."

The testimony of the Borden women was essentially what it had been at Bristol. Meribah Borden, examined first, spoke of "rash violence," and the others agreed with her. Mr. Mason failed to shake any of their stories, but he dealt with them condescendingly, as if they were too old and ignorant and female to bother with.

Elihu Hicks, the coroner, also tried the patience of the defense counsel.

"Why, pray," asked Mr. Mason, "did you allow the body to be buried if you were not satisfied with the verdict?"

"It was talked she could be dug up if it was necessary."

"And the verdict was not even legal," scolded Mr. Mason. "Two of the jurors were not freeholders, and only four of them signed it."

"Yes, but anyhow, I lost the paper," Elihu said.

"Step down," said Mr. Mason, shaking his head.

The testimony about the exact time when screams were heard, as well as the exact time when Avery had arrived at the ferryman's house, was inconclusive. All that seemed certain was that no two watches, clocks, or bells in the vicinity had been in agreement, and that this was a common state of affairs. Both sides gave up trying to prove anything about the time.

Mrs. Hathaway and her daughter, Lucy, repeated their Bristol testimony that Sarah was a quiet, well-behaved girl; that they had seen her with three letters; that she had planned to go out on Thursday, December 20, and seemed to have looked forward to it; and that there had been nothing in her behavior to suggest suicide.

"I knew her to be out of health," said Lucy, "and she said she had been out of health ever since she came from the camp-meeting at Thompson."

"Did she state the cause of her sickness to have been at the camp-meeting?" Mr. Greene asked.

"Yes, and she said, 'I never will go there again.' I asked why and she says, 'I can't tell you. I saw things that disgusted me, things which took place between a minister and a Church Member,' and then says, 'a married man, too.' "

After Lucy was excused, the crier adjourned the court until Monday morning. The jury had permission to walk about together and to speak to their families in the presence of an officer, but not about the case.

As the first witness to be called on Monday morning, May 13, Colonel Harvey Harnden, of Fall River, told the story of his pursuit and capture of the defendant. He also offered proof that the letter to Sarah Cornell, dated in Fall River on December 8, was written on a piece of white paper purchased at Iram Smith's store.

"And how do you know that?" asked Mr. Greene.

"I went to Mr. Smith and asked for what might be remaining of a ream of white paper that had been in his store on the eighth of December. There was a torn half-sheet, and I compared it under a microscope with the letter found in the deceased's trunk. One piece had been torn from the other. The fibers entered into each other exactly."

Over Mr. Mason's objections, the jury looked at the two sheets under a microscope, and saw that this was true.

Stephen Blodgett, driver of the Fall River-Bristol stagecoach, testified that on the eighth of December, he picked up Mr. Avery in Fall River and took him to Bristol. "He rode on the outside," Mr. Bartlett added. "He frequently was at my stable in Bristol and helped me hitch on. He told me he was very fond of a good horse—more fond than usual, I'd say. Fond of breaking horses, too.

"On Sunday, December 23, I called to see Mr. Avery in Bristol, because Mr. Bidwell had asked me to. Mr. Bidwell was going to Lowell to gather some information about the character of the girl that was hung. Mr. Avery said something to me about her being a bad girl, and that if it was known in Fall River, it would destroy the case against him. He thought if he could get the facts of her being a common prostitute, it would satisfy the people at Fall River that he was not guilty."

As Ephraim listened to this testimony, he fixed his eyes on the window back of the judge's bench, and tried to keep from showing any emotion. What Blodgett was saying was true enough, but the idea of contriving to make Sarah into a common prostitute stirred Ephraim's conscience. And as he stared at the window, he thought he saw her reproachful face. He had fancied seeing it several times, hovering above his cot at the jail, but this was its first appearance in the courtroom. He had to close his eyes, hoping no one would notice this behind his glasses. When he opened his eyes, the face was gone.

Attorney General Greene now called several persons who lived on the Island of Rhode Island and had *not* seen anyone resembling Ephraim Avery rambling about on the afternoon of December 20. One of these was Mrs. Sarah Jones, who lived near the coal mines. She told the court she had seen a stranger in the morning, but not in the afternoon. Before the Bristol hearing, Mr. Bullock, Avery's lawyer, had sent for her, and both he and Avery had asked her repeatedly if she could not remember a stranger in the afternoon. "Mr. Avery said his life was worth thousands of worlds to him," she testified, "and that it depended on my evidence. I told Mr. Avery that the man I saw was at half-past eleven in the forenoon. I do not doubt anything about it."

David Randolph, acting as one of Mr. Mason's assistants, inquired who had brought her to Newport. She said that it was Mr. Drake, a Methodist elder. He had asked her if it was not as easy for her to think she saw the stranger in the afternoon. "I told him because it was not so. He asked me what reason I had and I told him it was because I knew the forenoon from the afternoon."

Mr. and Mrs. Bailey Borden, a young couple from Fall River, testified that on Saturday evening, the 20th of October, they had been returning from Tiverton when they met two persons.

"The gentleman had on a cloak," Mr. Borden said, "and was rather higher than a common man. As near as I can recollect, he had on a black hat, with a pretty broad brim. I should think it was half-past nine. They turned into the main road leading to the bridge, a few rods from the old meetinghouse."

Mrs. Borden added, "The girl looked up and looked me full in the face. I said to my husband, it was Sarah Cornell and I think so now. I knew the girl's features. I worked in one of the mills, but not with Sarah. They were in close conversation. She passed me so near, her cloak brushed me."

Lucy Spink was a middle-aged Methodist of Fall River, who had been at the meeting on October 20, where Mr. Avery had preached.

"This is he, I think," she said, indicating the prisoner. "I came out of the meeting when he did. I saw a short young woman about five yards from the door. Her head was down toward the ground. I saw Mr. Avery go up to this young woman and I thought he spoke to her. He stooped over and looked her full in the face. I thought he broke up the meeting very early, and he was first out of the house. When he went out, there was no one outdoors but the woman."

Grindall and Nancy Rawson arrived from Woodstock next day, and with them came John Paine, the young man who had given Sarah a ride to the Thompson camp-meeting. Mr. Randolph, in cross-examining Paine, seemed to imply that there might have been something between the young man and Sarah.

"I was not particularly acquainted with her," Paine said. "No, there was nothing improper in her asking me to carry her to the camp-meeting, not in the manner in which it was done."

Mr. Paine was such an upright sort of young man that he did not seem to see why Randolph was questioning him.

Mr. Greene intervened: "I will put a question to you which you are not bound to answer. Do you have any reason to know who was the father of her child?"

"No, I do not," said Paine.

"Do you know of any illicit intercourse between Sarah M. Cornell and yourself or any other man?"

Paine finally understood. "I do not!" he exclaimed indignantly.

"We did not say there was such intercourse," said Mr. Randolph.

"I know it, but you seem to infer it," Greene said, "and I choose to settle that question now."

Mrs. Nancy Rawson was called next.

Greene: Do you do the washing?

Nancy: I do.

Greene: Do you know any fact, respecting the deceased being unwell as females are?

Nancy: A week and one day before the camp-meeting, she was unwell in that manner. I had the means of knowing because I did the washing. She remained at our house till the second of October. She did not have the regular recurrence at the time it should have come round after the camp-meeting. Before she left Woodstock, she told me what she feared might be her situation.

Mason: When did she first say so?

Nancy: On the twenty-first of September.

Mason: Did she speak of suicide?

Nancy: I never knew her to speak of it, or of any attempt on her part to commit suicide. I had not seen her for five or six years before she came to our house last June.

Another witness from Woodstock was Ruth Lawton, a tailoress, who had stayed at the Rawsons and slept with Sarah Maria.

Greene: Was she in August as woman usually are?

Miss Lawton: She was, a week before Thompson camp-meeting, to my certain knowledge.

Now came Grindall Rawson, who said that after Sarah Maria had told his wife of her suspected situation, he had consulted the Congregational minister in Woodstock and also a lawyer. "I thought it my duty to do all I could for Sarah Maria, but I did not know what. The lawyer thought it was best for her to come to Rhode Island and stay until certain what her situation was, and then communicate it to Mr. Avery.

Randolph: Why not wait in Woodstock until her situation was clear?

Rawson: If I had any thoughts upon the subject, it was that I should be unwilling to have her stay in my shop. I had two apprentice boys, and she would not like to be before them in that situation.

Randolph: Was there anything apparent?

Rawson: No, sir. But if such was her situation, it would come out and be known. My advice was founded on what the lawyer had told me respecting the law—that the father was bound to pay support for the child.

Randolph: What did she say concerning Mr. Avery at the camp-meeting?

Rawson: Do you wish to know the whole she said?

Randolph: Yes, the whole.

Rawson: She stated that one day while on the ground she saw Mr. Avery and he spoke to her. Mr. Avery had come there from Bristol. He said, "I should like to see you and talk with you, Sarah." He then said, "I will meet you to-night when the horn blows for preaching." He named a house, where several ministers were staying, but when they met he said there was no place to talk there, and told her to go on ahead, and he would overtake her. He did so, and they went arm in arm into the woods. He asked her to take her glasses off. They sat down. She asked if he had burned her letters. He said he had not, but would on one condition, and settle the difficulty. At that time he took hold of her hands, and put one of his into her bosom, or something like it. She said she tried to get away from him, but could not. She said he then had intercourse with her, and they returned to the camp. He promised to destroy the letters.

Randolph: Had the deceased seen or heard from Avery since she left Lowell?

Rawson: I never heard her say so.

Randolph: What was her character for chastity?

The attorney general asked, "What is the object of that question?" Randolph waived it. Instead, he asked whether the deceased had ever threatened suicide. Rawson said no.

Continuing under direct-examination, he said, "She had no friends or relations at Bristol. She spoke of none there but Mr. Avery. She always spoke of him kindly until after camp-meeting, and not even then as if she wished him any injury. The letters she asked Mr. Avery to burn, she said, were letters she had written to him just after she left Lowell."

After dismissing the Rawsons, Mr. Greene devoted the rest of his efforts to the three letters—pink, straw-colored, and white. As before, at Bristol, the steamboat engineer, Mr. Orswell, testified that he had carried the pink letter for Avery, whom he identified without hesitation.

"I thought at the time the man who gave me the letter might be a minister," he said. "He spoke polite and like a professional man."

Mr. Mason pressed his cross-examination hard. It was important to shake this witness's story, but Orswell was a hard man to shake. He was positive of the date—Tuesday, November 29, because that was when the *King Philip* had been in Providence. As for the time, they always began to fire up between eight and nine and he recalled that they were just firing up.

"You are under oath, sir," Mr. Mason said solemnly. "Do you still swear that this is the man?"

Orswell replied, "I am as positive that Mr. Avery is the man as I am that you are the man whose name is Mason."

The identification of the straw-colored letter was unclear, and Mason succeeded in having it kept away from the jury; but because of Harnden's detective work with a microscope, the white letter was admitted to evidence. Handwriting experts identified the writing on all three letters as that of Ephraim Avery.

Sarah's former landlord, Elijah Cole, testified that at the end of November, Mr. Orswell had delivered a letter, written on pink paper, for his boarder, Sarah M. Cornell.

"I recollect the direction: at Mr. Cole's. She had boarded with us eight weeks."

"Did she have any men visitors?" Greene inquired.

"No," said Cole. "No men ever visited her at my house."

"Did you mistrust her situation?" Greene said, using the circumlocution that meant, "Did you think she was pregnant?" Mr. Cole said he did not.

"Sometimes she was more cheerful than occasion seemed to require. More than was common in my family. At other times, she was lost in thought."

Cross-examining, Mr. Randolph asked about this "cheerfulness." What was it like?

"She seemed at times to use more laughter than occasion required," Cole replied.

Mr. Randolph asked hopefully, "Like a deranged person?"

But Cole disappointed him. "Oh, no, I wouldn't say that. Just more than common in my family."

As Ephraim listened to the sour-faced old Puritan's testimony, he remembered how sweet Sarah's laughter had seemed to him, and how refreshing her cheerful ways. Across his mind flashed memories of the two of them laughing together: and of the cold, sun-dappled brook; and the soft goose feathers in Mrs. Porter's barn.

The thought came to him: *Suppose I should now stand up and say, "Stop this farce! I am guilty!"* For an instant, he had a terrifying impulse to do this. But in the next instant he remembered Sophia and the children, the Methodists who trusted him, and his own horror of being executed. Tears came to his eyes, and, since he sat in full view of the judge, the jury, and all the lawyers, he dared not wipe them away. Instead, he took out his handkerchief and feigned a coughing fit.

X

The Case for the Defense

Next morning in the courtroom, an over-excited spectator called out, "Now we'll see Mason earn his fee!" The government had rested its case and it was time for Jeremiah Mason and his five assistants to take the center of the stage. *Stage*, Ephraim thought, was a good word for this courtroom, for the whole trial was being followed by the press and the public very much as if it were a play. As a matter of fact, word had reached Ephraim that there really was a play, based on the case, currently running in New York. It was called *The Poor Factory Maid*. He had also learned that a waxwork museum in Boston had added two new figures to its collection: Sarah Cornell being strangled by a black-coated Ephraim K. Avery. And a ten-verse poem, printed in the *Fall River Monitor*, read, in part:

> Poor victim of man's lawless passion
> Though e'er so tenderly caress'd
> Better to trust the raging ocean
> Than lean upon his stormy breast.
>
> On thy poor wearied breast the turf
> Lies quite as soft as on the rich.
> What now to thee the scorn and mirth
> Of sanctimonious hypocrites. . . .

203

Ephraim read the poem, but was mystified by it. How was it possible that people could be so against him, when his Methodist friends—and he spoke to almost no one else—seemed to think so highly of him? How the jury felt was beyond his ability to guess. Their Anglo-Saxon, Yankee, Puritan training had given them all an amazing skill in concealing their emotions. Ephraim could only put all his hope in Mason's powers of persuasion.

The judge banged the gavel for order, and Jeremiah Mason, elegantly dressed in a gilt-buttoned coat and a lace-trimmed shirt, arose and walked majestically toward the jury-box. Not for nothing had he been an attorney general of New Hampshire, a United States senator, and a best friend of Daniel Webster. He knew how to speak.

"The deceased was unrivaled in complicated wickedness," he began, in a slow, rather sad tone, as though no one could regret more than he the dreadful details he was about to unfold. "The history of abandoned females will hardly produce an instance of one so young being so adroit in all kinds of wickedness and obscenity—in lying, stealing, deceiving, both with her tongue and pen; in fornication and hypocrisy. Her deeds of lasciviousness, according to her *own account*, were sometimes committed on the Sabbath, and at noonday."

Mr. Mason here paused to allow this idea to make its impression on the jurors. Then he went on. "She was afflicted with a filthy disease, the abhorrence of all flesh; and her conversation was so obscene that the pen has never written it, nor the tongue pronounced it audibly.

"I will now state what we expect to prove of this unfortunate girl. That she was once a member of E. K. Avery's church in Lowell. There tried for fornication and expelled from the Church. That she was afflicted with an odious disease, to a great degree. And we will trace her for fourteen years in her lewdness and in this strangeness of conduct, and her tendency to commit suicide.

"There is a thought, which has been suggested somewhere, that if she were so abandoned she would care nothing about the

exposure of her guilt, and therefore would not have committed
suicide to escape it; but such was her strangeness, there is no
accounting for her conduct, by any rules of action ordinarily applied to human beings. Writers on medical jurisprudence tell us
that when a person is found dead and it is doubtful whether he
came to his death by his own hand or that of another person, we
should inquire into the moral character of the deceased, and into
his circumstances. If the character be vicious and the circumstances afflictive, there are arguments in favor of suicide. In this
case, there was scarcely a vice which the deceased was not in the
habit of committing."

Ephraim shuddered inwardly at this extravagant talk, and the
thought crossed his mind that if Mason were a member of his
Meeting, Ephraim would be obliged to expel him for telling lies.
Wasn't he going too far? Later, Ephraim heard someone in the
crowd remark that if the girl had really been so bad, how come
she hadn't been committed long ago to the House of Cor-
rection?

But Mason was as calm and authoritative as though he were
reading from the Bible. He went on to say that he intended to call
well over a hundred witnesses. Some would be Methodists, who,
being God-fearing people, could be confidently relied upon to tell
the truth. He made a point of disparaging the Fall River witnesses who had appeared for the government.

"Their minds are narrowed by the employment they are in.
They are the most excitable people in the world." And he added,
striking the jury-box railing for emphasis, "If you, gentlemen of
the jury, should convict Avery and he should be hanged, future
generations will regard the act with as much abhorrence as we
now do the hanging of the witches at Salem. The infatuation with
which Avery is pursued by the people of Fall River is the same
kind of infatuation."

His opening statement concluded, Mr. Mason began to call his
witnesses. Many of them were persons who had known Sarah
Maria Cornell and had nothing good to say about her. A young
man from Lowell, who had testified against Sarah at the Church

trial, said he "had heard" she was guilty of fornication and lying. When Attorney General Greene asked him why he had gone out of his way to complain of Sarah, he said, "Mr. Avery encouraged it. He wrote the charges down and preferred them in my name."

Mary Anne Barnes, a mill-girl who had testified at Bristol, repeated her story of Sarah's going to a tavern. "She drank so much wine she didn't know what she was about."

"Well, what *was* she about?" asked Mr. Mason.

Miss Barnes pursed her lips. "She did not tell me in so many words, but her face showed that there had been improper conduct. She wept, and said she thought the Lord forgave her, but that Mr. Avery had a hard heart and would not."

Lydia Pervere had been at the camp-meeting on Cape Cod. No, she had seen nothing improper about her there, but later, in Lowell, she had heard Sarah tell the story about the tavern. The tavern story was repeated by several more girls, and, as Mr. Greene pointed out, it was impossible to judge whether Sarah had been describing one tavern visit or many.

Sally Worthing, of Dedham, about thirty years old, remembered Sarah saying "that her sister had often told her she would come to the gallows; there were so many men after her." Sarah had also told her that Mr. Rawson had said she was more attractive than her sister, and had prettier eyes. Sarah, according to Miss Worthing, had kept cherry rum and brandy. She had confided that she had once been accused of stealing, and had gone out to hang herself. She had put the rope around her neck and was about to swing, but was deterred by thoughts of eternity.

"I considered her a very vile girl," concluded Miss Worthing virtuously. Nonetheless, the attorney general extracted from her the statement that in Dedham Sarah had been in good standing with the Church.

Mrs. Lucy B. Howe, a middle-aged Lowell woman, stated that Sarah had once come to her house and stayed, talking, until late. Sarah had told her she had made a humble confession to Mr. Avery and that she did not think he had treated her as became a gospel minister. While Sarah was at Mrs. Howe's, Dr. Graves came to the door and asked for payment. Sarah had said, "Not one cent for the old devil." Mrs. Howe added, "With a look that frightened me, Sarah spoke of revenge on Avery and all Methodists."

Miriam Libby, a Dover girl, said she'd heard Sarah say she could forge a Church certificate, imitating Avery's hand. "She said she could imitate most anyone's handwriting." But, added Miss Libby, "I never seen anything very bad in her conduct."

Caroline D. Tibbitts, of Lowell, testified that Sarah had once come into her bedroom and said she used to be respected, but her life was of no value now. "She threw her arms around my neck and wept so loud she could be heard down two pair of stairs. At other times, she would come into the mill and talk of her troubles and cry and then turn it off with a joke and laugh." She had told Caroline that Avery had expelled her, and that Dr. Graves had spoken to Avery. She also spoke of a young man whose courtship she had expected to lead to marriage.

"Did she speak of improper conduct with him?" Mason asked.

"She did," replied Miss Tibbitts.

Under cross-examination, Caroline Tibbitts added, "I was the most intimate friend she had. She said that Dr. Graves, in the office late, attempted improper liberties, which was why she wouldn't pay him. Also, he'd told Avery she had that disease, but another doctor said she hadn't."

Mary E. Warren knew Sarah in New Hampshire. She had once heard Sarah mention revenge on Avery, and also threaten to jump into the canal.

Mr. Greene, cross-examining, inquired, "Why did you not put Avery on his guard?"

"I guess I thought she would not do it," responded Miss Warren.

"Did she say it lightly?"

"Yes. I never told anyone until after the death. Then I told Reverend Dow, when he asked me what I knew."

Ann Cottel had boarded with Sarah at Dover. "She wept and said she'd drown herself because she was not admitted to a Love Feast at the Methodist meetinghouse. She said Mr. Avery had not treated her with common politeness and was hard-hearted and unfeeling."

Elizabeth Shumway, of Grafton, remembered Sarah as Maria Snow, at Slatersville. "She made confession in open church. She said Grindall Rawson had courted her, but her sister got him by art and stratagem." Miss Shumway claimed to have seen a poem that Rawson had written in Sarah's Bible. At Mr. Mason's request, she recited all seven verses of this poem. Mr. Greene remarked that her memory was amazing, since she had seen the poem but once, more than five years before. Greene also pointed out the wholly innocent nature of the poem, of which a sample verse was:

> Be careful, dear, in choice of friends,
> Take not the first that fortune sends;
> Until with scrutiny and care
> You find the character he wear.

Under cross-examination, Miss Shumway said that she had been brought to Newport by the Methodists.

"Did they tell you what to say?" Mr. Greene asked.

Mason objected, and the court upheld his objection.

Mary Hunt, of Jewett City, remembered Sarah's disappointment when her sister married Rawson, and that she had come to work dressed in white. "I told her one day she seemed crazy," Miss Hunt said. "She said she had been told so by others."

A remarkably bizarre tale was told by Ezra and Ruhamah Parker, who kept an inn at Thompson, Connecticut. They said that in 1826 a girl named Maria Cornell had come in at three in the afternoon, the last part of March, waiting for the Providence stage.

"She looked eight or nine months gone," Ezra testified. "I said to my wife I was afeard that woman would be sick afore morning. A young man named William Taylor came into the inn, and said,

'The devil, Maria, be you here?' Maria wrote out a paper and got money from him. She had threatened to swear a child on him." Later, Mrs. Parker had seen her undress and she had a blanket wrapped around her body. Next day, she was as slender as anyone.

"Where is this William Taylor?" demanded the attorney general.

"Oh, he's dead," replied Ezra Parker.

"And what proof do you offer that this woman and the deceased were one and the same?"

"Seems like," said Parker.

Thaddeus and Zilpha Bruce were the last witnesses of the day. They had known Sarah Maria Cornell at Jewett City and Maria Snow at Slatersville and knew they were the same girl.

Said Thaddeus Bruce, a man of about fifty, "I saw her come out of a storehouse in the evening twice between eight and nine, followed by a young man. I felt it a duty incumbent on me to talk to her, but she said there was nothing wrong. Later, in 1824, I saw her as Maria Snow. She told me she was starting over. She didn't want her former friends to know where she was, and she had taken the name Maria Snow because she had once known a very pretty girl by that name and she thought it had a pure sound to it. I saw her keeping company with a young man who didn't have a good reputation. Nothing criminal about it, as far as I knew, but I felt it a duty incumbent on me to admonish her."

Zilpha Bruce said that one day in Jewett City, Sarah Maria had come to her house and cried. "She had on a cloak and appeared to me to be larger than she ought to. She refused to take off her cloak. Soon after that, she went away from Jewett City."

Mrs. Bruce stepped down, and the jury was excused until Monday morning. It was the end of the parade of mill-people, and Ephraim felt relief. He knew that while some of the stories contained some truth, or half-truth, most were based entirely on gossip or were outright fabrications. The peculiar tale of the innkeepers from Thompson he was sure had nothing to do with

Sarah, for he remembered her telling him at the camp-meeting that she had never been to Thompson before; and surely it would have been pointless to lie about that.

Even though Ephraim knew his life depended on Mason's strategy, the systematic savaging of Sarah's character gave him a vague sense of nausea. The girl was dead. Was it really necessary to assassinate her mind, heart, and spirit and expose them to public scrutiny? Was it not enough to take apart her dead body? He sent word to Mr. Mason, asking if he could not desist from these attacks, now that he had made his point. But there was no reply. Mr. Mason did not seem much interested in his client's wishes, but only in winning the case.

The next move on the part of the defense was to explain and gloss over Ephraim's strange disappearance after the January hearing. Mason called the Bristol lawyer, Richard Bullock, who described the threatening crowds that had beseiged the Avery house on Wardwell Street.

"I was alarmed for his safety," said Bullock. "And I told him, 'It is foolhardiness to sleep at home.' I advised him to keep near-by, but where he would not be known. I felt that the man's life was in danger from the populace. On Christmas Day, a Bristol man came to my office, dripping with sweat and greatly concerned for Mr. Avery, to tell me that a boatload of Fall River people had arrived in Bristol."

A corroborating witness was Reverend John Bristed, an Episcopal clergyman of Bristol, who said he also had advised Avery to get out of town—not in order to escape from justice, but only for his own safety pending legal action.

Mary Davis, who lived on Wardwell Street, said she'd heard men in the crowd say they'd shoot him through the window.

"Did you see any guns, sticks, or other weapons?" Mr. Greene inquired.

"Well, no," said Mary Davis.

Character witnesses for Ephraim Avery were next on the stand. What an admirable person he was! A kind father, a faithful husband, a great Christian, possessed to an impressive degree of humanity, continency, peace, and good will. These recitals occupied most of an afternoon.

And was it at all strange that this exemplary person should wish to take a very long walk on a winter's day? A woman, Mrs. Le Barron, who had known Avery in 1825, when he lived in East Greenwhich, testified, "I have seen him pass my house walking north, where the scenery is very fine. He would be absent for hours. Sometimes he would walk on the seashore."

"From what you have seen has he a decided habit of rambling?" Mr. Randolph asked.

"I should surely think he had. Yes, sir."

An old gentleman of Bristol, who had known Ephraim's father during the Revolutionary War, said he had had a conversation with Ephraim about the coal on the Island, and Ephraim had said he'd heard it could be bought for three dollars a ton. "If that's so, I told him, go and get it."

As for the weather on December 20, Mr. Mason brought in several witnesses who had considered it pleasant. A Mr. de Wolfe, of Bristol, recalled that ships in the harbor had been readying for sea and unfurling their sails; and that the ground had been soft in the sun.

And who had seen Avery as he rambled about on the Island that afternoon? Here Mason's case was thin. Avery had said he'd met a man with a gun and a boy driving sheep, but these persons were not to be found. A stranger had been seen near the coalmines and on the Portsmouth road, but no one was ready to swear it was in the afternoon. Mason dwelt but lightly on this subject, and passed quickly on to two prestigious witnesses, Mr. Haile and Mr. Howe, who had presided over the Bristol examination. Both testified that the witnesses at that examination who claimed to have seen a tall stranger heading for Fall River on December 20 had all seemed rather vague.

Miss Betsey Hills, Sophia Avery's niece, now came to the witness stand, walking painfully on two crutches. She told the court that she was in the habit of staying with the Averys for extended

periods of time, and had been in Lowell on one occasion when
Sarah Cornell had called on Brother Avery. "She had her bonnet
on, and wept. I suppose she was pretending repentance."

"How could you tell it was pretended?"

"She shed tears."

"Are tears a sign of real or pretended repentance?" Mr.
Greene asked.

Miss Hills looked confused.

"Can you answer the question?"

"I did not see her shed tears, but she held a handkerchief to her
face, under her bonnet."

"But why do you say she was not sincere?"

Silence.

"Will you answer?" put in the judge.

"Well," Miss Hills said, "after we left we heard of her bad
conduct, and we did not think she could have been penitent."

"What did you hear?"

"Lucy Howe told us she did not seem penitent. I knew nothing
myself against the girl, but I heard she had been bad, wished
forgiveness, and asked to be recieved in church. Mr. Avery refused her and said he had had a great deal of trouble with
her."

Mr. Samuel N. Richmond, dry-goods store owner in Providence, testified concerning the shoplifting incident in 1819. Mr.
Greene objected that this evidence had no bearing on the case, but
the judge overruled him.

The rest of the week—this was the third week of the trial—
was devoted to alibi witnesses. Thirteen Methodists who had
been at the Thompson camp-meeting swore that Brother Avery
could not have had five minutes' free time there. Henry Mayo
and his wife, and Mrs. Patty Bacon, testified that they had
thought Sarah looked pregnant when they saw her at the camp-
meeting. Her clothes were tight and her bosom was full.

Nine Methodist ministers swore that in late-November, in
Providence, Avery had scarcely been out of their sight; certainly

not for the ten minutes it would have taken to deliver a letter to the *King Philip*.

The last three days of Mason's case were a murky mass of testimony from four doctors. All had impressive reputations, and although none had been present at the postmortem examinations of Sarah's body, they gave their opinions at length. In addition to the two examinations in December, there had been a third, thirty-six days after the second burial, when, because of public demand, the body had been exhumed again and reexamined by Doctors Wilbur and Hooper. They had found nothing new.

Mason hoped that his medical experts would swear that the bruises on the body were only the evidences of putrefaction; that the fetus was much too large to have been conceived at the end of August; and that the deceased had attempted self-abortion and had then hanged herself. But instead, the four doctors gave conflicting opinions and quoted conflicting authorities. It became clear that none of them was sure of the facts, and the chief effect produced was confusion and repugnance on the part of all present.

Ephraim resorted to small doses of an opiate, which helped him maintain that aloof dignity that Mason had recommended to him. As for the jury, most of them seemed restive. The case had gone on much longer than any of them had anticipated, and they were growing anxious about their own affairs, especially about planting summer crops. May was a bad time of year to be away from farms and gardens.

As for the prisoner, he had no garden to plant, but he felt as if his whole life were a ruined garden, a desert in which nothing would ever bloom again. When the defense at last rested its case, he was escorted back to his cell, where he vomited.

XI

Avery's Knot

It was time now for the summations, to which Mr. Mason and Mr. Greene each planned to devote an entire day. Mason was to speak first. As Ephraim was being brought in by his guards on that morning, a well-wisher whispered to him, "Mason could get the Devil himself off."

Ephraim did not care for the implied comparison, but he, too, felt sure that Mason could do anything. What he was unsure of was, what did he hope Mason would do? For it had now occurred to him that an acquittal would be another kind of condemnation: a sentence to a life of lies, pretense, and remorse for perhaps fifty years—for the Averys were strong and often lived to great ages. Fifty more years of nightmares and terrifying waking fantasies, of sudden nausea, and of seeing Sarah's face in unexpected places. A hanging death would be horrible, but, like Sarah's, it would be over in minutes.

As Ephraim watched his lawyer arise from his chair, take a pinch of snuff, and advance confidently toward the jury-box, he realized that Jeremiah Mason was performing for the benefit of Jeremiah Mason, and for no one else. The emotions of his client were of no importance to him.

Mason began by flattering the jury: "Most cordially do I congratulate you, gentlemen of the jury. For more than three weeks have you been confined to those seats. No trial for a capital felo-

215

ny, since the first settlement of the country, has ever so long engaged the attention of a jury."

Mason told them he knew they were above being influenced by the popular prejudice against the defendant, or by irreligious people who were behind this hounding of a clergyman. "But surely such a state of feeling could not prevail extensively in Rhode Island, a state originally founded on love of religious freedom and tolerance."

The first matter to be decided, Mason told the jury, was simply this: Was this a case of suicide or murder? Suicide, he informed them, was much more frequent than murder. *Vastly* more frequent. There were probably twenty to thirty cases of suicide to every murder. "An opinion prevails that there is a strong tendency to suicide in the people of this country."

Now for the reasons against murder: "The girl died by strangulation, and not one in a hundred, I might say one in a thousand, cases of murder will be found to have been effected by this means." As to the appearance of the body when laid out, "we have only the notions of three agitated old women. Suicide was the official verdict, let me remind you, according to that document of the coroner's jury, which Coroner Hicks has so inexplicably mislaid."

What altered this verdict? "The good women happened to examine a bandbox and there found this mysterious note in pencilmark: "If I am missing, inquire of Reverend Mr. Avery. He will know where I am gone." It was this little scrap of paper that put all this suspicion in motion, which has been fastened upon the defendant. This it was that created the fire that has since raged in the village of Fall River. It was found on Saturday and on Monday we hear of a town meeting of five hundred citizens, resolutions adopted, committees raised, subscriptions got up, and the whole community in a flame."

Mr. Mason's tone was wonderfully sarcastic. Who could be more silly than the three old women, or more hysterical than the people of Fall River? And what scrap of paper in the world could be more worthless than this one?

He went on: "How do we know the paper was *in* the bandbox before it was opened? Could not someone, filled with Fall River zeal, have slipped it in there? I bring no charge, but can you, in the absence of all satisfactory evidence, undertake to say what these people might do—especially the factory-girls—excited by the supposed commission of an odious offense?"

As to the three post-mortem examinations by Doctors Wilbur and Hooper, Mr. Mason dismissed these with a sneer. The two were only ill-trained country doctors. The first two examinations had not been thorough, and the third, after the body had been buried for thirty-six days, was surely worthless.

And why were the knees stained green? The deceased, despite her profligacy, had a religious tendency, and must have knelt to say a prayer before proceeding to the stackyard to take her own life.

And how did she tighten the knot? "She might have put one hand through the neck of the cloak, holding or pulling the cord in that way, and with the other hand passed through the opening in the cloak, below, have tightened the cord. That would account for the hand falling upon the breast, as it was found; and if that does not account for it satisfactorily, then the muscular motions in death might place the limbs in various positions."

And why were her clothes found smoothed down under her legs? In throwing back the feet, as she settled down upon the cord, her clothes might naturally turn in under her knees. Or the west wind, blowing all night, would drive them back under her. The wind would also account for the dishevelment of her hair. "No doubt it was kept in curls, as is the fashion with young women, and the night wind had blown them out."

Ephraim's aloof dignity was disturbed for a minute and he shifted in his chair. He remembered how, just as he was leaving the stackyard, some compunction had made him turn back and smooth Sarah's clothes down decently and arrange her shoes neatly side by side. But he had left the wild hair over her face, which he could not bear to see.

"Gentlemen of the jury," continued Mr. Mason, "in order to

come to the conclusion of suicide, it is not necessary to infer that the deceased left the house with a determination then to commit suicide. The history of her life shows that she was subject to violent passions."

This sentence brought him again to the task of attacking Sarah's character, and he settled into it in a sad-faced, unctuous manner.

"It is painful, but a necessary duty to perform—to describe a *woman*, to describe a woman who is *dead*, in a light as revolting as duty to the defendant requires. It is female character, when pure and unstained, which refines society. But in the same proportion as woman, when chaste and pure, excels the other sex, by just so much, when profligate, does she sink below them. And if you were to seek for some of the vilest monsters in wickedness and depravity, you would find them in the female form.

"What then was the character of the deceased? A strange compound truly. A woman at one time all piety, and at another—I regret to say—*all profligacy*. I admit that the profligacy of her character has nothing to do with the crime. If murder were committed, it is not mitigated by the wickedness of the victim."

When, afterwards, people accused Mason of trying and condemning Sarah, he disclaimed it by pointing out these last two sentences. He now went on to demolish her character:

"The first account of her finds her, aged about twenty, in Jewett City, Connecticut, in a state of pregnancy. You will recall the testimony of Mrs. Bruce, who told us she came to her house in tears, her shape much enlarged and hidden in a cloak. Next, Mr. and Mrs. Bruce found her at Slatersville using another name, Maria Snow. A change of name by a young woman to conceal herself is an occurrence extremely rare, in fact, almost unknown in New England. A young female who could do this must have been far gone in wickedness.

"Miss Shumway knew her at Slatersville, and was told the sad tale of disappointment in marriage and of wishing to be under the water. At Providence, we find her committing larcenies. At Thompson, she attempts to impose an illegitimate child upon

William Taylor, as related by Parker and his wife. These witnesses, undoubtedly, did not appear to very great advantage on the stand, but I appeal to you, from the honest simplicity of that old pair, that they did not come here to tell a falsehood. Clearly, a young woman who could contrive such a trick must be in the lowest state of profligacy.

"For the last ten or fifteen years of the life of the deceased, we find her lewdness and prostitution, falsehood and subtle hypocrisy continued habitually down to her death—ranging through all the manufacturing-villages in New England, and expelled as soon as found out from every factory she entered—keeping up the appearance and profession of religion as a cloak for her wickedness—artfully attaching herself to the most respectable females about the factories, as in the instance of Miss Hathaway at Fall River. I doubt, if on examining all the factory-villages in New England, you could find a character so abounding in vice.

"Yet, in the midst of vileness, her early religious training seems never to have been entirely obliterated, although it was strongly mixed up with gross hypocrisy, habitual sensual indulgences, and strange abstractions of mind. A creature of passion to which she gave unbridled license—screaming in the factory, and throwing her arms around the necks of her companions—coming into the mill, dressed up in a white gala suit—laughing and crying all in the same moment.

"We have heard a number of witnesses testify to attempts or contemplated attempts of suicide on the part of the deceased. It is not surprising. Suicide is so common among prostitutes that it might almost be called their natural death."

It was now twelve o'clock noon, and Mr. Mason came to a halt, leaving the words *suicide* and *prostitute* echoing in the jury's ears. But he was by no means finished, and at two o'clock he reappeared, refreshed by a substantial dinner, a good cigar, and a sound nap.

His client, meanwhile, had dined on warmed-over baked beans, cornmeal mush, and a few spoonfuls of new peas sent in by one of the Methodist women of Newport. He would have

welcomed a strong brandy and water; but of course, Methodist
clergymen were expected to be strict teetotalers.

He had lain on his dank cot and stared at the bars. He dreaded
seeing her face appear, but when it did not, he found himself
almost hoping it would. *Sarah,* he said, moving his lips silently,
*Why did you struggle? Why were you always so willful? Think of
it, Sarah, you might be alive today. It was your will against mine,
and you should have known who would win.*

But had he won? He buried his face in the pillow.

The judge convened the afternoon session, and Mr. Mason
returned to strutting back and forth before the jury-box.

"A murder must have a motive and that motive must be
proved. The government alleges that the defendant had had illicit
intercourse with the deceased, that she was pregnant by him, and
to relieve himself from the infamy of detection and the expense
likely to follow, he committed the murder. To begin with, there is
nothing in the character of the defendant (which, as you have
heard from numbers of witnesses, is blameless) to suggest illicit
intercourse. What possible motive can you conceive there would
be, for a man happy in his family, an affectionate husband, to
seek intercourse with such a woman—dangerous, offensive,
gross?

"The government says this act took place on Thursday evening, the 30th of August, at Thompson camp-meeting. Yet you
have heard any number of witnesses state the defendant was never alone or out of someone's sight for more than a few minutes. In
any event, the whole story is utterly improbable. Can it be
believed that a Methodist minister, conspicuous and well-known,
would fix upon such a time and place for the gratification of a
beastly appetite?

"As to the girl, you have heard testimony that several experienced matrons thought her pregnant. Rawson's shop, where she
worked, was frequented by fashionable young men, and you find
one of them taking no ordinary liberty with a young woman to
whom he had not been introduced—carrying her to the camp

meeting. You have heard evidence that she had been affected by the periodical indisposition common to females just nine days before the camp-meeting, but you have heard one of our eminent medical witnesses, Dr. Channing, declare that such events are possible even during the period of gestation. On the other hand, it is more probable that this unfortunate woman, depraved by ten years of profligate habits, has told a falsehood and that her sister was deceived. We are told on good authority that the fetuses of bad women are usually smaller than those of good women; and yet this fetus was so large that if it was only three months and twenty days advanced, it must have been a monster. You have heard much learned advice on this point. The government, before they can establish their case, must get over this difficulty.

"The next consideration is, whether the defendant had an opportunity and time to commit the crime. The government has produced a string of witnesses who *think*, who *have the impression*, who *believe* they saw a man something like the defendant, walking toward Fall River on the afternoon of December twentieth."

Mr. Mason reviewed each bit of this testimony and found it wanting: There were many people going about in dark clothing and broad-brimmed hats; Peleg Cranstoun had been heard later to say that he might have mistaken the day; the man served by Miss Hambley in the tavern was not wearing a hat; and so on. That the defendant had crossed over in the ferry was granted, but why was it so hard to believe that he had then gone for a ramble on the Island?

"Men possess different tastes and different habits," said Mason. "Some people love perpetual company. Others prefer being alone, indulging in solitary walks, exploring the various scenes of nature. It is in abundant testimony that the prisoner was fond of solitary walks and rambles.

"As to the witnesses who saw him in his rambles on the Island, it is unfortunate that no one swears to have seen him, but you are not to take this to mean he was not there. It is not for us to prove where he was; it is for the government to prove he was at the scene of the murder, and this they have not done and cannot do."

At 5:20 P.M., Mr. Mason asked for a short recess. He went to an inner room and had a light rum and water, combed his thick, white hair, looked in the mirror. He was pleased to find beads of sweat rolling off his brow, for he wanted to look like a man so devoted to the truth that he was willing to overexert himself in its behalf, even risking apoplexy. A man of sixty-five ought not to spend all day in a hot, crowded courtroom; he ought to be at home, taking his ease, but instead he was working hard to save the life of another human being.

At quarter to six he began to speak again, disparaging Orswell, the steamboat engineer, and reviewing Avery's alibi in Providence.

"But," he said, "since it is clear that Avery neither wrote nor sent the Providence letter, who did? Had this woman a paramour? Was it a part of the plot that a man resembling the defendant was employed to deliver that letter to Orswell? I admit there is a mystery about this letter. But Mr. Avery is not bound to account for it.

"We all draw some conclusion from the nature of an animal, when connected with any supposed act. The shepherd does not suspect his ox or his horse of destroying his flock; it is the wolf. The horse and the ox have the *power* to do it, but they have not the disposition. So of a man accustomed to teaching the peaceful doctrines and practices of the Gospel; it is not his nature to employ violent means, suddenly, to commit crime. No man goes the whole gulf of wickedness at one leap; it takes time to destroy the purity of a spotless heart.

"The defendant is a clergyman. So far as I know, a clergyman has not been arraigned at the bar in this country for murder, until now; I doubt if within the two hundred years of our history, a clergyman has been accused of that crime. This, I admit, proves nothing; it only shows the improbability of the commission of such a crime by the defendant; and should call for stronger evidence to convict him than might be required in some other cases. Although some look upon the Methodists disparagingly, I see not why the Methodist clergy may not compare advantageously with any other. It is a new sect, of most exact discipline.

"Gentlemen of the jury, I know you have been wearied by the great length of this trial, and I know how difficult it is for you to call to mind the essential facts in the case. I have endeavored to state them to you as briefly as possible. Whatever may be the result of your labors, gentlemen, I do, in behalf of this unfortunate defendant, render you his hearty thanks for the patience, the diligence, and the candor with which you have heard his cause."

Attorney General Albert Greene was not the orator that Jeremiah Mason was, nor did he have the commanding presence or the towering prestige; nevertheless, the general consensus in Newport was that he had a better case to work with. On the wharves and in the taverns, there was a great deal of betting as to the final outcome, and in Calvinistic parlors and kitchens, where betting was a sin, people predicted, foretold, guessed, and had premonitions.

Ephraim was impressed by his lawyer's talent for distorting the truth, but to him the truth was so obvious that it would have to prevail, even in the fumbling hands of Greene. He said to Mr. Randolph, who came to visit him at the jail on the evening of Mason's summation, "If I am convicted, I hope I may be executed as soon as possible."

"Executed, Mr. Avery? Are you dissatisfied with our efforts?" Mr. Randolph said, somewhat irritated. "We have labored long and hard for you."

"You have done well," Ephraim said gloomily.

"Mr. Mason has returned to Boston," Randolph said. "You may be sure he would not have done so if he had not been confident of the outcome."

"Are you?"

"Mr. Avery, nothing on this earth is certain," said Mr. Randolph, picking up his hat. "You clergymen know that and you know how to pray about it."

But Randolph had put his finger on Ephraim's deepest distress: he did *not* know how to pray about it—he no longer knew how to pray at all. He had tried, but something within him dispaired of being heard. To himself he could say, quite eloquently, that Sarah was a bad girl, that she was willful, and that she need not have died if she had only done as he said, but when he addressed the Lord, no words came.

Court was convened at eight in the morning, on Saturday, June 1, and Mr. Greene took the floor. He began by expressing his regret that he must prosecute anyone of fair and unblemished character, especially a minister. But the defendant must be tried, not as a minister, but solely for his own individual acts.

"The learned gentleman (he meant Mr. Mason) has censured the citizens of Fall River in a manner wholly unwarranted. There is (thank God) no armed police in this country, and it is therefore the duty of every citizen to aid the government in bringing to light hidden offenses. The people of Fall River have behaved very properly. They understood the value of circumstantial evidence.

"The prisoner crossed the ferry and went *somewhere*. If a number of people saw a man resembling the prisoner walking toward Fall River, and no one saw a man walking toward Newport, the circumstantial evidence that puts him on the Fall River road is very strong. There is no mystery about this kind of evidence. Men judge of it and act upon it every day in their concerns of business."

The jury, weary from trying to follow the flamboyant Mr. Mason all the previous day, was looking inattentive. Mr. Greene perceived this and moved to a more gripping subject:

"Allow me, gentlemen, to take a brief review of the character of the deceased. You have heard extraordinary stories about her.

For example, one witness has told us that at Jewett City in 1822 he saw her come out of a storehouse and also saw a young man come out after her, and that was all he saw! I will only say of this testimony that it shows the amazing industry with which every act of the whole life of this unfortunate girl has been traced out and brought to light, in order to make an unfavorable impression on your minds. At the very time when some of the defendant's witnesses swear she was at Slatersville, we have the farcical blanket story of old Mr. Ezra Parker and his wife, which they say happened in Thompson; a story of such absurdity and improbability as to render it unworthy of serious notice.

"The learned gentleman, the defendant's counsel, has given us the impression that the three months of her residence at Fall River was the only green spot in her life. He is mistaken. There were many calm and benign periods in her life, including the period between the time she left Lowell and when the prisoner again met her at the Thompson camp-meeting. You cannot doubt that if any evidence existed of a single act of vice, or even indiscretion during these periods, the friends of the defendant would have detected and exposed it.

"This young woman seems invariably to have confessed more than could be proved against her. Probably her contrition may have magnified her offenses. It is not uncommon in religious exercises. In the late-summer of 1830, the deceased left the vicinity of Lowell, poor, deserted, and friendless, her standing in the Church lost, and her reputation ruined. At the Thompson camp-meeting, the defendant and the deceased again met. Does the defendant repulse her? Does he cause her to be removed from the ground? Bad girls were removed from the campground, but Miss Cornell was not among them. Here you have it in proof that Mr. Avery, though, as it is said, well knowing her abandoned character, volunteered nothing against the deceased."

Ephraim felt every eye in the courtroom turn toward him, to see how he was reacting. He fixed his gaze on the stony-faced jurors and tried to look as they did. He also tried not to remember

how he had searched the campground over for Sarah, that hot
August day, and how elated he had been when he met her, coming toward him in her claret-colored dress.

"Was the death caused by suicide or homicide?" Mr. Greene
went on. "The defense had tried to show a tendency in the
deceased toward suicide, but there is no *recent* evidence of this—
either in Woodstock or in Fall River. And how do you find her on
the day and evening of her death? Unusually cheerful; providing
yarn for garments she intended to knit; purchasing material for
an apron; fearful of offending the overseer, lest she lose her job.
Furthermore, we know from the evidence of the white letter that
she had an appointment for that evening. We know that she went
out to see someone, and you are therefore obliged to exclude all
idea that she left the mill for the purpose of committing suicide.

"And what motive had she for suicide? If she had been pure
and chaste; subdued, in a moment of weakness by one in whom
she placed implicit confidence, and the author of her shame a
married man—under such circumstances you might indeed find a
strong motive for suicide. But the deceased had fallen long before,
and if that could ever have impelled her to destroy herself, the
period had long gone by.

"Let me also call to your attention that she had consulted with
Dr. Wilbur about the oil of tansy given her by the defendant. Dr.
Wilbur told her that it would be fatal to drink it. And she then
replied she would not take it, for she would rather have her child
and do the best she could than to endanger her life. It shows that
she had fully contemplated the consequences of having the child,
and had prepared her mind to meet them.

"Concerning the note found in the bandbox—'If I should be
missing, inquire of the Reverend Avery'—may I say that the
learned gentleman's suggestion that this note was forged by one
of the factory-girls in her zeal to see the defendant convicted, is
utterly absurd. Gentlemen, you cannot believe it. The learned
gentleman himself cannot have been serious in his attempt to

excite such suspicion. And, besides, you have heard an uncontra-
dicted witness—Mr. Durfee—say he saw it taken out of the
box.

"The learned counsel has contended that the deceased left this
note and forged the letters as part of a complicated scheme of
revenge. The idea is too absurd. How could she know that he
would be on the Island, or from home, on that day? And how
could she know, or imagine, that he would not be able to prove by
numerous witnesses just exactly where he was?

"We will now examine the physical evidence, which proves
homicide. There is no escape from the fact that the cord must
have been first tightened round the neck and the weight of the
body suspended upon it afterwards. Otherwise, the circle would
not have been horizontal. This evidence alone is conclusive. And
how could she, with her gloves on and her hands beneath her
cloak, have tied the cord to the stake and then made the clove-
hitch? I say further that she could not have replaced her arms
under her cloak if she had taken them out to draw the cord and
had drawn it so closely; and yet you find one arm is by her side,
under the cloak, and the other is also under her cloak, across the
breast, and raised in this manner."

Dramatically, Mr. Greene raised his arm nearly to his neck
and turned the palm outward. This position gave a striking appearance of fear and self-protection, and there was a murmur
through the courtroom.

"The clove-hitch knot," continued Mr. Greene, "is a knot
which women are not ordinarily acquainted with. There is no
evidence that the weavers in our factories are taught to make this
knot. It certainly is not the easiest, surest, or most natural one for
any person to use in the act of suicide by suspension.

"But there is other evidence showing the acts of another person
in this deed: I refer to the condition of the body. The three Bord-
en women were experienced in laying out dead bodies. They saw
the marks on the abdomen. If they were the ordinary discolorations, after death, would they have occasioned any surprise?

These marks corresponded to impressions of the human hand, in a position where the deceased could not have made them herself.

"Let me remind you, also, of the tall man and short woman seen in the lane that evening, walking toward the stackyard. And of the screams later heard. All these things contribute to show the presence and the action of some other person in this death.

"The circumstance of the feces as found pressed upon the body is very important. It appears to me very material to recollect that it was December, so that everything about the person of the deceased must have frozen in the twelve hours she hung there. In a perpendicular position, the feces would not have adhered to the body. To produce this condition, the body must have been laid horizontally, and therefore it must have taken place in the death struggle. This one fact, taken with other circumstances, is conclusive."

At this point, the court adjourned for noonday dinner, and did not reconvene until half-past two.

It was a warm day, and Ephraim could eat very little of his baked beans and mush. Even early strawberries sent in by the kindly Methodist women failed to tempt him. He kept thinking that very soon—perhaps tomorrow—he would know what his fate would be. He got down on his knees beside his cot, and tried to pray, as he had so often in this cell.

Oh Lord, you know I did not mean to take her life. She should not have opposed her will to me, so that I had to . . . had to show her . . . The words died out. The Lord was not listening. He tried again. *Oh Lord, forgive me, I was weak, I was a sinner, but I had to . . .*

Ephraim beat the cot with his fists.

Oh Lord, damnation, you know I am guilty, but you know I ought to be acquitted.

Ephraim felt ashamed. Now the words were not only failing him, but he was swearing at the Lord. In sadness, he remembered how eloquently and elegantly he used to pray. And now it was as if he scarcely knew the English language.

The jailer was at the door, rattling the keys.

"Time for court, Reverend."

As he rose to his feet and brushed off his knees, Ephraim mentally concluded his prayer: *Help me, Lord.*

This almost inarticulate prayer was the first he had prayed in many months that he thought might possibly be getting through. He prayed it all the way to the courthouse and all afternoon long.

Help me. Help me, Lord.

Resuming his summation, Mr. Greene spent at least an hour reviewing the three letters in minute detail. Unfortunately, the subject of what the letters said and what they meant and where they had been mailed and by whom had been gone over so much already that there was more than a little dozing in the jury-box. Greene did manage, however, to make a new and well-taken point about the pink letter:

"It is obvious that if the deceased forged all the letters, she could not have delivered them without an agent. *Someone*, beyond all doubt, gave the pink letter to Orswell. How could that agent so arrange it as to be in Providence precisely when the defendant was there? How could he be at Fall River the eighth of December and know the defendant would be there; and, above all, how could he have appointed a meeting with the deceased on the twentieth of December, knowing that Mr. Avery would at that time be on the Island, rambling all alone, no one seeing him, at the same time when a man who looked exactly like him was seen walking toward Fall River? Is not this an absurd idea?"

The jury came fully awake, and Mr. Greene pressed on.

"If the girl was conspiring with another man, why would they select a Methodist minister as their victim? There is no class of the clergy so scantily paid as Methodist ministers. Would they have selected the defendant, in the expectation of making it a profitable scheme? And since the man stands well and without reproach, such a charge would surely be unlikely to be believed. There was not only no hope of gain, but no hope of forcing a marriage, for the defendant was a married man. Where are all the fashionable young men who have been hinted at in this trial, as having been known to the deceased? They were in easy circumstances, perhaps affluent, and in a situation either to marry her, or to pay for it, to escape a doubtful charge of paternity. Why not charge it to them, if gain was her object? And one more point—if the correspondence was forged, would you not find the name of E. K. Avery signed to the letters?"

Greene now had to tackle the medical evidence, which besides being moot, was painful and embarrassing to listen to. He hated doing it, but he must, if he were to refute Mason.

"Whoever wrote the letters—and the evidence is irrefutable that the writer was Avery—knew that he was in a position to be charged with the paternity of the child. The age of the fetus he could not know; the fact of the connection, he could not forget.

"There is no greater diversity of opinion, on any fact in anatomy than upon the question of deciding the age of a fetus by its length. The doctors themselves differ, as you have seen here, and the best authorities differ, and who shall decide when doctors disagree?

"It is said there was no opportunity for the prisoner to have met the deceased on August thirtieth, at the camp-meeting. I agree that if you can rely on the memory of the witnesses, Mr. Avery was watched at that camp-meeting as never man was watched before. I do not doubt the honesty of the witnesses, but the pertinacity with which they have sworn to almost every moment of time to show where this man was on Thursday, August thirtieth, is to me most wonderful. I will admit that the act probably was not the result of deliberation. If this was his first error with the deceased, it might have been the temptations of place, circumstance, and opportunity which overcame him. He knew her frailty. There is no situation where a man of strong passions would be more likely to err than under such circumstances, with a female who was known to have departed from virtue, and with opportunity and secrecy offered.

"There is one part of the testimony I will allude to here, though I should not have done it if the learned gentleman had not seemed to place some reliance on it. I mean the statement of the curious Mrs. Patty Bacon. If the deceased was in the situation that this witness pretends she was, at the camp-meeting, by no possibility could she have been so for more than two months, when Mrs. Bacon saw her. At that period, the physicians all tell you, the fetus is about the size of a bee or a wasp. Gentlemen! What the difference would be in the ordinary size or appearance of a young woman who had swallowed a wasp, I leave you to determine! But they also have the testimony of a reverend gentleman on this point, who was satisfied of the fact because the young woman's clothes were tight behind! It is too ridiculous to be brought into the case. I do say, gentlemen, that this is going quite too far in the attempt to brand the character of that young woman. I do say that the attempt to introduce such *trash* here, to make an impression upon your minds against the deceased, merits a severe rebuke. I have now done with all I have to say of these extremely indelicate matters."

He said that with relief. As it was quarter after five, the court took a recess, and the attorney general resumed his remarks at twenty-five minutes before six. He now had to place Avery at the scene of the murder.

"We have traced the defendant to Thursday, twentieth December. All have agreed that on that day, shortly before noon, Ephraim K. Avery left his home in Bristol, crossed the Bristol ferry, and landed on Rhode Island at about two in the afternoon. We have the testimony of the ferryman, Mr. Pearse, that he was wearing a dark surtout, which he wears now, and a broad-brimmed, black hat. Since he was the only passenger on that ferry, Mr. Pearse had the fullest opportunity to observe him.

"Now. Where did he go from the ferry-landing? He either went to the Stone Bridge, or he passed on the road toward New-port. I will first show the way he did *not* go. Several persons, who

live on the Newport road, did *not* see him. No mortal saw him
pass that way. But on the road to Fall River, a tall man *was*
seen—and you have heard half a dozen witnesses say so.

"On that same Thursday, he was invited to Mrs. Gladding's in
Bristol, but excused himself. Does this look like intending to go to
Fall River that day to keep his appointment? His account of the
matter is that from a love of rambling and a taste for natural
history, he visited the Island, on a day extremely uncomfortable,
to say the least of it, for such an excursion; that he passed from
the ferry in a southerly direction, toward the coal mines; met a
man gunning and stopped and conversed with him; saw a boy in
a lot, driving sheep; passed by some Methodist households, without stopping; came out to the road at the Union meetinghouse, six
miles from the ferry and then walked back to the ferry. A most
strange and lame account, gentlemen. Where is the gunner?
Where is the boy driving sheep? They must have belonged there;
they cannot have disappeared! But they have never been found or
heard of. He is in the region of his friends, members of his
Church, but he passes by their doors and makes no calls. He says
he had the express purpose of getting information at the coal
mines, but no one sees him there. He says he was lame but he
never rested. His family at home was sick, and at ten o'clock we
find him exceedingly anxious to get to them; but at sunset he was
walking away from the ferry, and without possible motive, as far
as the Union meetinghouse. Only then did he begin to retrace his
steps to the ferry. The distance is six miles, and you have to
believe that he took from half-past four to half-past nine, five
hours, traveling a distance of six miles without stopping and in
great anxiety to return to his family! If they say he was so lame
he could not walk faster, I then ask why did he not stop at Brother Cook's, whose house he passed within a few rods and where he
knew he would be received as in his own house. If he was so lame
as not to be able to walk but little more than a mile an hour, is it
not unaccountable that he should hobble on and not stop anywhere? There was another man who stood in a near-relation,
Elder Drake, but his house was also neglected. No refreshment is

taken, he calls nowhere for a cup of water, and this man is thus rambling about in the midst of his friends and no one sees him. That, instead, he went to Fall River and met the deceased is to my mind clearly proved. That he contemplated murder I do not believe."

When Ephraim heard this last sentence, a great surge of relief swept over him. Here, at last, was someone who understood. Not that it would do him any good, but there was some strange sort of comfort in knowing that the man who was prosecuting him had grasped the situation and was willing to say so—unlike the man who was defending him. Ephraim continued his silent prayer, *Help me, Lord*, daring to hope that he was being heard.

"He did not intend to murder the girl," Mr. Greene continued, "but he was impelled to insure his own security by finishing the deed he had nearly accomplished anyway in attempting a lesser crime. Strange as it may seem, his regard for his family and the honor of his Church may, in a moment of desperation, have pressed him onward to the commission of that deed.

"The learned gentleman says that the suggestion of an attempted abortion is not proved. But is it not proved to be probable? The defendant was bred a physician; he was in a retired place with a female who charged him with being the father of the child to which she was to give birth, and he had every motive impelling him to relieve her from that situation and exonerate himself. The prints of fingers on the abdomen, in a position where the deceased could not have applied her own hands, raise a strong presumption of violence.

"The most charitable construction to put upon the deed is that the deceased fainted, and the prisoner was then placed in a situation where every motive that can impel the human mind to commit a crime was pressing upon him. The work could be quickly done—the pang would scarcely be felt by his victim. She might not recover from what he had already done to her and then discovery was inevitable. And it would relieve her and save his reputation for usefulness to Church and family.

"It is nine miles from the stackyard to the ferry, and it has been

said on the other side that the prisoner could not have traveled
this distance in the time at hand. But we have seen that no two
clocks agreed. There was a difference of three-quarters of an
hour among them. Furthermore, we cannot suppose the defendant traveled this route at an ordinary pace. If he had on his
conscience the murder of a fellow being, there never was a man
traveled that distance who had such motives for speed as he then
had, and the shortest time in which that distance could possibly
be traveled on foot, it was traveled by him. His object was to get
to Bristol that night, that he might avoid creating suspicion by his
unusual absence from home."

Ephraim could hardly restrain himself from giving Mr.
Greene a grateful smile. Greene was as right about that walk
from the stackyard to the ferry as if he had been there himself.
Walk!—it was almost a dead run, all the way. Ephraim had not
noticed the cold wind or his own fatigue. Propelled by the horror
of what he had done and the urgent necessity of getting home, he
had covered the nine miles in headlong haste, a black shape in the
blacker night, moving over the road like a cloud shadow.

Mr. Greene, of course, was wrong about the murder itself.
Sarah had not fainted; it was her screams and her resistance that
had forced him to kill her. *Forced?* he thought. Had he been
forced? Was it not, rather, an impulse? He looked the truth in the
face: she had screamed and he had killed her because in destroying her will and asserting his own, he thought he could put an
end to the chaos in his life.

Mr. Greene was finishing his summation.

"Your situation, gentlemen of the jury, is an awful one. You
are now to pass upon the life or death of that man. It was my duty
to strip the case of the ingenious doubts which have been thrown
about here by the able and learned counsel on the other side, and
to present to your minds the plain question of the guilt or innocence of the prisoner. What took place at the scene of death was
witnessed only by Him who has a knowledge of all things; but
you must decide upon the evidence before you. I have done my
duty and it now remains for you to do yours."

Twilight was falling. Everyone in the courtroom was tired and uncomfortable. Now that Mr. Greene had finally stopped speaking, there was a curious and solemn hush. The judge was silent for an instant or two before making a brief charge to the jury, in which he warned them against the tricky nature of circumstantial evidence, and reminded them that character must always be an important consideration.

Mr. Randolph turned to Ephraim and whispered, "You see? We've convinced him, and he's as good as told the jury: 'Don't hang a minister.' "

Ephraim disagreed. He had thought Greene's arguments wholly persuasive, especially since he knew them to be accurate. And he saw no change in the number of hostile and unfriendly faces as his guards led him away.

His own opinion now was that either verdict would be a condemnation. Even though a new law, passed by the Rhode Island legislature only that spring, forbade public executions, still the hangman's noose and the scaffold would be agonizing, ghastly, and ignominious. On the other hand, what would living be worth? Stretching ahead, perhaps far into the future, would be years of hypocrisy, years of dreading eternity, years of being haunted. And his will, his powerful, masculine will, in behalf of which he had committed murder, would be of no further use to him, because he would be driven by circumstances. Yes, either verdict would be a condemnation and—for the first time he was ready to admit it—either verdict would be deserved.

In his cell, Ephraim prayed for the first time since the night of December twentieth, *Thy will be done.*

The jury returned to the courtroom next day, Sunday, at about twelve noon, just as the church bells were ringing. A great crowd jammed in to the courtroom from the bright, sunny June day outside, and waited fifteen minutes for the prisoner to be brought. A number of people noticed that there was something different about him. He was still dignified, still rather aloof, but he did not have such an iron look.

The verdict was Not Guilty.

Afterword

The court discharged Ephraim Avery at once. With a large escort of Methodist clergymen, he returned to Bristol by ferry, and walked to the house on Wardwell Street.

When his wife saw him coming, she fainted.

In June, 1833, the Methodist New England Conference, in Boston, tried Avery and found him innocent.

Also in June, he preached at a Methodist meeting in Boston and was harassed by a menacing crowd. According to the *Boston Transcript*, "opprobrious epithets" were shouted, and he was removed from the area in a carriage, while the sheriff dispersed a mob of four or five hundred.

Newport Mercury, September 7, 1833:

Considerable excitement and disapprobation was created, as we learn, among the passengers on board of one of the Hartford steamboats last week by the report that Ephraim K. Avery was among their number. Order and quiet was finally restored, on the assurance of the captain that this highly unpopular individual should be landed at the first stopping place, and he was accordingly left on shore at Middletown, where it was not without difficulty that he made his way to the parsonage house in that place.

Newport Mercury, September 21, 1833:

Ephraim K. Avery preached last Saturday at Winchester, Connecticut. His appearance in that place produced great excitement and it was said that any further attempts of the kind would be visited with emphatic displays of popular indignation. The *Hartford Times* promises to attack him if he remains in the state any longer.

In November, 1833, Avery was reported to be back in Bristol with his family. He had been suspended by the Methodist Conference. In 1835, he "took a supernumerary relation." This meant he resigned from the ministry. He and his family then settled in New York State, where Avery became a farmer. In 1851, they moved to a farm in Lorrain County, Ohio, near Wellington. Avery occasionally preached in Methodist churches in Lorrain County.

He died in October, 1869.

So many of the curious came to visit the grave of Sarah Maria Cornell, on Durfee's farm, that the Durfee family caused the body to be disinterred once more and moved to an undisclosed and now forgotten place.

A few years after the trial, someone asked Jeremiah Mason whether or not he had thought Avery guilty.

"Why, as to that," Mason said pleasantly, "I don't believe I ever gave it much thought."